DEVIL'S CHAIR

STEFANIE JOLICOEUR

Keep the lights on!
Stefanie Jolicoeur

Original cover photograph by Skyler Smith via www.unsplash.com
Layout and final cover design by Delaney-Designs.com

ISBN: 978-0-9962121-3-7
Printed in the U.S.A.

The Happy Heart Studio
22 Danielle Lane
Dover, NH 03820

www.thehappyheartstudio.net

Dedicated to Tim
My man. My muse.
Love ya, baby.

ACKNOWLEDGMENTS

First and foremost, I'd like to thank my family for allowing me the time to write and work on all of my crazy projects. I appreciate your patience with the (occasional) late dinners and (usual) messy house (with four kids, that's no joke)!

I'd also like to thank all the friends and family who encouraged me to keep writing. Your support is appreciated more than you know.

Finally, to my husband Tim, thank you for letting me live my dream. In case I don't say it enough - you're the best! I love you!

Stef

Kate

Kate looked out the window of the rickety, wood paneled tour bus and sighed. *I'm here,* she thought and fought the sudden surge of emotion that prickled within her chest. The bus lurched to a stop as a cloud of dust kicked up under the balding tires. The door heaved open with a dry squeal and excited tourists descended the stairs into oppressive desert heat that enveloped their air-conditioned bodies with invisible waves. A few of the tourists coughed into clenched fists because of the lingering airborne dust.

Reluctantly, Kate pulled the ear buds from her ears, her protection from a chatty seatmate with way too many questions, and mentally prepared herself for the errand that had brought her so many miles from home. She stuffed her IPod into the new backpack that she'd bought specifically for this trip to Jerusalem, to the Wailing Wall. After zipping the pocket closed, she deftly removed a bottle of water from the mesh pocket on the side of her backpack and took a big, mouth clearing swig.

Kate returned the bottle to its mesh home and stood, finally ready to leave the bus. The driver stared at her in his oversized rearview mirror, impatiently tapping his fingers on the steering wheel. *No doubt he wants his break,* she thought and glanced in his direction with an apologetic smile.

Kate walked by the driver and nodded another apology. He nodded back, but didn't seem impressed with her remorse. She took the steps quickly, anxious to get away from the irritated driver. In her haste, she jumped down off the last step. A puff of brown dirt covered her white sneakers the instant she landed. She bent over and futilely tried to brush the settling dust from the surface of her shoes. It seemed to smear deeper into the creases of the white canvas.

"They will get more dirty when I leave, so you may want to move on," the driver hollered down from his perch on the driver's seat. He gave her a dismissive wave of his hand and slammed the door shut.

Kate nodded at him again through the grimy glass and realized he was right. She hitched her backpack into a comfortable position on her shoulders and walked toward the group of tourists from her bus that had formed a small, confused circle a few yards away.

As she walked, Kate surveyed the large number of vendors that had set up shop here. It struck her as odd for them to be so close to such a legendary and mystical holy place.

Why would a government allow such shady dealings to happen here? she wondered. But, a buck was a buck, she surmised.

Before Kate arrived at the group, a middle-aged man dressed in a dusty black suit approached her, hat in hand. Usually an unexpected encounter with a strange man made her uneasy, especially since she was alone, but this stranger wore a kind smile and had open, friendly eyes which instantly made her feel oddly serene.

"Excuse me, Miss? Are you an American?" he asked. His dry lips parted with a broad smile that felt welcoming, comforting.

"How could you tell?" she asked, still surprised for being so friendly to a complete stranger. But something about this place made her feel safe, as if nothing here could harm her. Plus, it was broad daylight and a bus-load of people stood a few yards away so that didn't hurt either.

"Americans always look so fresh when they arrive here," he said with an amused grin. Before Kate could respond, he continued, "Would you like a free tour of the wall? I'm a guide here and we had a bus break down so it will be an hour or so before my next official group is scheduled," he said, a glimmer of pride in his eyes.

"Free?" asked Kate, suddenly suspicious. She didn't know too much, but she was certain there was no such thing as free, especially here where everyone seemed to have an eager hand in your pocket, happy to relieve you of your vacation money.

"Honestly free," he said, and seemed to recognize her hesitation. "You'd be doing me a favor, really. I'm afraid I'd be rather bored if I had to wait much longer alone," he added, his smile pleading.

"I guess that would be okay," Kate agreed with a shrug. "But I've got to be back with my group over there in an hour," she said and nodded at the bewildered huddle of Americans still waiting for their own tour a few yards away.

"No problem," he assured her. "My name is Adam." He stuck his pale hand out toward her.

Kate extended her arm and took Adam's hand. His skin

was surprisingly cold despite the overwhelming heat and his dark suit. *His body must be acclimated the extreme temperature since he works here every day,* she thought. "My name's Kate. Kate Hart. From America," she joked, and smiled playfully at her new friend.

Adam grinned and gave Kate's hand a strong shake.

Kate tried to pull her hand away, but he held it for a second longer, seeming to enjoy the warmth of her touch. Reluctantly, he released her hand and nodded in the direction they would be walking. Kate smiled and turned the way he'd indicated so they were walking side by side. Adam held his hands behind his back, clasping his wrists with each hand.

"So, what part of America are you from?"

"I'm from the Northeast," answered Kate. She hesitated before continuing, not wanting to give too much information to a perfect stranger. After deciding it was probably safe since she was thousands of miles from her hometown, she continued, "Waterville, Maine, actually."

"Ahh," nodded Adam. "Is that where you say 'Live free or… die'?"

Kate shuddered involuntarily. Adam had drawn out the word 'die' almost as if he relished the word. She shook off the internal chill that was seeping into her subconscious and responded, "No. That's the motto for New Hampshire. That's the state next door. I live in Maine. I think ours is either 'The Pine Tree State' or 'Vacationland,' I'm not quite sure which."

"Vacationland sounds promising," said Adam, nodding.

"It is if you like beaches and lobster in the summer

and skiing and ice fishing in the winter." Kate laughed nervously and suddenly felt foolish for mentioning such luxurious things. She wondered if Adam had ever seen a snowy ski slope or eaten anything as fabulous as a freshly caught lobster.

Kate and Adam continued walking and started to make their way through the small market of vendors that littered the plaza with tattered canvas tents and shoddy wooden carts. Most of them yelled to Kate as she passed by, "Pretty lady, look here, you buy?"

At the end of the row, an aggressive vendor stepped directly in front of Kate and shoved a blue silk scarf into her hand. Startled, Kate tripped over her own feet and nearly fell into the dust.

"Whoa," said Kate. She grabbed onto the fabric that covered Adam's thin arm. *I hope I didn't damage his suit. It's probably his only one,* she thought grimly as she fought gravity and finally straightened.

With her footing back, she realized the vendor had quickly retreated from them, abandoning the bright scarf in a colorful heap in the dust. She turned to see where he'd gone. Squinting into the sun, she spotted him cowering behind his cart, his face partially hidden behind the rows of blowing scarves that hung from wooden rails, a rich canopy of vibrant camouflage.

Curious and with growing apprehension, Kate followed the frightened man's gaze. Bug-eyed and slack-jawed, he stared directly at Adam. Kate squinted at Adam, his silhouette blurred by the hot sun. Quickly, Adam broke his powerful gaze away from the shaking vendor and turned toward Kate. She'd missed it. Whatever had transpired between the two men, it was over. Now, his face relaxed, he was still the friendly, smiling gentleman who had initially greeted her.

"Don't be alarmed, Kate," he cooed. "These animals just need to be put in their place every now and again. It angers me when they attack our tourists in such a disrespectful manner." He continued, his tone soothing, "I wish they weren't allowed to be here, but unfortunately it is not up to me." He smiled broadly at Kate.

Hot and confused, Kate shook her head. Adam's hypnotic gaze seemed to calm the fear that had been growing inside her. He was so kind. *Maybe the extreme temperatures were playing tricks on me*, she thought and gave Adam a timid smile.

"Shall we continue?" he asked, raising his eyebrows, feigning innocence.

"Yeah, let's just get going," agreed Kate, suddenly desperate to get away from the claustrophobia that was starting to crawl on her skin from being surrounded by the buzzing vendors and throngs of dickering tourists. She wanted to move closer to the wall where the plaza opened and the vendors were not allowed to hawk their goods.

Kate and Adam resumed their tour, again walking side by side toward the wall. As Adam spoke about the origins of the wall back to its construction in 19 BC and continued through the history of the Roman Empire, the Middle Ages, the Ottoman Empire, British Rule and Jordanian Rule up to the current Israeli Rule, Kate couldn't help but notice how the remaining vendors they passed now seemed to be too frightened to approach her or even look at her. She sensed their eyes cautiously following her and Adam as they passed by their kiosks of trinkets. Oddly, she sensed fear and reservation in their hidden glances.

When they reached the wide expanse of the plaza, Kate took a deep breath and gazed at the wall about a hundred yards in front of her. Suddenly, she was overcome with intense emotion that was quickly bubbling to the surface. A sloppy tear rolled down her cheek, leaving a wet streak. As she wiped it away absently with the back of her hand, she remembered her mother's curiosity and longing to visit the wall. This had been her mother's trip—a trip that she'd never live to make.

Kate's anguish rapidly turned into a hot wave of anger when she remembered the phone call she'd received from her mother when she was admitted into the hospital. She'd told Kate not to worry and not to even bother coming to the hospital to check on her. They were planning on releasing her in a day or two and she didn't want to bother her with something so small.

Despite Kate's protests, her mother had convinced her that she was fine. Although she had reservations, Kate finally relented, promising that she would come to see her at home after she'd been released.

When she hadn't heard from her the next evening, Kate got worried. But, her mother had always been flaky about things like that, so Kate had tried to brush off her nerves. Kate had always been more the mother than the daughter in their backward relationship. This was probably why she didn't have any children of her own yet—already she was exhausted from being a parent to her own mother.

When the phone finally did ring at three in the morning, the news was not good. Kate's mother had a massive stroke around midnight and was gone.

When Kate was going through her mother's house a few days later, she'd found the plane tickets in a pile on her mother's wreck of a desk and decided that since her mother was unable to go on her fantasy trip, she'd go in her place and bring a pinch of her ashes to leave at the wall.

The idea of taking the trip herself had given Kate a great piece of comfort. She hadn't realized just how much until this moment, when she stood so close to the sacred wall that had eluded her mother.

Kate sniffed and wiped another errant tear from her cheek. After taking a few moments to collect herself, she realized Adam was no longer standing next to her. She looked to her right and then to her left and saw him standing a few feet away, waiting patiently for her to get it together.

"I'm sorry, Adam," she said, "I was just overcome. I guess I didn't realize how big this would be for me."

"Don't worry about it, Kate," he answered, nodding sympathetically. "I understand how being here in person can mean so much for so many. I consider myself lucky to be here every day."

"I'm a little embarrassed," she admitted. "I feel like I need to explain my sudden tear-fest," she smiled at Adam and wiped another tear from the corner of her eye.

"You don't have to explain, Kate," said Adam sooth-ingly, "but I'm all ears if you need a friend."

"Thank you," sighed Kate. She *did* need a friend. Being

an only child, she didn't have many confidants in her life. And, most of her friends had long been married off and were starting their families.

They walked quickly to and open bench and sat down. Adam, ever the gentleman, allowed Kate to sit first. She smiled up at him and squinted against the sun that blazed high in the sky. She shaded her eyes with her hand and couldn't help but notice how the sun made an angelic aura around Adam. He did seem like an angel to her. He had protected her from the aggressive vendor and now he was saving her from her own demons. He was saving her from her guilt and anger that had been building up over the last month since her mother's sudden departure.

Kate took a deep breath and started at the beginning. She told him of her youth in central Maine, growing up without a father and not much other family to speak of except for a grandmother who seemed to resent her very existence. She told him about her flighty mother, who was great at the fun stuff but not so great at the serious stuff. She spoke of her crushing grief and lonely nights spent sifting through her mother's dingy, unorganized house.

Kate talked for nearly twenty minutes straight, barely pausing to take a breath. Adam listened patiently, nodding thoughtfully in all the right places. After she was finished, she leaned back on the bench, spent. She mopped tears from her face with the collar of her shirt and looked at Adam. She smiled weakly at him, "Thank you."

Adam reached over and patted her knee with his cold hand. "Do you feel better now, Kate?"

Kate thought for a moment about his simple question.

She realized she did feel better—a lot better. The heavy feeling that she had been carrying in her chest had finally dissipated and now she could breathe easier despite being surrounded by blowing dust and overwhelming heat.

"I feel amazingly better."

"I'm happy for you, Kate," said Adam. "Do you want to continue? I did promise you a tour," he added with a smile.

"Yes, I'm ready. It's your turn to talk," she blushed.

Adam stood and said, "Follow me."

"Yes, sir," said Kate, giddy from her emotional release. She quickly got herself under control, wiping the smile from her face knowing that most people were here for somber reasons such as her own.

Kate was fascinated by the amount of knowledge Adam had about the Wailing Wall. She was equally taken with the wide variety of tourists who had come to see it. Some prayed, down on their knees despite the dust. Some greedily put their hands on the wall, searching the rough stones for comfort. Others faced the wall and swayed, yarmulkes perched precariously on the back of their heads, Bibles in their hands, their strange curled sideburns rocking back and forth in rhythmic waves.

Adam continued with his fascinating history lesson, pausing often to let Kate get a better look at certain areas of significance. As their hour together quickly faded, Adam grabbed Kate by the hand and led her to a corner on the far end of the wall, away from the majority of the crowd. Eyebrows raised, he looked at her expectantly.

"What?" she finally asked when she couldn't take his eager expression any longer.

"Come on, Kate," Adam urged. "Remember why you came here?"

Kate, unnerved by his impatience and the semi-secluded spot, started to question her judgment again.

As if reading her discomfort, Adam smoothed his tone and softly said, "The ashes, Kate."

"Oh! Right!" *How could she have forgotten? The whole point for this trip was to leave behind a handful of her mother's ashes.* Surveying the area, she realized he had led her to the perfect spot, away from prying eyes and walking feet, where she could say her last goodbyes with a modicum of privacy.

Kate slid her backpack from her shoulders and set it gently in the dust. She unzipped the front pocket and gingerly removed the black velvet satchel that held a portion of her mother's ashes. Cupping the satchel in her hand to protect it from the breeze, she realized she was crying.

Adam gave her a reassuring nod and a kind smile and took three large paces backward to give her some space.

Kate wiped her nose with the back of her hand and untied the knot that held the satchel closed. Suddenly, she was unsure how to proceed. Should she kneel? Say a prayer? The perfectionist in Kate was bubbling to the surface and was making this simple act of saying goodbye much more difficult than she had imagined.

Seeing her struggle, Adam stepped forward and put a cold hand on Kate's sweat-covered shoulder. "Would you like me to say a few words, Kate?"

Unable to turn around, she nodded once, sniffed and waited for his comforting words.

"Please, Lord, accept this woman, Mary Elizabeth Hart, into your sacred house. Hold her soul in your holy embrace. We thank you, oh Lord. Ashes to ashes, dust to dust."

Kate knelt in the dirt on one quivering knee and slowly emptied the satchel, careful to hold the opening close to the ground so she wouldn't risk an errant wisp of wind stealing away any of the ashes. Then, she took a handful of loose dirt from a few inches away and piled it on top of the small white hill. Gently, she patted down the fresh dirt and said, "Goodbye, Mumma."

Finished, Kate wiped her cheeks and the corners of her eyes with the collar of her shirt. She smiled at Adam and was relieved to see that he was smiling kindly back at her. His patient and understanding expression instantly calmed her. "Thank you for your words, Adam. They were just beautiful."

"You are very welcome, Kate. You look like the weight of the world has been lifted off of your shoulders."

"You know, it's strange, I do feel very light," admitted Kate, the giddy sensation returning.

"Unfortunately, I need to get you back to your bus, Kate." He nodded in the direction from which they came. "Our time is almost up."

They turned, walked across the plaza and through the myriad of vendors toward the meeting area for the tourists. Although they were mostly quiet on the walk back, Kate had a niggling feeling in the back of her brain that there was something important she needed to address.

As they made their way through the sea of vendors, Kate spotted a table filled with sparkling heaps of handmade jewelry. The items were obviously cheap, but she wanted at least one souvenir from her trip here, something to remember this profound day in her life.

"Adam, do you mind if I stop to look at this for a second?" She surveyed the table for something to her liking.

"Sure, Kate," agreed Adam. "Do you like silver?" he asked while watching her paw through the piles of silver rings and bracelets.

"No. I'm usually a gold girl," she said, a disappointed scowl on her face. "Ironically, this stuff is exactly what my mother would have wanted. She loved this kind of stuff. The cheaper, the better," she laughed.

"Maybe there is something else I can do for you, Kate."

She turned to see if he'd spotted a table with items that might better suit her. "Do you see a table with gold on it?"

"Not exactly. Let's get out of this claustrophobic spot and talk over there," he said and pointed toward an area clear of bantering vendors and tourists.

They walked quickly toward the open spot before it could fill up with waiting tourists. Adam seemed jittery which amused Kate. *Was he going to ask to see her again?* He knew she wasn't from here, so that notion didn't quite make sense. But, she'd seen her share of nervous suitors before and he seemed downright edgy.

They stopped walking and awkwardly faced each other. Forced to stand a few inches apart as the crowd grew around them, Adam seemed to get more anxious by the minute. Kate worried he would chicken out.

"You said you like gold, right?" he asked and reached inside his jacket.

"Yes, I tend to gravitate toward gold," she agreed, nodding, still wondering where this was going.

He smiled and, like a magician, pulled a gold chain from his interior suit pocket and displayed his gift to her on the palm of his shaking hand. "I have a souvenir for you."

Kate let out a low whistle. Immediately, she was taken by the beauty of the exquisite, ancient-looking key that hung from the gold chain. The key was about three inches long and was ornately etched along its length.

Although she had no intention of taking it, she was unable to resist and reached out to touch the key as it lay on Adam's extended palm. *Was it a family heirloom or God forbid, stolen?* Her fingers itched with an overwhelming need to hold it.

"Go ahead, Kate. Pick it up," said Adam, an eager smile on his face. He forced the key into Kate's reaching fingers.

"It's breathtaking," cooed Kate.

Adam stared intently into Kate's flushed face. "It's very old, but I feel like it belongs with you."

"Adam, I can't take this from you," said Kate. "I couldn't possibly…"

"Yes, you can, Kate," said Adam sternly enough to make Kate look up at his disapproving face. She hadn't expected such a forceful reaction to her refusal.

"But… it's yours and we just met. I've already taken so much of your time today, Adam."

He spoke in an urgent whisper, "Some things are meant to be, Kate. Don't you feel it?"

Kate hesitated for a moment and realized that it did almost feel like she was meant to be here, meant to meet

Adam and maybe meant to have this lovely trinket.

Adam smiled broadly and placed the shining key into the palm of Kate's hand. He curled her fingers around it and placed a cold hand over hers. "Don't you feel it, Kate?" he asked her again and squeezed her fingers into the cool metal of the key.

"Yes," agreed Kate, nodding slowly. Suddenly, she felt odd, queasy and lightheaded. *Was the heat was starting to get to her?* She longed for the wind generated by the movement of the bus and the small possibility of a working air conditioner. But at the same time, all she wanted was to take the gift.

"Wonderful," he whispered in her ear. He released her hand and slowly unlocked his gaze from hers.

"T—th—thank you," she stammered. She broke her gaze from Adam's imploring eyes and shook her head to clear it before she became too foggy.

Adam looked over her shoulder toward the growing crowd of tourists. "I think I see your group," he said.

Kate turned and recognized a few people from her bus starting to form a small circle near the pick-up site. Turning back to Adam, a wave of disappointment and sadness ran through her body. She was surprised for forming such a strong attachment to a total stranger. It was completely unlike her. Normally, she was a suspicious New Englander. She decided the combination of a foreign country, sleep deprivation, jet lag, intense heat and grief had rolled her into one big emotional meatball.

Kate felt an overwhelming urge to give her new friend a hug. This was also unlike her; she rarely hugged anyone.

She wasn't the touch-feely type, which was laughable considering she's a nurse. She could insert IVs and catheters, but hugs were few and far between.

Kate launched herself into Adam's arms. He enveloped her in a big bear hug, his arms strong in spite of his slight frame. "Thanks for everything, Adam, really. I haven't felt this good in a long time." She smiled, embarrassed.

"Likewise, Kate." He nodded his head and chivalrously tipped his black hat.

"Do you mind if I take your photo? Just with my phone?" asked Kate. Before Adam could answer, she slipped her phone from her pocket and snapped a keepsake. With a small wave of thanks, she stepped away from Adam and quickly moved toward her group. The bus pulled in front of them and Kate finally remembered the question that had been bothering her on their walk back. She turned to yell her thought toward Adam, but he had already disappeared into the crowd, his black suit blending easily into the undulating sea of conservatively dressed worshippers.

While in line, slowly shuffling toward the bus, her unanswered question for Adam weighed heavily on her mind. After she made her way onto the bus, she grabbed the closest available window seat and searched the surging crowd for him, desperate to spot the combination of Adam's black hat and dark suit.

Finally, she found him standing nearly fifty feet away, his eyes trained on her bus. Kate quickly pushed in the two metal tabs and slid the window down. She stuck her head out the opening and hollered, "Adam!" Adam's head twitched in her direction. *Good,* she thought, *he can hear me.* "Adam!" she yelled again.

Adam deftly made his way through the thick crowd and approached the bus. Already in gear, it had started to pull away.

"How'd you know my mother's name?" Kate shouted from the window.

A brief look of surprise spread across Adam's upturned face. Then, he shrugged and put his hand to his ear as if he hadn't heard what she'd said.

The bus pulled away. Instead of trying again, Kate waved goodbye to Adam through the open window.

Adam waved and quickly disappeared again into the crowd. Kate shut her window and leaned back. She shivered when her sweaty backside pressed against the cool vinyl seat.

Kate opened her hand and gazed at the fetching key that Adam had insisted she take. Her seatmate glanced over and smiled. "I bought a scarf," she said and held out a purple scarf, waving it proudly toward Kate.

"Nice," said Kate. "I was meant to have this," she said and held up her key. She placed the chain around her neck and let the key rest safely between her sweaty breasts. It was cool on her chest. *As cool as Adam's hands*, she thought and closed her eyes hoping to drift off. It would be an hour or more before they reached the hotel and she was exhausted from the emotion of the day, the wonderful day in which everything that had happened was meant to be.

Matt

Matt sat in the waiting room and glanced impatiently at his watch. *Thirty minutes and counting*, he noted and fingered the stack of tattered magazines on the table next to his chair. He'd been a pharmaceutical sales representative for almost ten years and he'd never gotten used to the waiting.

He stood and paced the room, glancing up every now and again when someone passed by, hoping it would be the nurse who'd absconded with his clipboard.

He pushed the power button on a remote control he'd found stuffed between two cushions and wasn't surprised when nothing happened. "Typical," he muttered and set the remote next to the magazines.

A nurse in rose colored scrubs hurried past the waiting room. He almost called out to her but then decided against it, certain she wasn't the right one. The nurse who'd taken his clipboard was bigger, *Maureen, no, Marlene*, he'd remembered and picked up a magazine about diabetes.

Another nurse passed by and Matt glanced up, hopeful. She looked up from her clipboard and causally glanced into the waiting area. She stopped just long enough for Matt to notice her taking a second look. He knew he looked handsome in his suit, a rarity in a sea of oversized scrubs and lab coats. He smiled warmly at her and nodded. She quickly looked down and continued her walk toward the nurse's station.

He had hoped she'd stop. *At least she'd be someone to talk to. An attractive someone*, he noted and went back to the sleep inducing article on blood sugar testing.

To his surprise, he watched as the pretty nurse turned on her heel and headed back to the waiting area. He exhaled as she approached him. His stomach twitched with nervous energy. She was quite beautiful, with brown hair and deep brown eyes that exuded a flicker of confidence. *Calm down*, he thought as she stopped near him and cleared her throat in an obvious attention-getting manner.

He fought a quizzical expression that threatened to spread across his face when she gazed down at him in the chair. He smiled at her, his white teeth sparkling, an amused twinkle in his brown eyes, "Um, is that mine?"

"Huh?" Her confidence dissipated and she clutched a key that had been bobbing loose on her chest.

"The clipboard?" He nodded at her hands.

"Oh, no, this one's mine," she said and smiled awkwardly, blushing pink.

"Oh, sorry." He gave her another beaming smile and sensed he was unnerving her. It was endearing. He liked her already.

"Are you waiting for someone?" she asked, looking over her shoulder.

He chuckled. "You could say that."

"Do you know who? I could track her down for you," offered the pretty nurse, obviously trying to salvage her dignity.

"I'd rather wait with you. If that's okay?" he asked. He fought the urge to wink; he didn't want to come off as cheesy or overly confident.

The nurse blushed again and looked down at her white sneakers. Then, she casually glanced at his left hand to see if he was wearing a wedding band. "Well, I'm supposed to be working," she said, "but if you need anything, you can ask for me. I'm Kate. Kate Hart. Some people call me Nurse Hart." She pointed at the name tag pinned on her scrubs near her left breast.

"Thank you, Nurse Hart. You're the first person here to treat me so kindly. Most hospital staffers treat pharma reps like they have scurvy or something." He laughed.

"Scurvy, huh?" She returned his laugh with an amused smile of her own.

"Yeah, you know, the adult version of cooties," he joked. This time it was his turn to blush.

"We probably have something for that here," she teased.

"I'm sure you do." He grinned. "My name is Matt Hopkins. It's really nice to meet you. Kate, did you say?"

"Yes." She blushed again.

"Well, I certainly hope to run into you again, Kate," he said. His heart surged at the thought of seeing her again. *Is there something here?* he wondered, hoped.

Kate nodded eagerly. "Um, would you want to meet me in the cafeteria for lunch today?"

"Oh." He sighed and his shoulders dropped.

"Never mind," said Kate and she started to turn away.

"Wait a minute," he reached out and caught her arm before she could retreat.

Kate seemed surprised by his touch and flinched automatically.

Instantly, he released her and felt guilty, like a kid who had snuck a cookie and gotten caught.

"Sorry," she said, her eyes pleading.

"There's nothing to be sorry for," he said. A broad smile spread across his face. "I only hesitated about lunch because I was trying to remember my schedule for today," he explained.

"Oh, okay." She seemed relieved that it wasn't a total rejection on his part.

"I have a lunch at another office across town today, but I'm free for dinner tonight. I mean, if you're free?"

"I think that would work," she answered, a smile spreading across her face.

He smiled and his heart swelled. He'd never had such an intense attraction to a woman before, at least not this early on. He could almost see the chemistry between them, like sparks from a fluffy carpet in winter-time.

"Do you want to meet at Rolando's? I think they serve Italian food there," he said.

"I know where that is. That sounds great. Will six work for you?"

He grinned at her. "That's great." He was enjoying himself immensely with this conversation with the cute nurse, and was disappointed when he looked beyond her to see the other nurse returning with his clipboard. He hated that he'd have to leave. *She probably has to get back to work,* he thought.

Kate followed his distracted gaze and saw Marlene

returning with his long lost clipboard.

"Here you go, Matty," she said cheerfully. She handed him the clipboard and gave Kate a sideways glance of disapproval.

"Thanks, Marlene," said Matt, without taking his eyes from Kate's.

"I'm here to help," she said between heavy, sucking breaths. She glanced at Kate again and scowled, clearly disapproving of the obvious connection between her co-worker and the handsome salesman.

"Well, I should run," said Kate. She looked away from Matt and gave Marlene an apologetic half-smile.

"I'll see you tonight, Kate," called Matt as she walked away.

"You bet," she said, waving her clipboard at him.
Marlene glared at Matt.

"What?" he asked, unclear if he'd broken some unwritten rule of the hospital.

"You asked her out?" she said, her eyes wet.

"Why? Does she have a boyfriend?" Matt asked, suddenly deflated.

"Well, no. But..." A crimson blush washed over her bloated cheeks.

Matt was confused. Then, it hit him. *Oh, God! Marlene likes me.* "Well, I'm sorry. I had no idea." He felt bad, but not bad enough to break his date with the intriguing and beautiful Kate Hart.

"Never mind," said Marlene. She left him alone in the waiting room.

Matt checked the clock. It was nearly lunchtime. He hoped the next six hours would pass quickly so he could see her again. He realized, smiling, that he'd have a difficult time thinking about anything else.

Kate

Kate could not believe how quickly the rest of her day passed. She flew through her to-do list and even added in a few extra chores to keep the next shift from complaining about how short they had left their supply carts. Before she knew it, it was time to head home and get ready for her big date with Matt.

On the way she hit way too much traffic for such a small town and barely had time to change clothes and throw a comb through her hair. She had planned on taking a shower and using makeup to cover the fading freckles that dotted her cheeks after her trip. She kicked herself for bothering to restock the carts for the moody night-shifters. *They wouldn't appreciate it anyway*, she surmised as she took a quick glance at herself in the full-length mirror and raced out the door.

She made it to the restaurant in plenty of time. Deciding she didn't want to look too desperate, she listened to a few more songs on the radio before going inside. Using the car's small lighted mirror, she gave herself a quick once over and was happy with what she saw. Despite not having time to take a shower, she thought she looked damn good.

When the song on the radio finished and the DJ started blabbing about an upcoming concert, Kate exited the car and walked toward the restaurant's entrance. Oddly, she noticed that the bouncing, nervous butterflies she normally had before a date weren't fluttering in her stomach. She paused for a moment and decided that they *were* there, they were just different. Something about Matt made her feel comfortable, like there was something deeper going on between them. She remembered his kind smile and twinkling, dark brown eyes and grinned.

She pulled open the door to Rolando's Italian Eatery and was greeted with a whoosh of warm air, scented with an intoxicating mix of garlic and freshly baked bread. Her stomach growled reflexively and she realized she hadn't eaten a thing since meeting Matt earlier in the day—she'd plum forgotten.

She approached the hostess table and waited patiently behind a young couple who had their hands tucked provocatively into the back of each other's pants pockets. A nervous twinge shot through her empty belly when the hostess scanned the list of names and frowned. *Was she wrong about Matt? Had he stood her up?*

Thankfully, the hostess interrupted her brief wave of panic, "Sorry, it was next to another name and I didn't see it at first. Is he your date?"

"Yes. He is," said Kate with a hint of pride. *He probably charmed his way into the best seat in the house*, she thought and smiled.

"He's a cutie," said the hostess. "If it doesn't work out between you two, give him my number, okay?" she teased.

Kate saw Matt at the table, sipping wine and peering out an oversized bay window into the growing darkness. He turned as the two women approached and stood. A broad smile spread across his handsome face.

The air in Kate's lungs hitched and she forced herself to breathe. He was even more handsome than she had remembered. Now she wished she had taken that shower and guessed she would be going home and taking a cold one later tonight.

"Hello, Nurse Hart," said Matt, a twinkle in his eyes.

"Hello, Sales Rep Matt."

"Touché." He smirked boyishly, a bit of a blush creeping onto his smooth cheeks.

Kate smiled and sat in the seat he had pulled out for her. "So, how was the rest of your day?"

"It got a lot better after I met you." He gave her a playful wink as he sat in his chair. "How 'bout yours?"

"Really good, but I've been away for a while so I was looking forward to getting back into the swing of things."

His smooth brow furrowed. "Were you sick?"

She hesitated, not yet sure how much to share with her new friend. "No, not sick exactly."

Clearly sensing her reluctance, he kindly let her off the hook. "Do you want to talk about something else?"

She sighed. "Yes! I don't want to bore you with the sordid details of my life. At least not yet," she said and smiled coyly.

"Oooh, sordid details, I can hardly wait," he teased.

"Don't get too excited, Matt. Believe me. It's not nearly as exciting as it sounds. But let's talk about something else for now." She gave him an assertive smile and a nod.

He grimaced. "Got it. Can we start over then?"

"Absolutely," she agreed.

He leaned back in his chair and took a deep breath. "I like you, Kate. There's something about you that feels…"

"Comfortable?"

He nodded. "Yes, comfortable is exactly the word I was looking for."

"I felt the same way about you today when we met at the hospital," she admitted. "Like we were destined to meet," she added. She gulped and looked down. *Don't scare him away*, she thought, instantly regretting her last comment.

When she finally dared to look up, she was surprised to see that he was grinning, almost wide enough for her to count each one of his beautiful white teeth. "I feel the same way, Kate."

Kate returned his smile and relaxed. "So, do you live here in town?"

"Yup. Born and raised. You?"

"I'm living in my mother's old cottage near the lake, but I'm hoping to change that soon."

Matt nodded. "Have you been looking already? Not moving too far away, I hope," he said, the red blush returning to his cheeks.

Kate shrugged her shoulders. "I'd like to be near work, but I'm flexible. A commute doesn't really bother me that much."

"Are you already working with someone? A realtor, I mean."

Kate shook her head. "Funny you should ask. My one contact at the hospital fell through so I've been looking for someone to help me find a new place and to sell my mother's cottage. Do you know anyone?"

Matt smiled and said, "Sure I know someone great! My college roommate married a gal that works over at Winslow Realty. I think her dad owns the place. They really know the area and could probably help you a lot."

"Do you think she'd be willing to work with a slightly neurotic perfectionist?"

Matt chuckled. "I don't see why not." He pulled out his thick wallet and dug through a pile of white business cards.

"Thanks, Matt. I really appreciate the help.

"No problem, Kate." He handed her a card. "Be sure to tell her you know me, that way they'll give you the royal treatment."

"Susan Poirier," she read from the card. "Sounds good to me." She smiled gratefully at him.

The rest of the evening was filled with a fabulous meal, stimulating conversation, and a lot of shameful flirting. Kate hated that the night had to end, but she had to work in the morning and so did he. She mulled over the idea of inviting him back to her mother's cottage, but something about that didn't seem quite right. If it was going to work between them, anything physical would have to wait. She'd had plenty of relationships that were based on a night of good sex, but none of them had lasted very long.

Matt, ever the gentleman, walked her to her car. He asked her out for another night and she quickly accepted. He also offered to help her with her house hunt which she gladly took him up on.

Worried he'd want a kiss, she ducked into her car before he could position himself to make a move. She couldn't bear to kiss the poor guy with the amount of garlic she had on her breath.

As she pulled out of the parking lot, she reviewed the events of the night. She scored a second date with a wonderful man who was a blue eyed, brown-haired hottie, got a referral for a real estate agent, and had a kick ass meal.

Life can't get much better than this, she thought and smiled.

***

Kate's sleep was full of odd dreams. Usually, her dreams were about being late to work or forgetting things, the things that drove her nuts in her waking life, but tonight her dreams were different. She saw her mother. It was the first time she dreamed of Mother since her death.

Mother sat quietly on a bench in a beautiful, lush park on a sunny summer day. She tilted her head toward the warm sunshine and let it wash over her face. She appeared much younger in the dream than Kate remembered in real life.

Kate felt the urge to approach her, to say "hello" and give her a big hug, but she was just a spectator in this dream. She wasn't to be seen or heard, much like Ebenezer Scrooge when he traveled with the three ghosts.

Her mother waved at someone who approached from behind Kate. Kate turned and saw, to her surprise, that the person advancing toward Mother was Adam. *Her* Adam. Adam from Jerusalem. She was confused. Mother and Adam hadn't known each other in life. *Why would they be together in a dream?*

Mother stood and gave Adam the hug Kate had wanted.

They sat down on the bench together and started talking. They looked animated as they spoke, although Kate was unable to hear their words. With a shudder, she realized she couldn't hear *anything*. No birds tweeting. No background noise. Her dream was devoid of any sound except for the constant thud of her beating heart.

Adam reached his hand toward Mother's face and held a single finger over her lips, shushing her like a child. Mother stopped talking and sat completely still. Her hands fell to her sides like limp noodles. She appeared to be falling asleep, as if Adam had put her in a trance with his touch. It reminded Kate of how she'd felt near the end of her encounter with him. She'd felt drunk, her head off-kilter. His intense gaze made her foggy, faint. At the time, she'd blamed it on the heat.

Back in her dream, Mother had become completely still. Adam removed his finger from her lips, jerked his head up, and looked directly at Kate. Kate smiled at him. *Could he see her?* She watched with curious fascination. Then, Adam's face began to change. Adam's cracked lips twisted into a wicked sneer. His exposed, aging teeth reminded Kate of an angry dog preparing to fight. The friendly brown eyes that had greeted her a few moments before had transformed into narrow black slits. He glared menacingly at Kate, his eyebrows creased and his forehead wrinkled when he tilted his misshapen head toward her.

An overwhelming wave of foreboding washed over Kate's body as she watched, helpless. *How could she have been so wrong?* Immediately, she was transported back to the market in Jerusalem—was this face the reason the vendor had been so scared of him? Stunned by Adam's sudden change in demeanor, she again questioned the intelligence of her decision to allow a complete stranger to show her around. During her mental flogging, she kicked herself for being so trusting. She needed to remember that she wasn't in Maine anymore.

A shudder rippled down her spine. She couldn't take her eyes off the wicked expression on Adam's twisted face. Suddenly, she could hear sounds. Desperately, she wished the dream had remained mute. Adam was breathing her name. At first, he whispered it, and then his voice grew louder and louder. He wasn't speaking it—he growled it between bared yellow teeth. His black eyes bored into her petrified face, deeper still, into her soul.

The Kate in the dream shook her head from side to side. She couldn't believe what she was seeing.

The real Kate woke up screaming and covered in a thin film of sweat despite the fact she'd thrown her covers onto the floor during the night. She shivered and scanned the room. Her eyes darted into every corner, inspected every shadow, and tried to convince her frightened brain she was safe and at home.

After a few minutes, her body relaxed and caught up to her conscious mind. A surge of guilt washed over her for having an intense, negatively-toned dream about her new friend. She was angry with herself even though her subconscious had dreamed it. In Jerusalem, he'd explained away his reaction to the vendor in a way that made Kate comfortable with him again. At one point in their time together, the sun bright in her face, an angelic aura appeared around him. For that moment, he did seem like an angel to her. He'd protected her from the aggressive vendor and he'd saved her from the guilt and anger that had built up over the last month since Mother's death.

Sitting in bed a few moments longer, she analyzed the details from her dream. *Was it a warning? Was Mother trying to communicate with her? And why was Adam with her?* Kate shook her head. Mother had always put a lot of energy into translating her dreams for hidden meanings, studying books and consulting psychics. Kate didn't want to start down that road. Not today.

After collecting herself, she noticed it was already sunny outside. On the cluttered side table, she lifted a stack of books to see the time on the alarm clock. It was almost 11 a.m.! She'd nearly slept the morning away. She hadn't slept this late since college.

She swung her legs over the edge of the bed and stood up. They were still wobbly from her intense dream. She rolled her eyes at herself for being such an idiot. She needed to get into the bathroom, take a shower and get started on her day.

As she stepped out of bed, she leaned over and craned her neck around a pile of books to read the cover of a magazine. A sudden, sickening realization hit her like a Mack truck. Something was missing. Frantically, she felt the skin around her neck. The key was gone! She hadn't taken it off once since she'd received it from Adam. She racked her brain wildly for clues of its whereabouts.

She forced herself to slow down, regroup. She walked calmly around the bedroom to search for her missing key.

First, she lifted her pillow off the mattress. It was still wet with sweat from her active night. No key. She climbed onto the bed on her knees and felt around with her hands. No key. She reached her hand between the mattress and headboard, shuddering at the thought of touching a cobweb or dust bunny. Still no key. She stood back and squinted at the bed, tapping her lips thoughtfully with one finger.

"The blankets!" she exclaimed. She ran around the end of the bed, grabbed the lump of damp bedding and shook them out. A soft knock echoed from the floor when her favorite new trinket slid out of the wet clump and landed on the satin trim on one of the blankets. She bent over, grabbed her key and held it up like a trophy. If anyone had been watching, they would've thought she'd just won first place in a scavenger hunt.

A strong surge of relief coursed through her body. *Was the missing key the reason Adam was upset with her in the dream?* As if he somehow knew she'd lost his gift and wasn't too happy about it. She laughed out loud for thinking such a stupid idea.

"Idiot," she muttered and ducked her head into the loop of the necklace, surprised the clasp was still intact. She must have been rolling around aggressively to lose the key over her head and not realize it. She held the key tight in her hand. It felt cold against her hot palm. It made her think of Adam's cold touch on that hot day. Kate shook her head and tried to focus on her busy day ahead.

* * *

After quickly getting ready, Kate checked the clock.

Today was a big day. After several successful dates with Matt, she had finally decided to meet with Susan, Matt's friend and realtor, to discuss the sale of her mother's cottage and find a suitable place for herself. Susan was due to arrive any minute and Kate was nervous. What if she thought the cottage was a total dump? She glanced around the small kitchen with a critical eye. It was certainly clean—she had seen to that. She'd scrubbed every inch of countertop and cabinet, surprised at how much black soot she removed. A person who didn't know Mother would've assumed she was a heavy smoker, but Kate knew the smoke was from the damn incense she insisted on burning, "cleansing the place" or some such nonsense. She could vaguely smell a hint of lavender and patchouli beneath the fresh scent of lemon cleanser.

Standing in the kitchen, she shook her head at the memory of her mother. The sound of tires kicking up gravel outside stirred her back to reality. She walked to the door and pulled it open. It squeaked obnoxiously. She made a mental note of the irritating noise, hoping she'd remember to oil it before the open house.

Susan climbed from her minivan then awkwardly reached back inside to pull out an armload of papers and a computer bag. She looked up when Kate opened the door and waved at her with the handful of papers.

Susan finished fishing in her passenger seat for paperwork and slammed the door. Kate flinched. Lost in her own thoughts again, the noise quickly brought her back to the present.

"Sorry! My husband is always yelling at me for shutting

the door too hard," said Susan, chuckling. "I swear, as if I could hurt it or something." She approached Kate with an outstretched hand.

Kate took her hand and shook it firmly. "That's okay, I needed to wake up a bit." She smiled.

"I hear you. I'm looking forward to sleeping in this weekend. It's been a busy week."

Kate led her into the small kitchen. She pointed at the little bistro table sitting neatly at the far end of the room. "We can sit and talk here if you want."

Susan nodded, sat at the table and flipped open her computer. "Perfect! So, what exactly do you think you want?" said Susan. She typed notes into her laptop as she listened.

They discussed Kate's likes and dislikes. She was impressed with how Susan was able to get her specific desires out of her so easily.

Susan reviewed the list of criteria she'd entered into her notes. "So, basically it looks like you're open to a fixer-upper if it means you can put your stamp on it," she summed up.

"Pretty much," said Kate. "I love decorating and I want the place to ooze my personality instead of making my personality conform to the place. If you understand what I mean."

"I totally understand. You seem like you're ready to take on a project."

"More than ready. I'm just sick of my life being on hold for one reason or another."

"I hear ya, sister," Susan said. Pawing through her stack of loose papers, she pulled together a handful of listings that applied to Kate's wish list.

Kate looked at the clock and was surprised to see it was almost one. She'd been with Susan for nearly an hour. It went by in what seemed like minutes.

"I hope you don't mind, but I've invited Matt to come along on the house hunt. He's never been here before either so maybe when he gets here I can give you both the grand tour?" Kate felt a blush spread across her cheeks as she said Matt's name.

"Sure, no problem," said Susan. "So, things seem to be going well in the Matt department?"

Kate could tell Susan wanted her question to sound casual, but was certain she was dying for some fresh dirt. "Yeah, he's great. We've only been out a few times, but I'm hoping for more."

"He seems pretty smitten with you as well. He's been off the market for a while so it's nice he might have hit a home run on his first time at bat." She gave her a knowing nod.

Kate didn't want to seem too eager for gossip about Matt, but Susan certainly had a way of making tantalizing comments that were hard to resist. "What do you mean 'off the market'?"

"I don't want to give away too many of Matty's secrets. But, since I'm sure he'd tell you this in a few dates anyway, I'll tell you." Susan leaned in close to Kate. Kate didn't quite understand why there was a need to whisper since it was just the two of them in the house, but she was dying to know the secret. She leaned in toward Susan.

"He was engaged, but the bi-yatch dumped him for a

wo-man!" Susan drew out the last word for shock value. Her bright eyes searched Kate's face for understanding.

Kate was stunned and unable to hide it. She'd assumed he had a past, but she never would've guessed that one. Not in a million years. "Poor Matt." She couldn't manage to say anything else.

Susan's eyes glistened with excitement. She seemed to enjoy Kate's reaction. "We were all shocked. His fiancée was gorgeous, too. Not like what you would picture for a typical lez-bo."

Kate had known a lesbian or two in college and unfortunately, they fit into Susan's stereotype of a typical lesbian; butch haircuts, plaid shirts, not a stitch of makeup. She started to dislike the way their conversation was heading. Maybe she should discuss this with Matt, if he even wanted to. At the very least, this subject would be fifth date territory.

Kate was about to attempt a subject change when she heard the sound of tires pulling to a stop on her gravel driveway. "Thank God," she muttered and glanced out the window to verify that the visitor was Matt.

"Remember," said Susan. She made a locking motion with her fingers over pursed lips.

"Got it," said Kate. She stood up to greet Matt at the door.

Kate pulled open the door and was greeted with another grating squeak. She cringed and looked at Susan. Seemingly oblivious to the noise, the realtor looked up from her paperwork and winked. Kate smiled back at her and turned her attention toward Matt. Already, he was out of his car and had bounded up the steps in front of her.

"Hey, gorgeous," he said. He stopped on the top step, inches from her surprised face.

She broke into a shy smile. "Hi, Matt." She struggled to keep from blushing.

"Hey, Matty," Susan yelled from inside the kitchen.

Matt poked his head around Kate and smiled at Susan. "Hey Susie-Q."

Kate took a step backward into the kitchen and motioned for him to step all the way inside.

"Nice place, Kate," he said, glancing around the room.

"Thanks, Matt. Do you guys want the grand tour?" She looked from Matt's beaming face over to Susan. Kate sensed Susan was sizing them up, eagerly taking in every awkward moment and inept flirtation to report back to her husband later.

"After you m'lady," Matt said to Kate. He swung his arm grandly and stepped aside to allow her to lead the way out of the kitchen.

"You're such a dork, Matt," said Susan. She followed behind Kate, punching Matt lightly in the shoulder as she passed him.

"That's Captain Dork to you," he said and laughed.

Kate tried to ignore their banter. By their body language, she imagined there was some history between them. Probably more than Susan's husband would ever know. She was pretty sure it involved a drunken night in college and some kissing. Maybe more. Those details could be kept between the two of them though, at least for now.

She led them through each of the small rooms and tried

to point out at least one unique quality afforded each room, doing her best to sell the plain little cottage. She thought it was probably unnecessary, but she didn't want Susan to think it was going to be hard to sell.

Matt and Susan looked around politely, neither of them saying much. Occasionally, Kate saw them exchange glances, but she tried not to be too paranoid.

As the tour winded down, back in the small kitchen, Kate turned to face them. It felt like facing a firing squad. Looking at Susan, she said, "Well?"

Susan looked at Matt, then back at Kate. Kate started to feel nervous again. She worried Susan hated the place and thought it was too hideous to sell. She dug her fingernails into the palms of her clenched fists in anticipation of bad news.

"Are you sure you want to sell this place, Kate?" Susan asked.

"Is it that bad?"

"Bad? It's freaking adorable! I have at least three clients who've been looking for a place just like this one. Are you sure you're ready to give it up? Because it's sure to sell fast!"

Kate exhaled. "Thank God," she muttered, relieved all her hard work had paid off. Despite the fact it was cleaned out, she still saw the little cottage as a dumping ground for Mother's odd ball collections. She was happy Susan had deemed it suitable for sale—in fact, better than suitable.

"This place really is nice, Kate," said Matt. "With all your history here, are you really sure you want to let it go?"

Kate relaxed her hands. "More than ready. This was

my mom's cottage and I need to find a place I can make my own."

"Well, let's go find your new house," said Susan. "Let me put this junk away in my car and I'll meet you guys outside." She gathered up her papers, snapped her laptop shut and deftly slid it into its case.

She hurried outside to give them a few moments alone winking at Matt as she passed him. With one swift movement, she was out the door.

After Susan left, and they were finally alone, Matt asked again, "Are you really sure about this, Kate? Susan can be pretty persuasive. I don't want her talking you out of this place if you decide you want to keep it."

"No. I'm sure. I'm ready for a fresh start. New place, new guy, new everything." She looked down at her shoes, blushing.

"I hope that 'new guy' is me," he said lifting her chin with his finger.

"Maybe."

"Good enough," he said. He leaned down and gently kissed the tip of her nose.

Kate was surprised he was being so bold. *Was he was comfortable because he had the added support from Susan outside the door?* She dismissed her worry and allowed herself to enjoy the sweet moment.

***

Susan's car door slamming home interrupted their tender exchange. "Sorry guys," she yelled into the open doorway. She flashed an apologetic smile.

"S'ok." Matt grinned. He took a step back from Kate and went out the front door. Kate followed behind.

"Do you guys want to jump into my 'mom' van and head to the first place? I can let you kids snuggle in the backseat if you want," said Susan.

"I'll let Kate have shotgun," said Matt. "This is her house hunt after all."

"Thanks, Matt," said Kate. She walked to the van and opened the passenger side door.

"Hop in the back, Matty," said Susan. She slid the back door open behind Kate's seat.

"Yes, Mommy." He passed Susan and ducked into the backseat. Kate couldn't be certain, but it looked like Susan gave his butt a quick swat as he entered the car. She turned to see if he appeared embarrassed or guilty from the goose, but he was busy buckling his seatbelt. He didn't seem too phased so she tried to put it out of her mind. She wanted to like Susan and Susan to like her. She decided to let it pass for now—they were old friends, after all. *But,* she thought, squinting at Susan as she rounded the van, *if it happens again, old 'Suzie-Q' and I will need to talk.*

Susan slid into the driver's seat. "I've got a few places for you to see today. At least one of them will suit you perfectly."

Matt

They climbed wearily into the van after leaving the last of the five homes on Susan's list. Susan was having a hard time hiding her disappointment in Kate's pickiness. By the last house, Matt could almost hear Susan's eyes rolling in frustration when Kate inspected it for imperfections. He hated for her to be disappointed but knew, his friend or not, Kate wouldn't want to compromise on an important and expensive purchase.

Susan started the van. "Well, I'm out of places for today. Well, except for…"

"Except what?" asked Matt. He leaned forward between the two front seats eagerly, like a kid on a road trip, trying to get a better view of a landmark.

"Well, there is one more that I can show you, but I'm sure you'll just hate it," said Susan. She gave them a defeated shrug.

"Why would you assume that?" asked Kate. Matt heard the defensiveness in her voice.

"Well, it's not as nice as the places we've already been to and you didn't seem too hot for those." Susan grimaced.

"I didn't hate them. They just didn't speak to me," Kate said.

"Well, this place has been abandoned for a while so it's a little more run down than you may want. It would probably be a waste of time," said Susan.

Matt could tell, even from that back seat that Kate was peeved. She didn't like to be dismissed. It made her stubborn side come out. "Let's go anyway. Unless you have somewhere else you need to be?" said Kate, unable to mask her annoyance.

"C'mon Susan," said Matt. "Let's give this place a try." He patted her on the shoulder.

"Okay, but don't say I didn't warn you."

"I'll keep an open mind. I promise." said Kate, holding her fingers up like a Girl Scout giving her pledge. Matt could tell she was trying to smooth things over. He hoped it worked. He knew she liked Susan and probably didn't want to risk pissing off one of his oldest and dearest friends.

"Okay. It's a bit of a drive. It's on the outskirts of Waterville. You might have a little jaunt to the hospital every day, if you bought it, that is," said Susan.

"That's okay with me," said Kate. From their earlier discussions on the subject, Matt knew she didn't care how far it was from the hospital. She actually preferred being away from town. That was how she grew up, all woods as far as the eye could see. None of the house upon house, typical neighborhood-thing Susan had been showing her.

"There is also a little, um, history that goes along with the house. Hence the abandonment issue," said Susan. She gulped loudly, doing a spot-on Shaggy imitation from a Scooby Doo cartoon.

"What is it?" said Matt, excitement in his voice, an intrigued twinkle in his eyes.

Susan hesitated for a moment. "There have been a few

deaths on the property, that's all," she said. A bead of sweat formed above her perfectly sculpted eyebrows.

"What kind of deaths? Murders?" Matt asked in a teasing, sinister tone.

"Not exactly," Susan said.

"What does that mean?" said Kate.

"There were a few suicides on the property. The last owner shot himself in the woods and I think someone else might have killed themselves or died under mysterious circumstances inside the house. But that first one was a *really* long time ago. The house was renovated by the last owners so I think they got out most of the bad juju. If you believe in that sort of thing, anyway," Susan said.

Matt was amused at how Susan was trying to make it sound like no big deal. "Bad juju?" he teased. He grinned and made a scary face at Susan.

Giving him the stink-eye in the rearview mirror, Susan said, "Shut up, Matty. You're just like my older, *dumb* brother."

"So, is that why it was abandoned? Just because of the deaths?" said Kate, ignoring their childish banter.

"Isn't that enough?" said Susan.

"Well, I could see how it might turn off some people. I don't think it would bother me that much. I work in a place where people die all the time. I guess I'm just used to it."

"Whatever floats your boat," said Susan with a shrug.

"Have you shown it to many people?" said Kate.

"No. Most can't get past the history. If you really like it, I bet we could get you a fantastic deal. It's owned by the bank since the last owner didn't have any family to leave it to. I'm sure they're dying to unload it."

"Nice choice of words, Susie-Q," said Matt from the backseat.

Susan shot him a dirty look in the rearview mirror. Matt made sure she could see his toothy smile, proud of himself for being a wise ass. "Keep it up, Matty and I'll drop you off right here."

"Sorry, Mommy," he said sarcastically.

Susan steered her minivan onto a narrow dirt driveway, riddled with deep puddles. They bounced on the shocks of the van. "Sorry about the terrain, guys," she said and braced for another impact.

"It reminds me of a ride at the fair," said Matt, the bouncing making him queasy. He hadn't been on a carnival ride since high school, and that ended with him barfing up a soft-serve ice cream and a giant pretzel. *And man*, he remembered, *that pretzel had hurt coming back up*. He cringed and held his stomach. He'd hate to puke in front of Kate. A nurse could probably handle it, but after his date ditched him at the fair, he'd always been nervous to be sick around anyone.

"Here we go," said Susan. She steered the van into a wide gravel-filled clearing surrounded by towering pines. The enormous trees had hidden the house from the road and blocked most of the sun.

The house was as run down as Susan had promised. The roof was covered in a thick blanket of mint-green moss. The wide farmer's porch tilted on one end, as if the supports had rotted underneath. The siding, once white clapboard shingles, was stained gray. Large chunks of it were missing, exposing dirty pink insulation. Despite the obvious flaws, Matt could see that Kate seemed pleasantly surprised.

The lingering silence was finally broken by Susan. "I warned you," she said.

"Can we get out and look around?" Kate said, breathless and clearly excited.

Susan hesitated and glanced at Matt. He gave her a shrug.

"Sure, if that's what you want to do." She pushed a button on her door's elaborate control panel to unlock the doors.

Matt opened his door and stood for a moment behind Kate, taking in the entire lot. History or no history, the house was genuinely charming. It glowed peacefully in the small amount of sunlight that filtered through the swaying pine trees. He was no architecture buff, but the front porch appeared to be made of intricately hand carved supports. Sure it had peeling paint and rotted boards, but he could imagine it gussied up. He knew Kate was a sucker for a farmer's porch and this one wrapped around the front and both sides of the quaint, two-story home. *Was it was a Cape-style?* He wasn't sure. At this point, the style of the home didn't matter. He could tell she wanted to get inside.

"Let's go in?" she said, not looking back to see if the others were out of the van yet.

"Go ahead," said Susan, "the door isn't locked."

Matt hurried to catch up to Kate. "Are you sure about this?" He looked at the cobwebs hanging over the front door. It looked like a money pit. As they stood at the door, he noticed it was eerily quiet. Maybe the sound of the bouncing van had scared away the wildlife, but he couldn't hear even a single bird tweeting in the forest beyond the house.

Matt turned and saw Susan still standing by the van. "Are you coming in?" He hoped Susan would stay outside. Observing Kate's slumped shoulders and occasional eye rolls at the other houses, he sensed she was tired of the meaningless features she pointed out while at the other properties. Kate didn't care about gas burning fireplaces or crown molding. She wanted a home, not a Home Depot showcase.

"Um, maybe you guys could start without me? I should check-in with the office. I'll catch up with you guys," said Susan.

"Okay," said Kate, obviously happy to have Matt and the house to herself.

Matt hesitated for a moment, and then reached for the doorknob. It was filthy. *How could so much dirt end up on one little handle?* As he reached for the knob, Kate grabbed his arm. He flinched.

"Sorry, Matt. Do you mind if I open it?"

By the grimace etched on his face, he was certain she knew he'd rather not touch it. He was surprised she wasn't bothered by the crud that had accumulated on the abandoned house. Normally, she freaked at the smallest mess and used a ton of hand sanitizer; probably her training as a nurse played a factor in her need for cleanliness. *She must think this place seems safe,* he thought and stepped aside. "Not at all. After you."

She giggled and grabbed the doorknob, and a small puff of dust erupted when she turned the handle. The hinges squealed in protest when she pushed open the heavy wooden door. She walked into the dark room and saw three clusters of furniture covered in dusty graying sheets, a stone fireplace on the far wall, and a wood floor in desperate need of some polish and elbow grease.

Matt whistled quietly behind her. "This isn't so bad," he said. "Smells musty, though." Kate nodded in agreement.

"I wonder if all of this furniture comes with the place?" she asked as she stepped further into the room and snuck a peek under one of the grimy sheets. "It looks really nice, probably some antiques." She dropped the soiled cloth back onto the floor causing another dramatic puff of dust.

"It sure does," said Susan from the doorway. Her voice startled them. They hadn't expected her to come in so soon. "It's pretty dark in here. Maybe we should open some shades?"

Matt nodded in agreement and walked over to the window closest to him. He pulled the string on the old roller shade and let it fly. As soon as the string left his hand, a hurricane of dust and grime covered him from head to toe. He held his breath at the last second and managed to avoid sucking in any of the filthy cloud. His dark suit was covered with a thin blanket of dust and a few chunks of something unidentifiable. Maybe pieces of wood from the aged window frame. Maybe mold.

"That'll teach you to manhandle things, you doof," said Susan. She went to the other window, gently tugged the string and carefully guided the shade up.

"Thanks for the sympathy," he grumbled

"I'll pay to have your stupid suit cleaned," said Susan.

"You bet your skinny ass, you will," he said.

Kate was oblivious to their whole exchange. She was busy looking around the room: opening doors on an old built-in cabinet, lifting more musty sheets to check out the furniture and admiring the craftsmanship of the wooden window and door frames.

"What do you think, Kate?" said Susan.

"I don't know. Something about this place feels right, you know?"

"I'm sure it'll be great with some new paint and a good cleaning. I can recommend some people to help you. We've used them at the office," said Susan.

"Sure," said Kate, although Matt already knew she'd rather do the majority of the work herself. He'd convince her to have a cleaning company do an initial once over to get rid of the dust and broken items, but knew she'd want to paint and decorate it herself.

"I can help, too," said Matt, laughing, "Just not in a suit."

"Can we check out the plumbing and wiring in the basement?" said Kate. Her eyes gleamed with excitement.

"Why don't you two do that and I'll poke around some more up here. Is that okay?" said Susan.

"Absolutely," said Kate. Her face glowed with an adventurous smile. "Are you up for that, Matt?"

He pointed at the dust on his suit and poked his thumb in the air, indicating he was up for more. "Why the heck not? I'm already disgusting. How much worse could it get?"

Susan pointed out the door to the basement. Kate and Matt disappeared into the dark. Carefully, they picked their way down the creaky stairs.

In the basement, the darkness swallowed the wooden staircase. The electricity was turned off, and they squinted in the miniscule light that streamed in through the very small rectangular windows on either side of the stale basement. The sun was beginning to set and they were going to lose the remaining light quickly with the thick forest that surrounded the house.

Matt kicked something hard with his left shoe and picked up a new-looking flashlight. He clicked the black button. The light bulb cut sharply through the growing darkness.

Kate turned to see the source of the light. "That was smart of you to bring a flashlight," she said.

"I wish I could take credit for it, but it was already here on the floor. As if someone dropped it here."

"Well, however it got here, we need it," she said.

"Yeah, I'd hate to think what I'd get into if I was flailing around in the pitch black."

She laughed. It echoed hollowly off the stone walls. "Could you use your light to check out the pipes? And watch out for any loose wires. I'd hate to have you shocked into next week."

"Just don't leave me down here if I do."

"You got it," she agreed. She turned her attention toward the far wall. "I'm going to look over there," she pointed to the opposite side of the basement.

At the wall, she touched crumbling bricks with her

hands. They felt moist. The whole place needed a check for mold.

Matt watched Kate for a moment as she touched the bricks. The existence of the brick wall seemed peculiar to him. It didn't quite fit into the rest of the house. He turned and looked across the basement. The other three foundation walls were constructed out of stones. *Why would one wall be made of brick?* On the brick wall, he noticed a few spots where the mortar had disintegrated. He watched Kate as she tried to peek inside one of the cracks, but she didn't say if she could see anything.

He turned and moved the flashlight across another wall, searching for the pipes. From his side of the basement, Matt said, "What the hell is this?"

"A leak?"

"Come over here, Kate. You've got to see this."

"What is it?" She approached him from behind. He had the flashlight's beam trained on a protrusion on the wall.

"I don't know what the hell that thing is. But it sure is ugly, isn't it?"

She leaned in closer. "It looks like a figurine. No. It's a gargoyle," she said.

"Why the hell would they put that down here? Look at it. It's cemented between the stones. I'd guess it's been here since they built this place."

She reached out and touched the curious creature. "He's not ugly. He's kind of neat. Like a protector of the house. I like him," she said, a satisfied smile spreading across her face.

"You do? If you think that thing is attractive then I

guess I shouldn't worry if I look like a dog."

She laughed. "I don't think he's attractive. I'm intrigued by him. By his history. Like you said, 'Why the hell would they put him down here?'"

"I don't think I'd care to know. Are you ready to go?"

"Yeah. But, would you think I was a nut if I bought this place?" She looked at Matt, hope gleaming in her eyes.

He knew she'd buy it anyway, but was glad she wanted his opinion. He sighed. He'd hoped the disturbing gargoyle would send her in the other direction, but what did he know? He'd only known her for a few weeks. Maybe she was into all that Gothic stuff. *"Lady in the street, freak in the bed,"* he'd thought involuntarily, remembering a lyric from an old song. "Do you really think you could be happy here?"

"I think I can be," she said.

"Then I think you should go for it. And with the money you save on the mortgage, you can really fix this place up."

Kate launched herself into his arms, and embraced him with a tight hug. A cloud of dust puffed from his ruined suit. "Thank you, Matt! That means a lot to me," she said, clearly relieved by his support and the hope that he'd be a big part of her new life in this house.

Kate

Kate sat in the glass-walled office in the center of Susan's real estate agency, exposed, like a fish swimming in her see-through tank. Everyone seemed to gawk at her. A few even pointed at her, whispering. The office staff stared at her slack-jawed, obnoxiously curious. *Is my imagination running wild?* They probably wanted to catch a glimpse of the cuckoo bird who bought the ramshackle joint with a terrifying history.

She tried her best to ignore them, but she was having a hard time containing herself. She was a wired bundle of nerves, giddy with excitement. She squeezed Adam's key as it dangled from a chain around her neck. It seemed to soothe her growing nerves while she waited for Susan, trying to be patient. She couldn't wait to hold the keys to her new home and begin her new life in her new place—a fresh start.

After signing an inch-thick pile of papers, Susan presented her with the keys. The small silver keys felt light and cool. After she got up to leave, she felt she should take a bow. She heard high fives being smacked behind her as she exited the main door.

***

Matt had offered to meet Kate at the house so they could go through it together, but she had turned him down flat. She wanted her first time there to be just for her. She figured she'd have a few minutes to wander around before the power company showed up to reestablish a connection.

In the weeks leading up to her purchase, she'd had a multitude of professionals checking the house out top to bottom. The electrician had been pleasantly surprised by how well preserved the wires were despite the home being vacant for nearly five years. She had received glowing reports from just about everyone she'd hired to inspect the place, except for the plumber.

The plumber had spent exactly two minutes in the basement and then suddenly had some mysterious emergency he needed to attend to elsewhere. He promised her that everything looked okay at first glance and if she happened to have any problems after the water had been turned back on, he would send his best guy out to fix it, free of charge.

Well, a leak in the basement wouldn't make her renege on the home. Not much would have kept her from buying it. The feeling she got from it was unexplainable. She had tried many times to tell Matt why she loved this place, but she couldn't quite put her finger on it. The closest explanation she could come up with was that deep down, the dilapidated little house reminded her of her mother, unkempt and battered by the elements, but really a gem in disguise.

The sun shone brightly as she headed down the driveway. "My driveway," she said aloud.

She liked the way that sounded. She smiled when her car dipped into the rutted path. It would be something she'd need to fix soon so she didn't lose a wheel or bust an axle. She could fill holes with gravel until she could afford to pave it. It was a long driveway, secluded from the main road. She'd have to save up at least a year.

So what if it took ten years to fix it? She liked the rustic charm of her driveway. It would keep people out. She'd always hated people dropping in unexpectedly. A few people had stopped by Mother's cottage looking for her mother in recent weeks. She cringed at the memory of having to tell a few long lost friends that their buddy had died and had been dead for nearly six months.

She pulled to a stop in front of her new house. It looked brighter in the afternoon. It seemed happier than when she had been here the first time with Matt and Susan. She almost wished she had asked Matt to come so he could see she wasn't crazy, that this place had some redeeming qualities.

She pictured cute little window boxes filled with bright colored flowers. *Maybe purple? Yes! It's my favorite color.*

Now walking toward the front door, she was surprised again at how quiet it was here. She could barely hear any vehicle from the nearest street. The barrier of thick pine trees served well as a buffer to the outside world. *But no birds? Were the acidic pine trees keeping the birds away?* She wasn't an ornithologist, but there was something here they didn't like.

Her hand shook a bit when she put the gleaming key into the old, rusty lock. Ironic that such an old house would have such a shiny key. A house like this should have an ornate key like the one Adam had given her.

Reaching into her blouse, she pulled the key from the safety of her cleavage. She'd barely taken it off since she'd nearly lost it in her blankets a few weeks before. She'd been surprised at how much anxiety the missing key had caused her.

She admired the intricate etchings in the sunlight and held it up to her new door half expecting them to match— but no luck. Tucking her key back into her shirt, she took a deep breath of the pine scented air. Turning the new key in the lock, she heard a dry scraping sound as the lock popped and the door opened.

Immediately, she was hit with the overpowering scent of dust and abandonment, but knew it was temporary. She had the maid company scheduled for 9 a.m. tomorrow. She could manage to survive one night of discomfort. She'd snagged a few surgical masks from the hospital and would make do.

The room was nice and bright since they'd left the shades rolled up. She loved the way the light seemed to hit the room in all the right places. She stared at the beauti-ful, hand-hewn built-in cabinet, the stone fireplace and the unique, wide planked wood floors. She ran her hand along the sloped slab of rustic granite that served as the mantle to the fireplace. She picked up an old blue teapot with hand-painted white flowers and admired it before setting it down gently on the dust covered stone. The hidden details would all look great after being tended to properly with broom and polish.

She walked across the room and gently tugged one of the protective sheets off a small group of furniture anxious to see what she had bought along with the house.

The sheet peeled back slowly, reminding her of a

magician performing a dramatic trick. She hoped to find some magic under the grungy cloth. Surprisingly, there was almost no dust on the dark wood of the three small tables that emerged into the sunlight. Two were side tables for a sofa and the shortest one would be great as a coffee table.

The newly discovered tables were just as ornate as the trimmings of the home. Heavy and perfectly imperfect, she could tell that they were all very old and appeared to be hand-tooled rather than manufactured by a machine. She wished she had paid closer attention watching Antiques Roadshow on television. A Keno brother would come in handy right now for an appraisal.

She ran her hands along the edges of the coffee table, feeling the intricately carved designs with her bare fingers. She was amazed at the minute details of the tiny carved flowers, vines and leaves that stretched along every side of the table and down each leg. The foot of each leg was not forgotten; she could see they were carved into claws, like an old-fashioned bathtub, perfectly engraved right down to each pointed fingernail.

She was eager to see the other pieces hidden under their protective cloths. Just as she was about to pull the next one off, she heard a short rap on the front door. It made her jump and she scolded herself for being such a dork when she went to answer the door.

"Afternoon, Ma'am. I'm here to hook up the electricity for a..." he looked down at his clipboard, "A Miss Hart. Is that you?"

"Yup, that's me."

"Sign here, please." He pointed at the dotted line on the

bottom of the form marked with an oversized X.

"Sure. How long do you think it will take?"

"Hmmm, not too long, I don't think. It's basically throwing a switch or two," he answered, taking a good look around. "So, did you just inherit this place from a wacky aunt or something?" He smirked at her, as if proud to be so clever.

"No. I just bought it."

"You *bought* this place? Really?"

"Do you have a problem with that?"

The man snapped his head back toward her. He seemed to be a bit scared of her. "Uh, no. Sorry. I was just kidding. I'll just get to work." He retreated out the door to his idling truck.

"You do that," she called after him. She swung the door shut between them. "Wacky aunt?" She couldn't believe how rude he was. She turned back to face her new living room and got busy removing more sheets. "That guy doesn't have a clue," she mumbled. "Not a freaking clue."

***

The boor from the power company was in and out in a little over an hour. After he was gone, she walked from room to room flipping all the switches along the way. She was more grossed out by the level of dirt and cobwebs than she'd ever admit. She had brought a sleeping bag and intended to spend the night on the floor, but now that she'd seen the grime in the soft glow of light bulbs, plans changed.

She figured she could go back to Mother's cottage, but most of her stuff had been packed. A charming older couple had jumped on it before it had even been officially listed. Since they offered her a smidge above what she wanted to ask for it, she decided it was best to let them have it right away. It would save her a ton of stress in keeping it clean for showings and having to make herself scarce as strangers wandered through her home, touching her things with germy hands.

After seeing her new place in the light, the germ phobic part of her was screaming out again. She had seen a number of large, hairy spiders dangling from intricate webs and dust bunnies as big as her fist in nearly every corner. She would camp in her car. Since the cleaning ladies were due to arrive first thing in the morning, she'd rather stay on the property.

She was a little disappointed with herself for chickening out and spending her first night in her car. But no one would have to know that detail. If Matt asked her how it went, she could just say 'fine' and leave it at that. She didn't think he'd pry. Thankfully, with her, he was pretty laid back.

They had been on quite a few dates in the last few weeks and Kate was beginning to really like him. Maybe even borderline love him. She was trying to keep herself from getting too excited. She'd been let down a few times in the past after getting too jazzed about a guy early on in the relationship and she didn't want to be hurt again.

He seemed to feel the same way about her, too. He'd told her on their last date about his fiancée who'd left him for a woman. His cheeks had become flushed with embarrassment when he told her how he caught them doing nasty things to each other on the couch when he came home early one day from work. He'd been blindsided.

Kate was sure his hesitation in the intimacy department directly related to how hurt he had been from the cheating ho-bag. Sure, they had done some kissing and touching, but he always pulled away when things started to move horizontal.

When she got her new place cleaned up and he got more comfortable here, she hoped things would change. She wished he were here now. Maybe then she'd be able to stick it out inside the house if he were here to protect her from the crawling spiders and humongous dust bunnies.

Kate spent the rest of the afternoon and evening meticulously mapping out where she'd put every piece of furniture after the place had been scrubbed. She wanted no question as to where each chair, table, and lamp needed to be placed when she brought her stuff over tomorrow or the next day.

She had been so busy that, when she rolled up the shade in the kitchen, she saw it was pitch black outside. She was mesmerized by it. She had never seen woods that dark. The tall pines barely allowed a hint of moonlight to shine through to the ground.

Why, it's 9:30 p.m. already! The day had buzzed by in a blur of organization. She realized she'd better get to her car and get some sleep.

She walked across the small kitchen and reached for her car keys she'd had left in one clean spot she'd made on the dusty countertop.

Kate looked down at the countertop in disbelief: The

clean spot was empty! *Did I move my keys?* She remembered going to her car for a granola bar for dinner a few hours ago, but dammit, she'd set the keys back down in the clean circle.

She looked under the small ledge of countertop and scanned the floor. She kicked aside a good sized dust ball, assuming she'd hear the sound of jangling keys as her foot scraped across the floor. But nothing. Nothing.

She straightened and stared at the clean spot again. It mocked her with its glaring emptiness.

She decided to retrace her steps from the moment she'd believed she left her keys until now. She'd been in her bedroom for probably an hour. Maybe, out of habit, she'd had taken the keys and left them up there. She took the steep stairs two at a time. She flipped on the light hoping to see her keys. On the side table? Lying on the musty mattress? Nothing. Despite the sinking feeling in her stomach, she kneeled and looked under the bed. They could have fallen under it while she was making plans in her notebook.

Nothing.

She never lost things. In the middle of the room now, she patted down the pockets of her jeans. Empty.

Kate went back down the stairs, shaking her head for being a forgetful fool.

Wait! Mother had always been one to leave keys jammed into the front lock. Many times she'd seen her keys hanging sadly, forgotten in the key hole. It made sense: she'd been excited, unlocked the door, pulled it open, and went inside. She hoped she wasn't becoming like Mother. She ran to the front door and yanked it open.

Now outside, she looked at the doorknob. Zippo. It was empty.

Back inside, Kate scowled at the room. She had no idea where to look next. She hadn't been in the basement today and she couldn't have dropped them outside because she would've needed them to open the door. She paced back and forth in the living room, racking her brain for ideas. The keys had to have fallen somewhere, and the thick dust cushioned their landing enough so she didn't hear a sound. She probably wouldn't have heard them even if she had kicked them.

She went into the kitchen and stopped mid-step, frozen. Right there, lying on the counter, in that freshly cleaned spot, were her keys. She couldn't believe it. She gulped and rubbed her eyes as if starring in a Saturday morning cartoon.

Leaning toward the counter, she stared at her keys, confused. Bending her head down she inspected the countertop for any signs of them being moved; a slide mark in the dust or footprints left behind by a stealthy mouse. There wasn't anything out of the ordinary. Just her plain old jumble of keys. In the clean spot.

Hesitantly, Kate picked up her keys. They were cold to the touch, colder than she would expect them to feel on such a warm night. She held the weight of them in her palm, bouncing her hand up and down as if doing a mental calculation.

A faint sound echoed from the basement. It could have been a machine kicking on, but it was enough to get her heart racing even more.

It was time to call it a night. She hurried from the kitchen, not bothering to turn off the lights. She sailed through the living room and out the front door, shutting the door firmly behind her. She locked it with a loud click using her newly found keys.

She hesitated for a moment on the front porch and strained her ears toward the eerie silence of the woods. She couldn't get over how quiet it was out here—not even the rustling of a chipmunk or squirrel could be heard in the underbrush, and no bird called to its friends. Kate hurried down the steps and beeped her car locks open, preparing them so she could open the door as soon as she was next to it.

In five giant steps she pulled open the door. She looked back at her house. It looked alive again as light blazed from the windows with open shades. She longed for the comfort of her car, of something familiar in such a strange place.

The key thing had freaked her out. *Good grief, am I losing my mind or something worse?* Mother had always been forgetful and before her stroke, Kate had worried she'd succumb to dementia or Alzheimer's. *Do I now face the same fate?*

She tried to shake off the waves of dread. Laying in the backseat of her car, she made herself comfortable. She pulled the sleeping bag over her shivering body. *Look*, she told herself, *it was just the newness that freaked you out.* She'd never been one to embrace change. She promised herself she would try better tomorrow. There was always tomorrow. Finally, she fell asleep.

***

Kate was dreaming. She was deep in the dark woods, wandering aimlessly, barefoot. This surprised her; she wasn't one to go traipsing in the woods without shoes, not even in a dream.

A strange fog rolled into the woods, surrounding her. Her heart raced. *Was she being chased? Was she lost?* The universal feeling was fear. Suddenly, she heard a faint tapping in the distance, like a woodpecker's incessant drumming, or maybe tree branches hitting each other in the swirling mist.

She stood motionless in the thickening fog, her heart racing at an alarming rate. The tapping became louder, sharper. She spun around, confused by the fog. *Which way is left and which way is right?* She was about to scream for help when a voice called her name.

Kate licked her dry lips and leaned forward, craning her neck toward the voice. "Mumma?" she yelled into the fog. There was no response. The tapping sound became louder still, now a frantic rapping. She covered her ears with her hands to drown out the noise, shook her head back and forth, and wished the sound away. She wasn't ready. *Ready for what?* She didn't know.

A loud voice screamed at her through the fog. "Miss Hart. Are you Miss Hart?" The voice was concerned.

Kate stirred in the backseat of her car. The fog from her dream vanished. She straightened her body and was startled by a small, dark haired woman peering at her curiously through the steamy glass. She'd been knocking on the window by Kate's feet, trying to wake her.

The woman wore a yellow 'Happy Maids' shirt. Kate couldn't believe she hadn't heard the woman's car bouncing up the pitted driveway.

Kate held a hand up to the woman to show she'd heard her and she could stop knocking. The woman smiled and waved. She took a few baby steps away from the window. Kate held up her index finger to let her know she'd be out in a minute. The woman nodded and stepped further back from the window to give Kate privacy as she pulled herself together.

Kate pulled on her jeans. She'd slipped them off in the middle of the night. She'd gotten hot in the car, but didn't want to open a window and risk a mosquito invasion. She stepped out of her door on the opposite side of the cheerful woman, buttoned her jeans, and slipped on her sneakers.

After smoothing her hair and straightening her shirt, Kate walked around her car and approached the woman with an outstretched hand. "Sorry about that. It was too dirty to sleep inside. You'll see what I mean when you get in there." She hoped to divert the woman's speculation, if she even had any.

"I know, we saw the door open when we arrived and went in already. I already have two girls working upstairs. I hope that is okay with you?" She nodded toward the front door. It was wide open.

"That's odd," said Kate. She distinctly remembered locking the door last night. She remembered the click of the lock when she turned the key. She had even given it one last turn to ensure the lock took before she'd bolted to her car.

"I can have them come out, if you want," said the woman. A look of confusion spread across her round face.

"Oh no," Kate said, "They're fine. I thought I'd locked that up last night. Guess not." She shrugged at the woman.

"Okay, well, I'm Gloria. I'm the team leader. You can give any instructions to me and I can pass them along to the girls. Unless you speak Spanish?"

"It's nice to meet you, Gloria." Kate tried to shake off the cobwebs of sleep still nestled in her brain. She was confused. *Am I starting to lose it? Was the incident with my keys last night real? Now the opened door? No*, Kate told herself. *It's stress. Stress could make anyone do stupid things.* "And, no, I don't speak Spanish."

"Well, shall we go in and get busy?" Gloria had enough enthusiasm for both of them.

Kate smiled at the petite woman. She envied her energy. It was barely 9 a.m. and here she was, raring to go. Kate longed for a cup of coffee, but her coffee maker was buried in a box somewhere at Mother's cottage. She kicked herself for not planning that one better. She started to long for the days when the moving and cleaning would be done and she could settle back into her usual routine of sameness. She thrived on normal. What others called a rut, she considered perfection. "Let's get to it," Kate said. Gloria took the lead into the house.

"It's not so bad," said Gloria. A hint of sympathy hid behind her smiling eyes. "I bet we could be done by lunch if we really moved our butts."

"That would be great." Kate wanted to get done early so she could bring the rented moving truck over from

Mother's cottage and begin to unload her possessions. After he got out of work, Matt was due to come over, and she'd love to have some things put away before he arrived. She sighed at the long to-do list that started to run through her tired mind.

"Don't worry, honey, we'll get there." Gloria gave Kate a motherly pat on her drooping shoulder.

"Thanks Gloria. I hope it ends up as great as I picture it in my head."

"Are you kidding? My girls could make the Statue of Liberty shine."

"I sure hope so." Kate looked wistfully around at the dusty living room.

"Do you have any special instructions, Miss Hart? Or should I just tell the girls to get to it?"

"Just get rid of all the dust, cobwebs and anything else that doesn't belong. Save the floors for last," said Kate.

"Good enough. I'll go tell Cecelia and Margarita. We'll probably work from top to bottom, if that is okay with you?"

"That's perfect. I'll be down here removing shades if you have any questions for me."

Gloria nodded and bounded up the narrow staircase to give instructions to her co-workers. Kate heard her speaking to them rapidly in Spanish, her foreign words spraying out like a barrage of bullets. Kate didn't know too many Spanish words, but she was sure they'd do a wonderful job. She could barely wait to smell the fresh scent of the powerful cleansers they'd use.

***

A few hours into cleaning, Kate had removed all of the dusty, mildewed shades from the downstairs windows. The house was remote so the added privacy wasn't necessary, plus they were disgusting. She couldn't wait to be rid of them. Matt would be glad to see them gone, too. It cost him a bundle to get his suit cleaned. He was still after Susan to pay the bill, but she had skillfully avoided his calls so far.

Kate stood in the bright living room and breathed deeply. Although the ladies hadn't made it to this room yet, the sharp scent of chemicals floated in the air. It reminded her of the hospital. She loved that hospital smell, so clean and sterile.

This place needs a good sanitizing, she thought.

Gloria bounded down the stairs with one of the Spanish speaking women who'd been working diligently in the upstairs bedrooms. They had been jibber jabbing in Spanish on the way down and stopped as they approached Kate.

"Miss Hart, there is a problem in the upstairs bathroom," said Gloria. She glanced at the other cleaning woman.

"What is it, Gloria?" Kate assumed it was a bug or mouse or some other wayward creature that needed to be removed.

"Miss Cecelia here says there is no water coming from the sink. She'll need some water to clean the bathroom and refill her mop bucket." Cecelia nodded.

"Oh, right. The plumber turned it off when he was checking the pipes. I can go down to the basement and start it back up for you," said Kate.

"No, no, we can do it," said Gloria. She nodded at Cecelia who marched over to the basement door, pulled it open, and squinted into the darkness. After visually confirming the door led to the basement, she disappeared into the black void. Her thick-soled shoes barely made a sound on the narrow wood steps.

"How's it going up there?" said Kate.

"Wonderful! You should come up and take a look. After the bathroom is done, we'll be ready to move downstairs." Gloria beamed at Kate.

"Really? You guys are quick."

"Thank you. We try to be efficient and quick," she said. She pointed to the motto printed on her t-shirt.

"Right." Kate nodded, amused.

Cecelia stumbled through the basement door. Hair disheveled, her eyes were wide with fear and her body shook uncontrollably.

Gloria turned toward Cecelia. Her cheerful face dropped at Cecelia's obvious distress and panic. "What happened, Niña?"

Cecelia fell into Gloria's outstretched arms and began to speak excitedly in Spanish. She wavered between hysteria and tears. Kate had no idea what she was saying, but it sounded bad. She could make out a few words. Gloria smoothed her hair and tried to calm her. Cecelia repeated, "muertos, fantasma, y Diablo."

Kate listened intently as Cecelia repeatedly moaned the foreign words to her boss. Although Kate had never taken Spanish in high school, she knew from nursing school that muertos meant dead or death. Diablo might mean devil.

She wasn't one hundred percent sure on the other word, but would ask Gloria after Cecelia was comforted.

Gloria pulled Cecelia close to her chest and patted her back, trying to get her to relax. "Do you mind if I take her outside for a moment?"

"Sure. No problem." *What could have scared Cecelia so badly? There wasn't much to see in the basement except for... the gargoyle!* Kate slapped her head as Gloria and Cecelia walked toward the front door. Gloria used all her strength to hold Cecelia upright and assist her out of the house. Cecelia's knees had officially turned to Jell-O. Kate watched them hobble down the porch steps.

Should I go outside to explain to Gloria about the stupid gargoyle statue built into the wall in the basement? Should I apologize for not remembering it was down there? Even with the power on, Kate was sure the little guy could freak anyone out, especially someone who was probably extremely religious and might read negativity into such an ugly and unexpected totem.

Kate heard their voices in the driveway. They'd neglected to shut the front door in their haste to exit so it was possible to overhear. So far, Gloria wasn't having much luck calming Cecelia. She seemed to become more agitated as Gloria spoke to her softly in her native tongue.

A car door opened and closed. Kate took a step away from the front door so she wouldn't get caught eavesdropping on their private conversation. Gloria returned to the living room alone.

"Um. Cecelia will not be coming back in today," said Gloria.

"What happened to her? Was it the statue?" Kate was genuinely concerned about the poor woman.

"Statue? No. She didn't say anything about a statue. She thought she saw something, but she is a little loco. You know what I mean?" Gloria forced a smile and twirled the air by her ear with her finger.

"What did she see exactly?" said Kate, unable to hide her curiosity.

"Nothing to be worried about, Miss Hart," she said. "The good news is she did get the water turned back on before she saw, um, what she said she saw. We, Margarita and I, should finish up in no time." She patted Kate's arm and worked her way past her toward the narrow stairway leading to the second level.

"Wait! What did she see? I need to know. Please tell me exactly what she said," said Kate.

Gloria hesitated for a moment with her foot perched on the first step. "She'll be fine, just fine." She bustled up the stairs, leaving Kate alone in the living room.

***

A few hours later, Gloria and Margarita finished cleaning the entire house. It was passed three o'clock when they were ready to leave. Kate glanced out the window periodically at Cecelia to check on her well-being. She could see the poor woman sitting in the backseat of the station wagon, rocking back and forth with her knees pulled up to her chest and her arms wrapped tightly around them. She'd been doing the same soothing motion for hours. Although it was hard to tell through the glass, she still seemed to be mumbling to herself, repeating the same mantra over and over again. *Was she losing her mind? Praying? Maybe both?* Either way, she wouldn't be "just fine" anytime soon.

"We are finished, Miss Hart," said Gloria. Finally, she seemed tired after her long day of cleaning.

"You did a beautiful job, really," said Kate. She looked at the gleaming floors, dust-free furniture and spotless walls.

"Thank you." An exhausted smile spread across her face. "Good luck to you. I wish you much happiness in your new home." She glanced sideways at Margarita who nodded once.

Kate hadn't missed their exchange. Gloria's raised eyebrows told Kate she'd obviously filled Margarita in on what Cecelia saw in the basement.

"Adios, Miss," said Margarita. "Buena suerte y que Dios los bendiga," she added and walked out the front door.

Kate nodded and smiled as she walked by. "What did that mean?" she said to Gloria after Margarita shut the door, leaving them alone.

"She said, 'Good luck and God bless.'"

"Oh. How nice," said Kate.

"Call us again if you need help keeping up with cobwebs."

"I'll do that. Thanks, Gloria." Kate opened the door for her.

Gloria hurried down the front steps. Kate remembered she'd forgotten to ask the Spanish word Cecelia had been repeating earlier.

"Hey! Gloria!"

Gloria stopped and defensively shrugged her shoulders as if expecting to be hit. She turned slowly to face Kate. "Yes, Miss Hart?" Her voice was hesitant.

"When Cecelia was upset she kept saying 'fantasma.' What does that mean?"

Gloria pursed her lips and shook her head. She took a few backward steps toward her station wagon. Her hand fell on the handle behind her and she yanked opened the front door and said, "'Ghost,' Miss Hart. She said 'ghost.'"

Gloria slid into the driver's seat, put the yellow station wagon in gear, and sped out of the driveway.

"Crap," Kate muttered toward the silent woods. "Crap, crap, crap." She turned on her heel and went back inside her freshly cleaned house.

Matt

Matt stopped by Kate's new house every few days. She hadn't convinced him to spend the night yet, and he could tell she was starting to take it personally.

Every time he went to Kate's he felt antsy and uncomfortable. Kate said he reminded her of Daisy, the abused Scottish terrier her mother had taken in from the local animal shelter when Kate was a child. The poor dog always shook and seemed to expect trouble around every corner. Matt acted the same way; peering suspiciously around doors and down hallways almost as if he expected to be assaulted by someone, something. Although he couldn't articulate exactly what it was, he sensed it wasn't good.

Kate had told him about the mystery with her car keys—how they'd disappeared and then magically reappeared in the clean spot, without a trace of evidence pointing to an answer for what happened. His face turned ashen and he got lightheaded while she related the story. Clearly, she was fascinated by it all. Matt was not.

Now, nearing the house, Matt imagined Kate pacing nervously in the front room. Over the phone, she'd indicated that tonight was going to be *the* night. She'd ask him to stay over. If he said no this time, it might be the end of their relationship. She said she didn't want to play games and he needed to get over what was bothering him if he expected to date her.

Matt's tires crunched to a stop on the gravel out front. His stomach twisted into a nervous knot. He hated confrontations, especially when it might end with getting hurt or hurting someone else. And he dreaded hurting Kate. He knew she had really deep feelings for him and she'd be so hurt if they ended things now. But, he also knew that she wasn't planning on moving to a different house anytime soon. He'd need to accept her *and* her house into his life if he expected their relationship to move forward.

As he approached the front door, Kate, impatient, whipped it open before he had a chance to rap on it. She caught him with his hand raised in the air in preparation to knock. He stumbled back, startled by the door's quick movement. Instantly, he wished she'd waited the two seconds to allow him to knock on the stupid door. All he needed was to be an anxious mess before he even walked in the house.

"Sorry, Matt. I didn't mean to startle you. I just couldn't wait to see you," she said, a hint of impatience in her smile.

"It's okay." He knew his worried expression belied his statement and although he tried to hide it, Matt knew Kate sensed he was getting worked up already. She'd mentioned on his last visit that it was strange to see him like this. When they were in a restaurant, he'd be his fine, charming, confident self. Here, in her house, he turned into a bowl of cologne scented Jell-O.

Kate grabbed his sweaty hand and dragged him into the living room pulling against the resistance in his body.

If life were a cartoon, Matt imagined, he'd be leaving

drag marks on the floor from digging in his heels. Her annoyance at his uneasiness erupted in a flash of angry heat in her face.

"Come on, you big baby," she said. She yanked on his hand again and sat him on the couch beside her.

"Baby, huh?" A boyish smile broke out across his handsome face. His heart skipped a beat when he squinted flirtatiously at her with his deep blue eyes.

"That's what I said."

He hated knowing their relationship might end. She made him honest-to-goodness weak in the knees. He wanted the physical side of their relationship to progress. Lately, he'd had a few dreams that made him want to be with her even more. He blushed as he allowed his mind to float to a particularly hot dream where they made love on a beautiful, white sand beach. He'd woken that morning covered in sweat. Desperately, he'd tried to fall back asleep, hoping the dream would continue. But, he was unable to return to the erotic fantasy. The rest of the day he was massively frustrated, mentally and sexually.

He knew a good looking gal like Kate could get any guy she wanted into the sack and knew it was amazingly frustrating for her that Matt had her wait so long. They'd been together for nearly six months now and he hadn't even put his hand up her shirt. Nor had he dared try. He knew why he was waiting, but he couldn't tell her—he didn't know how.

"What's with the red cheeks?" Her playful tone pulled him back from his racing thoughts.

"Are they?" He absently rested a hand against his left

cheek, feeling the heat throb under his fingertips.

"Penny for your thoughts?" she said, amused by his sudden change in temperament.

"I think my thoughts would cost a bit more than a penny." More heat flashed through his face and prickled on his chest and down his arms.

"Oh, really?" She scooted closer to him on the couch. She reached out and grabbed the hand he'd rested on his cheek. She kissed the top of it gently, barely brushing her lips across his flushed skin.

His whole body tingled from her tender kiss. He leaned toward her and kissed her mouth. He loved how soft her lips felt against his. He'd shaved, too. This was good. Usually he had enough scruff on his chin to grate cheese.

She kissed him back and set her hand on his thigh. He reached over and held the back of her head with a strong hand and pulled her closer, pushing his tongue into her mouth.

She kissed him back passionately and moved her hand up his thigh, toward his hip and pulled him close. For the first time, he didn't pull away. He was into the moment as much as she was.

Suddenly, he stopped kissing her and pulled his head back to catch his breath. She pushed him down on the couch and climbed on top, straddling him, and pressed her hips into his.

Matt pulled her torso down on top of his. He kissed her forcefully. Through his thin pants, he let her feel that he was aroused. Very aroused. He desperately wanted to be inside her. It'd been a long while since he'd had sex. He hoped tonight would be the first time with Kate.

She pulled away from his grip and lifted her shirt over her head. She grabbed his hands and put them on her breasts, over her bra. He pulled her back down by the satin cups and kissed her again, groping her breasts with eager hands. He reached around her back and fumbled with the hook on her bra.

Realizing he was having trouble with her clasp, she leaned up a little and reached behind her back to undo the tiny eyehooks. She playfully shrugged her shoulders out of the white straps, holding the cups in place over her breasts. Matt smiled, enjoying the show.

He reached up and took one of her hands away. Then, he took her second hand away. Her bra fell on his chest with a plop. They both laughed. He picked up her bra and tossed it onto the floor.

He took in the full view of Kate's exposed breasts, inches from his blushing face. "Wow," he said.

"Thanks." She unbuttoned his shirt and bent down, laying her bare breast on his burning chest.

They kissed again. Matt rubbed her breasts and massaged her nipples between his fingers. She moaned with pleasure.

He pushed her up with his strong arms and kissed her breasts, licking her nipples with the tip of his hot tongue, enjoying the sounds she made when he sucked them.

"Do you ever take that thing off?" he asked and swatted the dangling key out of his face.

"What?" Enjoying his caresses so much, she was clearly oblivious, confused by the randomness of his question.

"Your necklace. Do you ever take it off? It's kind of in the way," he said and tugged gently on the chain that held the key Adam had given her.

"I hadn't really thought about it." She slid the chain out of his grip and held the cold key in her hand. "Is it bothering you?"

"A little bit," he said.

"Well, off it goes then," she said. She lifted the key and chain over her neck and set them on the small table next to the couch. "I don't want anything to interrupt all of your hard work." She leaned back toward him.

He cupped her breasts in his hands and smiled. He wiggled his eyebrows seductively. "Let's get back to it then," he said and leaned up to kiss her.

They kissed and fondled each other for a few more passion-filled minutes. Kate reached for the belt on his pants. He let her unbuckle it. Her firm breast swung slightly as she tugged on the belt, dropping it on the floor. It landed with a metallic thud. She reached for the button that held his fly shut and pushed it through the hole. When she started to unzip his pants, he saw the excitement of the moment grip her, taking her breath away. Oddly, he imagined she was a pirate digging for buried treasure.

Worried he'd insult her with an ill-timed smile, he looked out the window and focused on what he was allowing to happen.

Suddenly, he forcibly grabbed her hands, stopping her mid-unzip. "What the hell was that?" Fear filled his voice.

"Did I hurt you?" she said, obviously confused by his negative reaction to her seduction.

"No, it's not you. I just saw... someone. Outside that window," he said and pointed to the window that flanked the front door.

"What are you talking about?" she said, frustration echoing in her voice.

"I swear I just saw a face. A man's face. In that window." He lifted her from his lap and set her roughly on the couch. He stood and sprinted to the window to search for the mysterious stranger.

"This is a first for me," she mumbled and rolled her eyes at his backside. She reached down on the floor and grabbed her bra, fixing it over her exposed breasts.

Matt turned to her and knew she felt very silly. And angry. And, he knew she wouldn't believe a stupid story of a man in the window. She would think it was just a ploy to keep from having sex with her.

"Really, Kate," he insisted, willing her to believe him. "He was wearing a black suit and a black hat. An old fash-ioned-looking one." He squinted and looked from side to side out the window into the growing darkness.

Kate's entire body began to vibrate with anger and re-sentment. She bent over to pick her discarded shirt from the floor, snagging the fabric with her fingertips. She snatched it from the ground with a disapproving grunt. She stomped to the table next to the couch, picked up her key necklace and shoved it defiantly over her head, not bothering to tuck the swinging key into her shirt.

"Kate, I totally saw someone out there. Please don't be mad at me." He took a step toward her.

"Forget about it, Matt," she said. She bit her lip and

held a shaking hand up to keep him from approaching her. "I don't think this is working for me anymore."

"This what?" Shock spread across his handsome face. His forehead creased and then smoothed. He gasped. "Do you mean us?"

"I mean us," she said. She stared coldly into his warm blue eyes.

"Don't do this," he said. He turned his head toward the window, and tried to blink away tears that squeezed from the corners of his eyes. His lungs tightened making it hard to breathe.

"It's always the same with you." She softened her tone. "You don't seem comfortable with me and I can't accept that." She walked toward him, and looked into his eyes.

He turned away, hiding his face, feeling anger rise in his chest. Suddenly, he jerked his head up. "It's not you I'm uncomfortable with. It's *this* fucking place!" He swept his arm dramatically around the room.

Her face reddened and she grabbed the key that dangled on the outside of her shirt. She squeezed it in her sweaty palm. "This *fucking* place is my home and I'm not going anywhere." She clenched her teeth, clearly fighting a torrent of angry words that threatened to erupt.

"Well, I can't help that this place gives me the creeps, Kate." A well-timed shudder rippled through his muscular frame. "I mean the deaths, the missing keys, the gargoyle statue in the basement, *and* the completely silent woods. It freaks me out. Something is not right here."

"I said I'm not leaving." She stuck her chin out in defiance.

"Please come home with me," he begged. "I'll give you what you want—just not here." He walked toward her and grabbed her hands. They still clutched the key. He squeezed her hands and looked into her eyes. He could see her tears and was glad she had some, too. "Please, Kate. Please come home with me."

She shook her head from side to side. Between sobs she cried, "I can't Matt. I need to be here. I can't explain it. I *need* to stay."

He hung his head, released her hands and dropped his arms to his sides. He turned away from her and wiped his face on the sleeve of his shirt. He stooped by the couch, picked up his belt and held it in his hand. That was it then. Clearly, it was time for him to leave.

"Are you sure you won't change your mind?" he said as he walked to the front door and turned the knob. "I don't feel right leaving you here when there is a strange man skulking about."

She snorted. "Skulking about? At least *he's* not afraid of this place."

She was being rude and condescending, but he didn't care. He knew she was frustrated beyond belief. *How could this night end with me leaving with my tail between my legs while I blame it on something as benign as a house?* "It's not you; it's your house."

Kate stifled a cynical laugh that threatened to escape her pursed lips. "I'll be fine, Matt. Just go." She pointed toward the door with a shaking finger.

He paused, closed his mouth, and shook his head. He stepped onto the porch and started down the front steps, into the silent night. She slammed the door behind him. As the gravel crunched under his feet, he paused and looked back at the house, the stupid house that ruined his chances with her. He should have told her the truth. He wished he'd been brave enough to tell her everything. But, he needed more information to back up his suspicions. Only then would he try to win Kate back.

Kate

A few days after the blow up with Matt, Kate was close to devastated about her loss. She muddled through her work days, and tried to keep her mind off their conversation and how it went wrong so fast. *Why am I being inflexible about my new house? If I wanted to, I could sell it and make him happy. But, is the 'creepy' house bit just a line? An easy way to make his escape rather than tell it was* me *who repulsed him?* She wasn't sure. Besides, she was too stubborn to relent to his wishes.

She sat at the nurse's station reviewing her patient list, when a familiar voice pulled her from her distant thoughts.

"Kate, did you hear me?" said Marlene. She stood on the opposite side of the counter, impatiently tapping her heavy foot.

"What?"

"I *said* you have a phone call on line two. Been staying out too late with lover boy, have you?" She snorted.

"Something like that." Kate forced a smile. "Do you know who it is?"

"Who else would it be? It's Matt." She sneered, rolled her eyes, and started to stomp away. "Line two," she said gruffly and waddled down the hall, leaving Kate alone with the blinking telephone.

"Matt?" she said aloud. *Why the hell would he call me*

at work after what happened the other day? She stretched her arm across the cluttered desk and picked up the phone's receiver. She put it to her ear and pushed the flashing red light.

"This is Kate." She tried to make her voice sound official, as if she hadn't been informed who was waiting on the line. And Marlene could have been wrong. Marlene would like to think she knew Matt well enough to recognize his voice, but she could be mistaken. It could be a patient or another drug rep. She couldn't wait to find out if it was really him.

"Hi, Kate," said Matt. He sounded relieved, as if worried she might not bother to pick up the phone after their ugly fight.

"Matt? What do you want?" She tried to keep emotion out of her voice. Instantly, she wished she hadn't sounded so cold, but she was living on fumes and had a hard enough time being nice to patients, let alone the guy who'd dumped her over a house.

"I was wondering if I could see you. Maybe get some lunch today? I've got some stuff I need to tell you."

Kate thought about his request for a moment. Could she mentally take another fight? Had he come to his senses? Maybe he was going to man-up and decide her new house was okay or at least not the real reason he'd left. Finally, she said, "Okay, I guess so. Do you want to go to the diner?"

"That's great!" he said, clearly excited. "Can you do 12:30?"

"Sure, sounds good." She was about to hang up, but

heard him clear his throat as if he had something to add.

His voice wavered, "Um, Kate, I, I miss you."

"Yeah, I miss you, too, Matt," she whispered into the receiver. Her stomach flipped as his words washed over her.

"See you soon." He hung up quickly.

"Yup. See you soon," she said to the dead line and set the receiver in its cradle.

Checking her watch, she saw she had an hour to finish her morning rounds and get presentable for lunch with Matt. She hustled through her list, checked off the completed tasks and had just enough time to check her makeup in the bathroom mirror before leaving for the unexpected lunch date.

She grabbed her keys and purse from her cubby in the nurse's station. Marlene sat at the desk eating a huge salad. It was smothered in a white, creamy dressing—blue cheese, by the smell of it.

"Check me out, Kate. I'm on a diet." Clearly proud, she pointed at her monstrous salad with a dripping fork.

"Looks good, Marlene," Kate said, mentally calculating the calories in her co-worker's lunch—easily 900, maybe more. "By the way, I'm meeting Matt for lunch so I might be a bit late getting back. Can you cover for me?"

Marlene sighed. "Okay, but when I get all skinny and meet my boyfriend for a nooner, you'll have to cover for me. Okay?" She grinned at her, obviously pleased with her joke.

"You got it." Kate giggled and headed for the door, trying to imaging a skinny Marlene. That was almost as likely as moving out of her house. She headed out into the sunlight.

***

Matt was already at the diner when Kate arrived. She wished she'd had time to change her clothes before lunch. She was in her plain blue scrubs today while Matt wore a handsome black suit. Already, she was at a disadvantage. She pushed the silly thoughts out of her head and approached the table. Matt was looking down at his cell phone, nervously pushing buttons. He hadn't seen her come in yet.

She walked to the table in her cushioned nursing shoes and plunked down on the puffy bench, startling him. *Still skittish*, she thought and fought the urge to roll her eyes at him.

He fumbled to put his phone in his suit pocket and greeted her with a weak smile. "Sorry about that. You jumped me." A sheepish smile spread across his handsome face.

"I'm used to it." She smirked back at him.

"Yeah, I guess you are." He looked down at his hands. They were clenched tightly together on the table.

"So, why did you want to see me?" Her patience was already wearing thin and she wanted to get this whole thing over with. She could tell by his nerves that he wasn't here to beg for forgiveness.

"I need to tell you some things that I haven't been totally honest with you about." He looked nervous, sick.

"Great," she muttered. She leaned back on her seat, and steeled herself for his revelations.

"I hope it will explain a lot. I ordered you a drink and asked the waitress to leave us alone for a bit."

Kate looked at him squarely, her eyebrows raised. "Can we just get to the point, Matt? I'm getting tired of these games."

Surprise washed over his face, his brow furrowed, "I'm not trying to play games with you, Kate."

"Whatever." She crossed her arms across her chest.

"Well, I wanted to bring you here to talk a bit about my past so maybe you'll understand where I'm coming from. At least in regards to your house." He paused, obviously anticipating an angry outburst.

Kate fought every muscle in her body to keep from rolling her eyes. Despite her irritation, she'd give him a chance to explain. Maybe it would be helpful in her next relationship. Arms still crossed, she leaned in to listen.

"When I was growing up, my grandmother, Betty, was considered to be sort of, um, psychic. Although, she liked to be called a 'sensitive'." His words fell awkwardly off his tongue, clearly his nerves were getting the better of him.

Kate leaned in closer, intrigued. She hadn't expected this. She'd thought his story would be about his lesbian ex-fiancée or a bad childhood experience, not a psychic grandmother.

With her rapt attention, Matt continued, "Grandma Betty told my mother I was a sensitive, too. Of course, as a kid, when she called me a sensitive, I thought she meant I *was* sensitive. I was offended by it. Anyway, I didn't know what she meant until much later when I'd grown up and recognized I was having visions or visits or whatever you want to call it." He exhaled loudly, obviously relieved from his long-held secret.

"So... you're psychic?" She wasn't sure if she believed him.

He nodded. "I guess so. I prefer to call myself a sensitive like Grandma Betty. But psychic works, too."

"Please go on," she said. She unfolded her arms, reached across the table and grabbed one of his shaking hands. She patted the top of it to reassure him she'd try to understand whatever he told her, no matter how insane.

"Thanks, Kate." He looked at their coupled hands. Then, inhaling deeply, he glanced into her eyes and said, "So this is where you might get angry with me." He ripped his eyes from her steady stare and looked at their entwined hands again.

"I've been getting bad vibes from your house. I have from the very beginning. Susan's admission about the two deaths there sort of explained it away for me, but it didn't seem reason enough for the feelings I've been getting from the property. So, I went back to find out if there was more she'd left out. She hadn't been avoiding my calls about the dry cleaning bill, she just didn't want us to ask any questions about the house." Cautiously, he looked up again.

She stared at him wide-eyed, mouth agape. "So, what is it?" She almost didn't want to know the truth.

"Susan lied to us, Kate. She lied to *you*. There were not two deaths on the property. There were *seven*." Matt paused briefly to allow the staggering number to register in her overloaded brain. "And they were all suicides, Kate. Every person who's owned that house over the last century has killed themselves either in the house or on the grounds."

Kate was dumbfounded. She shook her head in disbelief. "Seven?" Her voice quivered.

"Seven."

"Fucking Susan," she moaned.

"I know," said Matt. He nodded and gave her trembling
hand a reassuring squeeze. He stayed quiet for a moment
allowing the horrifying news to sink in. After a few minutes, he wiped a tear from her cheek with his finger and
asked, "Kate?"

"What?" She sniffed.

"There's more."

"There's more?" Her shoulders sank. She looked small
in the oversized booth, like a scared child.

"The land that your house was built on has a Native
American connection, too." His eyes searched her tear-
streaked face for understanding.

She felt stupid, like her over-worked brain had melted
her intelligence away with each new secret. "Like Indians?"

"Yes, like Indians."

The blood drained from her face. "If you tell me my
house is built on an ancient Indian burial ground, I think I'll
vomit right here," she said and took a swig from the drink
Matt had ordered for her, wishing it was something much
stronger than iced tea.

"No, not a burial ground exactly."

Kate sighed. "Thank God for that." At least there was a
small glimmer of hope in the mess that was her life.

"Well, don't go thanking Him yet," he cautioned. "The
native tribes around here called your land the Devil's Chair.

That's all Susan would tell me, but I have an idea on where you could find out more information."

"Devil's Chair?" she repeated. "Great, just freaking great."

"There's a bit more, Kate. Do you think you can handle a bit more?"

"Lay it on me, Matt." She sniffed, shook her hand free of Matt's grip, and wiped her wet face with a paper napkin. "I want to hear everything." She mustered as much confidence as she could, and prepared for the next absurd detail he'd reveal.

"My Grandma Betty had a stroke a few months before she died. She was able to function physically, but her speech was really hard to understand. So, a few days before she died, she pestered my mother to have me visit. I came home from college and she made me write down a vision she'd had that was keeping her up at night. It was about me. From what I could understand, she said, "Beware of what the kind heart brings." He pulled a tattered sheet of paper from his suit pocket and laid it on the table between them, smoothing out years of wrinkles.

Kate picked the piece of paper up and studied it, holding it inches from her face. "What does this have to do with me or my house?"

"I think I misunderstood her. Her speech was so garbled at the time. I think she was trying to say, "Beware of what Kate Hart brings." He looked down at the table, clearly unable to look into her bewildered, tear-filled eyes.

"What?"

"I know. It's crazy. I'm sorry." He looked up briefly and

nervously ripped apart the edge of his napkin.

"So you're telling me your 'sensitive' grandmother warned you about me, like, ten years ago?"

"Yes."

Kate pushed back from the table and sat stick-straight in the booth. *Was she going into shock? Actual physical shock?*

"I'm sorry, Kate. I shouldn't have told you."

She shook her head. "No. I'm glad you did. I don't know what to do with all this, but I must admit I'm glad you told me." She forced a smile.

Matt exhaled and pushed the remains of his shredded napkin to the side of the table. "Susan gave me the name of an old Indian Chief who might be able to give us more information on the property. If you're interested, that is."

Her expression eager, she replied, "I'm more than interested."

Matt slid handwritten directions across the table toward her. "Chief Redbird. He's your guy."

She studied the information on the paper and nodded. "Chief Redbird, it is."

"Do you want me to go with you?"

"No thanks. I think I should start looking into some of this stuff for myself," she said without glancing up from the paper.

"Okay." His shoulders dropped, obviously feeling defeated and unneeded.

Kate looked up from the directions on the paper and saw she'd inadvertently hurt him. She reached across the table and patted his hand, "We'll figure this out, Matt." She gave him a kind, reassuring smile.

"I hope so, Kate. I hope so."

***

Kate's head reeled after leaving the diner. She barely knew where to begin with the truckload of unbelievable information Matt had dumped on her lap. She recapped the news in her head as she drove back to the hospital. Basically, her boyfriend was a psychic with ten year-old warnings about her from his dead Grandma. Her new house was haunted with at least seven ghosts of suicide victims and her property was located on or near the mysterious, Native American area called "Devil's Chair." No matter how she worded it, it sounded utterly loony, ridiculous.

"Shit on all of it," she said aloud. She entered the parking lot to the hospital, "I should just save myself some time and check into the psych ward right now," she mumbled, turning into the nurse's lot. She laughed out loud in her car, her voice echoed in the small space.

If I didn't laugh about it, I'd probably be on the ground in a sobbing heap, she thought as she pulled into her parking spot, readying herself for her return to work—to the *real* world.

Kate didn't know how she'd make it through the rest of her shift. If she could concentrate hard enough on her tasks and hurry through her afternoon rounds, then she might have some time to surf the internet for more information about her house. She might also have time to call this Redbird character and schedule a meeting with him. He'd probably think she was a loon, too. She mentally ticked off the things she hoped to accomplish before leaving for the day.

She was able to get through her rounds faster than anticipated since two of her patients had been discharged while she was away at lunch. She only had to deal with three others and do some research.

After bustling through her list of must-dos, she retreated to the nurse's station and logged into the hospital computer. She hoped to prove Matt's information wrong, but deep down, she knew he wouldn't lie. There had to be some basis for what he had told her.

Kate tapped her finger on the computer's mouse impatiently as she waited for the system to connect to the search engine. Resting her face in her hands, she watched the little blue circle grind away. She felt tired. Bone tired. All of the stuff Matt had laid on her at lunch made her feel heavy. She imagined this was probably how Marlene felt on a daily basis, carrying around all that extra weight. She vowed to eat a light dinner to balance out the cafeteria ice cream she'd inhaled to soothe herself after her eventful lunch date.

Finally, the search engine popped up and happily asked, "Where to?" She clicked her mouse in the empty white box, scrunched her fingers into tight fists, and then relaxed them on the keyboard. She typed "Devil's Chair" into the glaring box and inhaled deeply before hitting enter.

A list of matches compiled slowly on the screen. Some of them could be eliminated immediately. She scrolled down the list and found a website with good possibilities about eight options down. She clicked on the attached website and waited again.

The link brought her to an old newspaper article from the Waterville Daily. That was the name of the local newspaper when she was a child. They'd been bought out by a bigger franchise a few years ago, but must have kept the archives active for people to research. She was glad about that. This site looked like it could be just what needed.

The title of the archived article was: "Devil's Chair: Fact or Fiction?" She scanned the article for any tidbits that stuck out to her. She noticed the author had interviewed a Chief William Redbird, Sr. He must be the father of the man she was supposed to contact. Otherwise, he would be over one hundred years old by now. The article had been written in 1967.

She glanced up from the computer screen and saw Marlene and one of her cohorts walking toward the nurse's station. Kate quickly hit the print button. The old printer rumbled to life. She hurried to it and waited for it to spit out her pages, grabbing them off the printer just as Marlene and Nancy crossed the threshold into the nurse's station.

"How was lunch?" said Marlene with fake curiosity.

"Pretty... interesting," Kate said. She folded the article into a small square and slipped it into the front pocket of her scrubs.

"I bet." Marlene snorted and gave a knowing glance to Nancy who blushed and turned away from Kate, stifling a giggle with her hand.

Kate sensed she must've been the main topic of conversation at the nurse's lunch table today. She knew firsthand how much the ladies liked to gossip. She didn't have the time to mind. She'd let Marlene have her fun. She had bigger fish to fry, Indian Chiefs to call, the usual evening activities.

The article was already starting to burn a hole in her pocket. *Could she wait until the end of the day to read it? No.* Her best bet was to close herself into a stall in the ladies restroom and finish it before anyone noticed she was missing. Based on the length of the piece, it might take five minutes. Marlene was known to take twice as long in the can—more pipes to empty and more surface area to clean. She headed to the bathroom, stifling a giggle of her own.

"What's with the grin, Kate?" said Marlene when Kate stepped around her on her way into the hallway.

By Marlene's tone, Kate sensed she was looking for trouble. But, Kate knew when to walk away. The newer nurses would have to entertain her today. She turned the corner and retreated toward the ladies restroom. "Just happy, I guess."

The bathroom was empty. She chose the stall with only one neighbor and a wall on the other side. Why was she being so secretive? Anyone who happened upon her would have no idea what the article meant. She simply didn't want anyone to ask her any questions. She wasn't ready to talk yet, and if someone asked her about it, she risked launching into an emotional tirade on all the weirdness that was her life lately.

Kate put the lid down on the toilet and wiped it with a wad of fresh toilet paper. Of course she picked the grimiest place in the hospital to read her article. She should've thought it through and locked herself in a janitor's closet or an empty patient room. Already safely tucked away, she sucked it up and sat on the seat to find out what the article had concluded all those years ago.

She unfolded the article and smoothed the creased pages on her thigh. She licked her lips and began to read:

Devil's Chair: Fact or Fiction
By Malcolm Childs

Many of us have grown up hearing stories of Devil's Chair. I remember my grandfather spinning yarns about it when we were children. He would hold me and my cousins captivated by the fireplace on cold winter months, amusing us with terrifying stories of ghosts and Indians. As a child, I always believed every word that my grandfather had ever spoken. He was my hero. Now, as an adult, I am less of a believer of his wild stories, but decided I needed to find the truth, to console my childhood fears, and see how farfetched Grandpa Eddy's stories really were.

I started my search for the truth with a meeting with the much revered Chief of the Penobscot Indian tribe, Chief William Redbird, Sr. We met at his home, much more a log cabin than wigwam, to discuss the history of Devil's Chair and to sort through rumor and truth.

Chief Redbird was a very pleasant fellow. Aged in the face by weather and years of experience, he surprised me by being as normal as you and me. I childishly expected him to be wearing a feather headdress, lavishly beaded chest plate, and leather moccasins. That was how I pictured Indians in my mind when my grandfather regaled us with his stories.

*The Penobscot Indian tribesmen hold very strong be-
liefs on the history of Devil's Chair that date back to the
beginning of their written records which, although closely
guarded, are believed to be over 500 years old.*

*The myth of Devil's Chair started having some legs
among us white folks in Waterville back in the 1930s when
two male teenagers got lost in the woods while hunting for
squirrels. They recounted a fantastic story of being lured
in a trance-like state, deeper and deeper into the woods by
a red-eyed man. They claimed to be led through the trees
and underbrush to a stone structure near the river that had
been long hidden deep in the woods. It resembled a throne.
The boys claimed to have witnessed the Devil himself sitting on the throne, staring at them with his piercing red
eyes. They were able to pry themselves from his gaze only
when they heard the search party calling their names many
hours later. They turned toward the voices to signal their
position and when they turned back to face the red-eyed
man, he was gone. He had vanished into thin air as quickly
as he had originally appeared.*

*The Penobscot Indians, as told to me by Chief Redbird,
believed the red-eyed man the boys had claimed to see was
likely a Loks, which the Indians believe to be a wolverine
with a malevolent spirit—also known as an Indian Devil.
The other option offered by the Chief was that they could
have seen a wildcat that the Indians refer to as a Lucifee
and is sometimes confused with the Loks. According to
folklore, both are known to have brilliant red eyes and are
cunning creatures.*

The Penobscot Indian population has avoided the Devil's Chair area like the plague since their people were massacred there many years ago by the military that wanted to confiscate their land. The stone structure the boys had claimed to witness was probably the stone structure the Indians had built to honor their fallen tribesmen. Weather and the elements had possibly changed the architecture of the temple, making it appear like a chair to their inexperienced eyes.

After the report from the two boys, the police searched the area for a man in the woods, but were unable to find any evidence of his presence. Nor were they able to confirm the existence of the structure the boys claimed they'd discovered. They were also unable to find evidence of animals of significant stature that would fit the size or description the boys had described.

In my opinion, Devil's Chair does not exist in the paranormal sense as we were brought up to believe. Until I have concrete evidence to prove otherwise, I'll have to believe that my Grandpa Eddy was pulling my leg, or if you prefer, pulling the wolverine over my eyes. Please excuse the bad pun and catch my article next week when I explore the myths surrounding the Loch Ness Monster.

Kate shook her head at the piece of paper she held in her hands. *What a ridiculous ghost story! Had I missed something?* She reread the article for anything she might have overlooked.

Giving up, she thought about her next step. She should contact the current Chief Redbird, just to know her house wasn't located on their burial ground or death site or whatever else could connect her house to the scourge of suicides. And, just how close was her house to the supposed 'Devil's Chair' the Indians had built? Maybe it held some secrets she could use to rid her house of whatever was creeping out Matt.

The opening of the outer door to the bathroom brought her back to the present. She'd been lost in the 1930s, picturing two frightened boys hopelessly lost in the woods. She refolded the paper and stuffed it into her pocket.

Kate had been reading for almost eight minutes. Marlene would start nosing around soon so she went back out on the floor to finish her shift. She'd call Redbird from home and make an appointment. She had the day off tomorrow and would ask if she could see him then. She wanted to resolve the nonsense that was frustrating her life.

Her meager amount of research left her unsatisfied. She had so many more questions now than when she'd started. She stomped to the nurse's station and grabbed her clipboard. She needed to complete one more round of vitals before she could leave for the night.

After Kate clocked out, she was tired and lumbered to her car. She hoped to gather enough strength to call Chief Redbird. Even though she wanted to go straight to bed, she had to schedule time with him. After all, the early bird gets the worm.

She turned on her road and bumped along the driveway, saddened by the horrible things that had happened here, on her land, in her house. She wished things could be different, that she could have her happy little home, handsome man and decent job. God knew she needed normalcy, to have her boring old life back.

She pulled to a stop on the gravel driveway. Tears streamed down her cheeks. She hadn't realized how heavily this weighed on her. It'd been hours since Matt had come clean with his secrets, but deep down, she'd known there something was going on even though she couldn't put her finger on it. Of course, Matt's psychic ability wasn't anything she would have guessed. Not in a million years.

Wearily climbing out of her car, she slammed the door a bit too hard. She paused for a second and looked up at her house expectantly. *Will it look any different now that I know the secrets it holds?* So far, it looked like the same place. Nicely fixed up, too. She searched the façade of her home for signs of paranormal activity: a specter of an Indian, a suicide victim's transparent mist, or a red-eyed man. She shuddered and shook her head to clear it of the awful thoughts oozing into her mind. If she intended to stay here, she'd have to forget about a lot of this stuff. Somehow. Someway.

With gritted teeth, she marched up to the front porch, defiant in the face of whatever might lurk there. Kate rolled her eyes. She had begun to sound like paranoid, psychic Matt.

She inserted the key into the lock and let the door swing wide open. She took a quick peek inside and reached around the door frame to flip on the light switch. To her relief, the lights illuminated the room. Nothing appeared to be amiss.

She walked into the living room and shut the door. She

set her purse and keys on the couch and grabbed the portable phone off the side table. She dug the note Matt had given her out of her purse, and dialed the numbers he'd written in his neat block printing.

The phone rang once, twice, three times. About to hang up, she heard a click on the other end and got an earful of labored breathing.

"Hello?" said a man after moments of hesitation. He was still breathless from whatever he'd been doing.

"Um, hi, you don't know me. My name's Kate Hart. I was told to call you about information you might be able to give me regarding a property I bought off Shady Lane."

The man recovered his breath enough to respond. "Shady Lane? Did you say Shady Lane?"

"Yes. The old white place."

"Hmm." The man grunted thoughtfully on the other end of the phone.

"Are you the Chief? Chief Redbird?"

"Yes, Ma'am. I'm Chief Redbird. Who'd you say this is?" He sounded confused. Kate worried he was older than she'd imagined. *Was he forgetful? Maybe he was.*

"I'm Kate Hart. I got your name from my real estate agent. Maybe you know her? Susan Poirier?"

"Oh yeah, I've met Susan once or twice. I know her father from town."

"Well, I bought this place from her and she thought you might be willing to give me some history surrounding the house and the land up here." She crossed her fingers and laid them on her leg.

"Sure, sure. I'd be happy to tell you anything you want

to know. I'm *very* familiar with where your house is."

"Ah, would you want to come here so we can talk? Like, maybe tomorrow? If you're available." *Was she pushing him?*

"Sorry, Ms. Hart." His voice was matter-of-fact. "My people don't go on the land up there."

"Oh." The newspaper guy had mentioned something like that in his article.

"You're more than welcome to come to my place," he said.

"That would be great!" she said, unable to hide her excitement. "Does tomorrow work for you?"

"Yup. Seems fine. Noon-ish would be good. You can find me at the Winding Winds trailer park. I'm the last one on the left."

"Thank you so much, sir, um, Chief. I really appreciate your allowing me to pick your brain."

"See you tomorrow, Ms. Hart," he said.

"Yes, tomorrow around noon." She placed the phone on its base and leaned back on her couch. She felt much better now, in shape to get a good night's sleep and figure this mess out tomorrow.

She reached over and picked up the phone again, about to dial Matt's number, and then stopped halfway through dialing and beeped the phone off. Her heart sank. She'd almost forgotten they had called it quits for now. If he was using his psychic powers right now, he would know she was thinking about him and missing him desperately. If he was really good, he would know she needed to hear his voice right now.

She stared at the phone, expecting it to ring at any moment. It would be Matt, calling to tell her "goodnight." She stared at the phone for a few minutes, sighed and stood up. Better get ready for bed—it could be a big day tomorrow. She went upstairs to her bedroom.

***

Kate woke up early and cursed at herself for not replacing the moldy shades. On work days, she enjoyed morning sunshine in her window. On an off day, such as today, she'd hoped to sleep later. After tossing and turning for half an hour, she bit the bullet and got up. She could take her time drinking coffee and showering. Then, in no time, it would be late enough to go to the Chief's trailer.

"Trailer park," she grumbled as she dragged out of bed and went down to the kitchen.

Whatever happened to a reservation? she wondered as she poured a scoop of coffee grinds into a fresh filter.

She hated it but she couldn't help being a snob about these types of things: trailer courts and the curious mix of elderly, poor, and criminals who usually inhabited them. Mother had her living in a trailer park for a short time while she was in junior high school and Kate was tortured by it. She knew why, too. In her limited experience, most inhabitants of trailer parks had seemed to march to their own drummers and she hadn't wanted to be lumped into that bunch by her friends at school.

She hoped the Chief wasn't an oddball. It would be just her luck to be stuck in a tin can with a freak.

Why am I being a bitch about someone who was taking

time out of his day to help? At the very least, she owed the guy the benefit of the doubt. *And who am I to judge?* She was one bad relationship away from being committed. She shook her head.

About an hour before she was supposed to leave, she gathered her personal items in preparation for her departure. To her surprise, her car keys that she'd left in the living room with her purse, were on the kitchen counter. They were splayed out on the counter, as if someone had deliberately separated out each key, making a fan out of the small pieces of metal. She shuddered. She hadn't done it. No one else had been here today.

Finally, she had an inkling of what poor Matt had been experiencing. Although she would never know what it was like to have a vision or a psychic feeling, she was pretty sure her rapidly beating heart and instant cold sweat would measure close to his level of anxiety. She hated to admit it, but maybe he was right about leaving this place.

Quickly planning her escape, she calculated that if she left now and grabbed lunch on the way, she'd be over at Winding Winds close to noon.

Kate snatched her keys off the counter and noted that they were freezing. The metal almost stuck to her clammy hand like a kid's tongue on a frozen pole. Grabbing her purse from the couch, she went outside. For the first time since she'd moved in, she sensed a heaviness in the house. Now outside, the pressure lifted like a dark cloud.

She shuddered again and climbed into the safety offered by her car. Her heart thudded in her chest as she pulled out of the driveway, spewing gravel behind her. She barely braked over the bumpy ruts in the road. "Don't break an axle or flatten a tire in your haste to leave," she mumbled.

When she pulled out onto the main road, her heart rate slowed. She took a deep breath and blew it out between puckered lips. All of this was getting to her and she started to replace fear with anger for being a boob.

The Chief would help her. He *needed* to help her. She hoped he would be lucid and willing to share information.

"Please help me, Chief," she pleaded to her windshield. "Please."

***

After her lunch, about five minutes before "noon-ish," she turned into the Winding Winds trailer park. Carefully, she followed the narrow drive lined with trailers. Occasionally, she turned the wheel fast to avoid an errant tricycle or muddy pothole. There seemed to be a large number of both in here. She turned by another bike that was tipped on its side in the road.

When the road came to an end she immediately recognized the Chief's trailer. Quite frankly, she would have been able to easily pick his trailer from all the others. Most yards had the appearance of effort being made to care for their sparse lawns. His yard looked more like a field. A clothes line hung from his dented metal porch up to the telephone pole that leaned on the left side of his driveway. It was heavy with animal skins in all shapes and sizes.

She took a good look at the drying pelts and recognized a squirrel skin and another that looked like a raccoon. The others? She didn't know and she really didn't want to know which poor critters had met their demise at his hand.

The dented overhang of his porch, held up by three weather-warped two-by-fours, was covered with a large animal skin. More were tacked to the side of the trailer, flanking each side of the dirty screen door. Kate stepped from her car and approached. Getting a closer look now, she realized the soft brown color and white spots on the skins decorating his trailer were from deer—two fawns, she surmised by the spots and the small size of the twin hides.

At the door, she expected to see a feral dog, pulling viciously at his chains, waiting to pounce on her. She surveyed the lawn and quickly determined he probably didn't have dog. If he did, there would be chewed animal skins and mounds of feces littering the dry, unkempt grass.

She knocked twice on the aluminum door frame which rattled unpleasantly under her knuckles. She paused, listening. The inner door was ajar so she assumed he had to be home or at least close by.

"Hello?" she called into the darkness beyond the screen door. "Anybody home?"

She heard a grunt of exertion from deep in the trailer, beyond the sun's reach. Finally, she recognized the protesting squeak of overused springs and shuffling footsteps.

"I'm coming," called the Chief. "Hold your horses." He grunted his way to the front door.

Kate was nervous. She'd never met an Indian Chief. The article description of his father had stuck in her brain. She imagined him in an outfit made of fresh animal skins and feathers decorating long black hair. Her heart was nearly beating out of her chest when Chief Redbird stepped out of the darkness and into the square of sunlight that peeked through the dusty screen door.

"You Kate Hart?" he said and pushed the screen door open with one large hand.

Kate nodded at the Chief, wide-eyed. She couldn't speak. She stepped forward into the small trailer, following his lead. He wore a faded, red flannel shirt buttoned halfway, a ribbed, graying wife-beater tank top or t-shirt was hidden underneath. His blue jeans were probably as old as she was. His fabulous black hair, peppered with gray around his face, was the only indication of being an Indian. It was pulled back into a low pony tail, tied with a scrap of leather or maybe an old shoelace.

"Have a seat, Ms. Hart." He pointed to a worn checkered sofa on the far side of the living area. He sat down in a well-loved recliner and pushed the lever to elevate his feet. Kate glanced at them, disappointed he wasn't wearing moccasins. Instead, he wore a pair of white gym socks. *Well, they were probably white when he bought them,* she thought and fought the urge to cringe.

"Mind if I smoke?" he asked, holding up a cigarette.

"It's your house, Chief Redbird." Being so proper with him seemed foolish, but she didn't know what else to call him. He didn't correct her either. She waited for him to light the cigarette with a silver lighter, engraved with a picture of a soaring eagle.

The Chief sucked greedily on the cigarette and the end burned a bright red. He snapped the lighter closed and set it delicately on the side table, nodded and winked. Kate was surprised how nimble his large fingers and hands were.

He squinted at Kate through a cloud of smoke. "So, little lady, you had some questions for me?"

"Yes, sir. I, I mean, Chief." She looked down at her lap. Should she have looked further into things before she came and talked to him?

"How 'bout you call me Red and I'll call you Kate," the Chief said with another playful wink.

She smiled and nodded. "Thank you, Red. I'm sorry I'm a nervous wreck. I'm not usually like this."

"I make all the girls quiver." He gave her a broad smile showing his straight teeth, yellowed from the years of cigarettes. They reminded her of a fresh ear of corn on the cob.

She relaxed a bit, grateful for his joke. She was surprised he had such a handsome smile and charming demeanor. She bet he did make the ladies quiver. Ladies his age, anyway. "I'm sure you do, Red."

"So, ask away, Kate," he said and inhaled another long drag from his cigarette.

"Well, as I told you on the phone, I bought that old house off Shady Lane. The one that had been unoccupied for a while. I've been having some issues with it. I was hoping you might fill in some of the blanks for me. I was led to believe the history of the area might be the cause of it," she said. She looked at her hands folded on her lap. *Would he take her seriously? Or think she was a crack pot?*

After a minute of silence, he exhaled and she looked up to gauge his reaction. His smiling face had turned to stone. He looked his age, mid-seventies, as he mulled over Kate's words. Slowly he brought the cigarette to his mouth again and let the smoke out in small puffs.

Finally, he spoke. "I'll tell you what I know." He flicked ash off his cigarette into a leaf-shaped ashtray. "But I'll need to start at the beginning." He took one long last drag from his cigarette and mashed it out on the ceramic leaf.

"I'd be grateful for anything."

"Before the white man came," he started, sounding like the Indian Kate had initially expected, "When our people roamed these lands freely, a fable was passed on from generation to generation about a red-eyed creature in the woods where your property is now located. My people called it the Loks Niz Mekwi Nsizegw. This means a wolverine spirit with two red eyes. Many warriors from my tribe had seen it on hunting trips. Some claimed to hit it with arrows, only to have the creature disappear into the underbrush, unscathed.

As the white man trespassed on our hunting grounds, they too saw the red-eyed creature. Although, they claimed it was a man, not an animal, as our people believed."

"I read in an old article," Kate said, "about a massacre and Devil's Chair. What was that about?"

"Was it that article by," venom filled his voice, "Malcolm Childs?"

She nodded yes, startled by his reaction.

"That man made my father sound like a fool. He played down the massacre, belittled it. He'd told my father the article was going to be his chance to set the record straight about the killing of his people and that, that *lying jerk* turned it into a ghost story. He glossed over the injustice against our people." He slapped the worn fabric on the arm of his chair.

"Tell *me* the truth, Red." She worried he was too angry to continue.

Red shook his head, his pony tail swishing on the back of his flannel shirt and continued. "My father's father was Chief of the Penobscot tribe here in Maine. He was a powerful man and highly regarded by our nation. The white man knew he was very important to our people. He was revered like no other Chief before him.

"After the white man came and started to build on our lands, my grandfather went to their courts to demand they stop. He fought hard to save our sacred lands, meeting with crooked politicians, playing their tedious games. When he wouldn't go away quietly, the locals lured my grandfather and his council to a tract of woods that had been cleared by the white men. They were told they brought them there to witness them fixing all the damage they'd caused. Instead, right there on the spot, in those ruined woods, they shot my grandfather and every member of his council. They threw their murdered bodies off the rock formation near the river, known by our people as Devil's Chair. Ever since then, the red-eyed creature was commonly seen there, perched upon the rocks or 'chair.'

"Anyway, my grandmother was pregnant with my father at the time. She went into labor when she heard her husband had been murdered. My father was born a Chief. He had to be a strong leader, recognized it as a small child. It was a burden on him. It was more responsibility than any child should bear.

"Meanwhile, the white man continued raping our lands and building their fancy homes on our hunting grounds.

They even turned the red eyed creature, the Loks, into a red-eyed man, to match their own image.

Intrigued and nearly breathless, Kate leaned forward, unwilling to miss a word.

"My father was a great man and a great Chief, but he never trusted the white man because of what they'd done to his father.

"The first white man who he decided to trust was that slimy reporter. He'd promised to highlight the massacre and in the very least, let the world know how our people were mistreated, murdered for their land.

"The jerk trivialized the whole thing. This made my father so furious. He never again spoke of the massacre to a white man. He didn't want to give them another opportunity to make a mockery of his people." Red paused and shook his head from side to side. "My father died a broken man." His dark eyes filled with pain. He stared into Kate's watering eyes.

"I'm so sorry, Red. I had no idea your people were treated so badly." She blinked away tears. She'd read about the massacre in the article, but the enormity of it didn't hit home until she saw the deep sadness in Red's dark brown eyes. She understood why they were insulted by Child's depiction.

Red continued, "After the massacre, our people deemed the land surrounding Devil's Chair as cursed. With the murders and sightings of the red-eyed creature, they declared that no Penobscot would ever set foot on that land again. Too much of our people's blood had been spilled there. They didn't want to risk a confrontation with the red-eyed creature. Folklore tells us the Loks preys on sadness. A Penobscot tribesman, with his heavy heart, would be easy prey."

"So, you think my house is cursed then?" She wiped an errant tear from her cheek with her shirt collar.

"I can't say for certain. But it would make sense to me. Any home on those lands could be cursed or have my ancestor's spirits passing by. There's also the red-eyed creature or red-eyed man to be concerned with. Anyone or all are possible." He nodded, his lush pony tail swishing again.

Her voice was squeaky, scared, "Can I do anything about it?"

"Not really. The spirits will always be on that land. And, I don't know how to battle a creature I can't put my hands on. But, you could try an offering of sage. The sage might calm the spirits. They might leave you alone, at least from time to time." He gave her a tired smile.

"What do I need to do?"

"Get a bundle of sage and burn it. Carry it from room to room. Like a blessing. The spirits will know you mean them no harm."

She nodded her head. "Okay."

"But, Kate," he said, leaning toward her, "*Do not* go out to Devil's Chair. Many white men have gone out to Devil's Chair, either on purpose or from getting lost in the woods. Most never come back. Those lucky enough to return… are never the same."

"Like the teenagers?" she said.

"Yes. Those boys were lured into the woods by their red-eyed man. Although they were lucky enough to be found in time, they were never the same. One of them died in a motorcycle accident a few years later. The other was lost in a haze of drugs for many years. He was finally claimed before he turned twenty-five. The curse follows you out of those woods. Please. Just *do not* go out to Devil's Chair. Kate. Do not."

"I won't," she said. She didn't like being told what to do, but given the facts and possible threat lurking in the woods, his request seemed reasonable. "I promise."

"Good." He put his hands on the arms of his chair. "Do you need some sage? I think I have some growing out back in a pot. I'm like an old Indian Boy Scout. Always prepared." The twinkle had returned to his brown eyes.

She laughed and nodded. She liked Red and hoped to keep in touch with him, maybe even become friends.

Red pushed himself out of the old recliner with an audible grunt. "Uh. These old bones aren't what they used to be." A pained grimace spread across his lined face.

Unable to keep her nursing skills contained, she asked, "Do you have arthritis?"

"Yup, down to every bone." He stretched his arms over his head. His undershirt shifted with his reach and she saw he wore a necklace made from a leather string, adorned with wooden beads that appeared to be hand carved. A black and white spotted feather hung in the middle of the beads.

She pointed at his necklace. "Did you make that?"

"Yup." He lifted the necklace from his chest and looked down at it, clearly proud. "I can't get that detailed any more, with the arthritis and all, but I was quite good back in the day." He beamed at Kate.

"It's just beautiful." She reached up to touch one of the intricate beads.

"Do you want it?" He pulled it over his head. "I've got a million of these things lying around."

"I couldn't take that from you." She held up a hand to stop him from putting it around her neck.

"Consider it payment for spending an afternoon with a crazy old man." He hung the necklace over her wrist.

"Are you sure? You must've worked so hard on it." She admired the necklace and fingered the ornate carving of a wolf's face on one bead and an eagle's profile on the other. "It's absolutely beautiful."

"Just tell your friends where you got it and tell them you paid handsomely for it." He winked at her.

"You've got it," she agreed.

"Let's get out back and get you that bundle of sage." He lurched forward, got balanced, and ambled slowly toward the screen door.

"Thanks, Red. Thank you so much for all of this." She held up the necklace and smiled.

"Glad to be a help to someone. There's not much use for an old Indian Chief these days."

"I'm sorry about that. It must be hard to see things change so much over the years."

"It's harder to see myself age." They went outside and walked through the knee-high grass to a small circle of shrubs in wooden buckets. He broke a handful of branches off a small bush and deftly wound it into a bundle, using a loose piece of twine to wrap it tight. He handed the collection to her.

"Thanks, Red." She smiled gratefully at her new friend.

"This should burn long enough to go through the whole house. Make sure you hold it up into the corners and do every room. Even the basement. If you have any left, you could do the outside, too. That should do it. At least for a while."

"Thanks again, really Red. I finally feel like I can do something about all of this stuff that's been happening at my house."

"Well, I hope it works."

"Me, too."

***

Kate drove home. She peeked repeatedly at the tightly wound bunch of sage that rested on the passenger seat. *Would a little bundle of sticks help?* She wasn't convinced. But, with nothing more to lose, she'd try it as soon as she got home.

She pulled down her familiar road and bounced along the rutted drive. The unrestrained sage bundle launched from the seat, onto the floorboard and rolled away. Kate tried to grab it before it disappeared into the darkness under the seat, but her reflexes weren't fast enough. It disappeared into the void.

"Crap!" She yelled at her misfortune and reluctantly turned her attention back to the view outside the windshield. In the dusky light that filtered through the tall pines, a dark figure loomed ten feet in front of her car, blocking her path. Immediately, she stomped on the brake with both feet. Her car veered toward the edge of the drive, nearly hitting a sapling before lurching to a stop. Glancing down, she was momentarily relieved to see the sage roll out from under the seat. She shifted her gaze once again and peered through the glass to verify she'd stopped in time and hadn't nailed the figure on the road. Blinking and squinting, she leaned forward, her gawking stopped only by the restrictive seatbelt. She was dumbfounded. The figure had vanished.

Craning her neck, she searched the landscape outside the rear window of her car to make sure she hadn't passed the figure when she'd looked down at the rolling bundle of sage. Her eyes searched each tree, paused on each flickering shadow.

After her careful survey of the woods around her idling car was complete, she shuddered. A thought from the recesses of her memory suddenly occurred to her. *Had she just seen the red-eyed man?* She hadn't gotten a very good look at whomever or whatever was in her path, but it appeared to be a man dressed in black from head to toe. If it had been a real person, he was overdressed for the season. The hairs on the back of her neck prickled, her heart, already accelerated from her near collision, raced even more. Her mind pondered the possibilities.

She thought back to her last ill-fated encounter with Matt. He'd claimed to see a man wearing a black hat outside her window. Her near miss, coupled with the fact he'd seen a man in a black hat, might equal the red-eyed man! She held a shaking hand up to her mouth. It hung open like a cabinet door that had freed itself from the confines of its hinges.

She gulped at the air. Beads of sweat tingled on her forehead. She pressed the gas and straightened the wheel to get her vehicle back onto the rutted path. She pressed the gas pedal harder, down to the floor, wanting to get home and get her Indian blessing started. *Would it work against the red-eyed man who stalked the grounds around her house? Who knew? Was he the one moving her keys?* This last thought made her shudder again, a thin stream of nerve-induced sweat trickled down the middle of her back.

She pulled to a grinding stop on the gravel in front of her house. Reaching down, she rescued the bundle of sage from the floorboard and hurried out the driver's side of the car. She slammed the door shut and ran up the steps of the front porch. She stopped for a moment and listened to the silent woods beyond her driveway. For the first time since she moved in, the unearthly silence gave her the creeps.

She shivered, turned to unlock the door, and pushed it open, her key chain left dangling from the lock. She'd be safer inside the house despite the fact the red-eyed man might have been in here, moving things, messing with her. So far, his actions had been benign. *But... was this the beginning of more?* The mental burden of seven suicides began to weigh heavily on her mind. *Had the red-eyed man caused those people to go crazy? Crazy enough to hurt themselves? No, to* kill *themselves.* Her body convulsed with another fear-induced shudder.

After yanking the key from the lock, she hurried through the living room and went straight into the kitchen. She dropped her purse and keys on the countertop and pulled open her junk drawer, organized neatly, of course, and grabbed an old book of matches from the back of the drawer. She hoped they would still work properly, even though they were a few years old. She ripped a match from its paper base and closed the cover to expose the black strip.

Upon a quick inspection, she saw that the head of the match was still intact. It hadn't crumbled off the stick when she'd pulled it from the flimsy book. *A good sign.* She dragged the head of the match across the black strip and expected to hear the familiar popping sound and catch a whiff of sulfur. To her displeasure, the match didn't light. Hoping more friction would get it started, she folded the cover back open and pinched the match between the cover and the black strip.

"Here we go," she said aloud and pulled on the match. This time, she heard the telltale snap as the match came to life. The flame danced rhythmically on the tip of the match in the darkening room.

Instinctively, she cupped her free hand around the flame and held it to one end of the sage bundle. It was dry and lit easily. She scooped the bundle from the kitchen counter and blew out the match in one flowing motion.

Red had told her to burn the sage for a minute and then blow out the flames. The smoke would continue to emanate from the bundle for ten minutes or more if she'd done it correctly. She looked at the clock on the microwave oven and decided it had burned for long enough. She blew gently on the bundle, extinguishing the flames.

Just as Red had told her, a thin wisp of smoke radiated from the tightly wrapped bundle. The smell of the sage re-minded her of the incense Mother had used at her cottage when Kate was growing up. The smell comforted her. It gave her hope this would work, would cleanse her home, and keep the red-eyed mystery man at bay along with any other random spirits who might come her way.

She tucked the matchbook into the front pocket of her jeans and walked around the kitchen, lifting the smoldering bundle of sage into every corner. She waved her hand at the bundle, forcing more smoke to billow out, hoping that more smoke would make the blessing last longer. *Red wasn't specific about volume—he wasn't even certain it would work*, she remembered. She left the kitchen and went into the living room, walking slowly, deliberately, with her wafting bundle.

She made the rounds through every room on the first floor. After relighting the sage, she covered the entire second floor with its wispy smoke and strong odor. The bitter smoke swirled up the walls and collected in misty tufts on the ceiling. It seemed to cover her with a protective barrier.

She had enough sage left to cover the basement and spread some around the perimeter of the house. She looked out the window and noticed the sky had become dark. She'd wait and do the outside cleansing in the safety of the morning sun, not wanting to risk running into anything, anyone, at night, alone, with just a bundle of smoking sage to defend herself.

She opened the door to the basement and walked down the narrow staircase, each ancient step creaking under her weight. *Had they squeaked that much before?* She carried the wafting bundle of sage in front of her, away from her face. She'd already snarfed up enough of the pungent smell for one day. Her mind drifted to images of a patient she had who'd died a miserable death. He suffered from lung cancer after years of inhaling cigarette smoke. Inadvertently, she thought of Red.

By the time she reached the bottom step, the sage had almost stopped smoking. The mugginess of the basement had dampened her smoldering sticks.

She dug into her pocket for the matches. With only a few left in the book, she hoped she could get it going again to complete the basement and still have enough sage and matches left to cleanse the outside in the morning.

She set the bundle of sage on an old workbench left by the previous owner. Kate eyeballed the pegboard wall covered with rusty tools and shuddered. *Had one of those hanging implements been used for one of the suicides?*

She shook her head, clearing her mind of the morbid, horrible thoughts. The basement was creepy enough with its dirt floors and sneering gargoyle statue leering at her from its cement perch. She didn't need to induce panic with thoughts of people hurting themselves with random, crusty tools.

She finally retrieved the matches from the recesses of her pocket and greedily pulled them out. She hunched over the bundle of sage and yanked a match out of the tiny booklet.

She struck the match and her hand flailed wildly, as if it wasn't attached to her own body, setting the precious bundle flying across the room. "You clumsy fool," she muttered aloud.

Knowing it would take a moment to find the missing

sage in the poorly lit basement, she blew out the match before it could burn the tips of her fingers. She hated to waste such an important and dwindling resource, but she had no choice.

She'd seen the bundle of sage roll across the floor, into the shadows on the far side of the basement. It had stopped near the strange, crumbling brick wall—a vivid reminder of her trip to the Wailing Wall. Absently, she fingered the key that hung around her neck.

Walking briskly to the wall, she searched the darkened floor for the sage. Her eyes had trouble focusing in the darkness. She scolded herself for not bringing a flashlight.

Despite her aversion to anything dirty, she got down on her hands in knees and felt her way to the bundle. She crawled along the length of the wall and swept her hand from side to side in a three foot radius. Finally, in the darkest corner of the basement, where the light from the single bulb at the end of the stairs would never reach, she found her prize.

"Gotcha!" she said into the darkness. Righting herself with the bundle, she brushed the dirt floor from the knees of her jeans. As she rose, she found she was face-to-face with a new hole in the brick wall. *Was it new?* She hadn't noticed it the last few times she'd dared to venture down here.

Glancing at the dwindling book of matches in her hand, she thought it might be worth using one to see what was on the other side of the wall. She imagined it was another wall. There wasn't enough room for it to be anything other than a brick façade, covering the old stone foundation. Probably, it had been put up as extra support for a foundation that might've had structural issues from years of neglect and harsh New England winters.

Carefully, she struck a match, noting she only had three left in the pack. She held the small flame to the hole and tried to peer beyond it into the darkness. No good. Straining her tired eyes, she peered deeper into the blankness beyond the brick wall and scolded herself for not leaving a flashlight on the workbench.

Although she couldn't see beyond the hole, the diminutive flame did reveal that the mortar between the bricks was woefully dry. She touched it with her spare hand, holding the newly-found bundle of sage between her thighs. The mortar easily turned to powder between her fingertips. The match had now burned far enough down to cause pain. She blew the flame out just before it singed her pinched fingers. She sucked on them briefly to ease the burning sensation and quickly removed them from her mouth, remembering she'd just been crawling around on the packed dirt floor.

She shuddered again. This time she shuddered against the germs she could almost feel seeping into her body instead of against the dankness of her gloomy basement.

Kate stopped for a moment to regroup and decide what to do next. If she used one match now to relight the bundle of sage and cover the basement, then she could use the remaining two matches tomorrow to take care of the outside. Or, better yet, she could use them now to look in the hole. Tomorrow morning, she could go to the store to buy more matches or, better yet, a cigarette lighter and use it to relight the sage and cleanse the outside.

She struck another match, re-lit the bundle of sage and walked around slowly, holding it up to each corner of the basement, wafting the ribbon of smoke with her free hand. She covered everything, stopping briefly to pay special attention to the statue of the gargoyle.

"Breath deep, buddy," she said to the sneering creature. She held the sage under his skinny, upturned nose.

She also made certain to cover the mystery wall. She angled the sage into the open hole, lightly blowing the smoke inside the dark crevice behind it.

Finally, Kate was satisfied she'd completely covered the basement. The white smoke swirled lazily around the single, bare light bulb at the end of the staircase. She tapped out the glowing embers of sage on the dirt floor and set it on the work bench. She eyed the tools again. One of them might help her make progress on the brick wall.

The small pickaxe, looking like it could have been used by one of the Seven Dwarfs, would easily crush the powdery mortar. She lifted it carefully off the dusty pegboard and walked back to the dimly lit wall wishing she'd thought to pay the electrician to string a light bulb over here. She squinted at the small hole in the wall.

She tapped lightly at the mortar surrounding the hole. As she'd expected, it crumbled easily from the force of her hand and the weighted point of the sharp metal. She spent the next ten minutes working a single brick out of the wall, using the eye-level hole as a starting point.

When the brick was almost free, she set the pickaxe onto the floor and used both hands to wiggle it. The more she wiggled the brick, the looser it became. The motion reminded her of a wiggly tooth in a child's mouth. Dust from the broken mortar covered her face, hair, and the front of her shirt. Determined to remove the brick, she barely noticed the mess on her skin and clothes.

She gave the brick one last hard tug. It came free in her hands and sent her reeling back a few steps. "Take that, bugger," she said smugly to the brick. She looked it over for markings. After finding none, she set it down on the floor.

Using her fingers, she cleared away more mortar and peered into the hole. She noted with an annoyed grunt that the modest glare from the light bulb behind her was completely blacked out by her head when she moved into its path.

For exploration's sake, she decided she would sacrifice one of her last two matches. She dug her dirty fingers into her pocket and pulled out the matchbook. She ripped off one match and lit it with a satisfying pop. She breathed in the strong scent of sulfur, enjoying the smell. It was a heck of a lot better than the musty old basement and floating mortar dust. She reached toward the hole she'd made from the removed brick.

In order to see anything beyond the hole, she'd have to reach her hand through the opening and look through the small space that wasn't filled with her arm. Grimacing, she pushed her hand through the hole. It reminded her of an Indiana Jones movie. He had to reach into a hole filled with large insects waiting to take a bite from his flesh. The idea of coming into contact with bugs made her cringe, but she pushed her hand further into the hole.

Knowing that soon the match would burn her finger-tips, she scowled and pressed her forehead against the cool bricks and peered into the hole. To her dismay, she only saw another wall a few feet away. It appeared to be the stone foundation, as she'd expected.

As the disappointment registered in her mind, she was startled by the match that was still pinched between her fingers. It went out. But it didn't just sputter out. It had been *blown* out. It wasn't the sensation of wind or air flowing from vent. She'd distinctly felt hot air exhaled onto her fingers. The unmistakable feel of air exhaled from lungs. Human lungs.

Quickly, she withdrew her hand from the hole and inspected the match. It had been blown out just before it would've burned her fingers. She looked back at the hole and caught a fleeting glimpse of a shadow passing the opening.

She backed away from the wall. Her mind reeled with nervous energy and trepidation. *Is my tired mind playing tricks on me? There couldn't be anyone behind the wall. There was no way in. And, it couldn't be an animal; the shadow was way too tall.*

Kate continued to retreat from the wall until she bumped into the workbench. She looked down and grabbed the small bundle of sage from the countertop and turned toward the stairs.

Hesitating on the bottom step, she took one last glance at the brick wall. Suddenly, the most horrible noise she'd ever heard emanated through the hole she'd created. It was a pain-filled, dreadful, bird-like screeching. Soft at first, it continued to grow louder and louder. She stood on the bottom step, frozen, her mouth agape in shock and horror.

The last screech Kate heard before she ran screaming up the steps was so loud and so full of angst that she almost felt bad for whomever or whatever was making the wretched sound. Although the nurse in her sensed the sorrow and pain exuding from the maker of the noise, she wasn't planning to stick around to help it. She didn't even want to see it.

She bolted up the stairs and out the front door, grabbing her keys and purse on the way. Mentally, she flogged herself on the way out the door. *Why did I remove the brick? Burned the sage?* The creature or whatever she'd woken up didn't sound happy to be disturbed, it sounded miserable and scary. *What on earth have I done?* Now, she knew Matt had been right. He'd been right all along. She was going to need more than an old Indian Chief's sage-burning trick. Exactly what she needed, she didn't know. But it would have to be a great deal stronger than sage to rid her house of whatever had overtaken her basement. Much stronger.

Matt

The doorbell to Matt's condo was pushed again and again. "Coming!" he yelled as he hurried to the door. He swung it open and smiled, surprised to see Kate. Then, concern spread across his face when he realized she was crying. She grasped the metal railing with her free hand to support her quivering legs. "What happened to you?" He took a step outside the door and grabbed her.

She fell into his arms, clearly weakened from her ordeal. She tried to form a sentence, but was unable to utter anything understandable between spastic gasps for air.

Unable to walk on her own, Kate let Matt wrap his strong arm around her waist and half-carry her inside. He noted that in addition to her body's uncontrolled shaking, she was covered in dirt.

He sat her on the couch and grabbed an afghan from the arm of his reclining chair. Shaking it out to its full size, he wrapped it around her trembling shoulders. He wanted to ask what had happened, but knew she needed to calm down first. Still, questions floated urgently in his mind. *Had she been assaulted? Something worse?* He fought his imagination from wandering into a very dark place.

He grabbed a handful of paper napkins from his cluttered coffee table and held them out to her. Weakly, she took them from his hand with fumbling fingers and pressed them against her eyes. After a few moments, she removed them and used the damp wad to wipe tears, mucus, and dust from her face. As she calmed, her breathing slowed back to normal and after blowing her nose on the lump of paper napkins, she seemed more like herself again. Finally, she looked over at him sheepishly.

Matt, anxious, sat on the edge of the couch, waiting for her to speak, uncertain if he should comfort her or leave her alone.

She smiled feebly. "Sorry, Matt, I didn't know where else to go." She looked away and stared down at the bright afghan draped over her shoulders, falling into a colorful puddle on her lap.

"It's okay, Kate," he said, gently patting her back. "Do you want to tell me," his voice cracked, "what's going on?" Incredibly worried, his handsome face was somber, dark eyes concerned.

Kate gave him another forced smile.

He smiled back, but confusion remained in his blue eyes.

"Don't you know why I'm here?" she said, clearly trying to be playful.

"Are you serious?" he sputtered. "For God's sake! Is this some stupid joke? To test my psychic skills?" His mouth opened in disbelief.

"No... no, it's not," she stammered. She swallowed hard. "Something did happen," she said, her tone serious again.

Brushing off his lingering feelings of betrayal, he said, "Tell me about it."

"It's about the house." She searched his face. "Do you want to hear it?" she said cautiously, obviously not wanting to piss him off again.

He nodded. "Absolutely."

"Okay. Let me begin by saying you were right and I was wrong. So wrong." She shook her head from side to side. Dust from her mortar-covered hair fell in wispy tufts onto the afghan.

"That's probably the first time I've ever heard those words from a woman," said Matt. He appreciated the comment, but thought it was a feeble attempt at trying to lighten the mood.

"I know and I'm sorry, Matt." She pulled her left hand from under the bulky afghan and grabbed his hand.

"Go on," he said.

"Well, I met with Red this morning." She paused to take a deep breath.

"Who's Red?"

"Chief Redbird. The Indian Chief you told me about. He asked me to call him Red."

"Should I be jealous? One meeting and you're already using a nickname?"

"Well, he's riddled with arthritis and is close to eighty years old so I think you're probably safe on that one." She laughed, clearly flattered at his feigned jealousy. "Oh yeah," she laughed, "and he smokes like a chimney and has an extensive collection of dried animal skins all over his property."

Matt laughed heartily. He loved to hear her laugh. It gave him hope that maybe their precarious relationship could be salvaged. "Sounds lovely," he said, grimacing. "Please, continue."

"Well, Red gave me some sage to burn. The smoke is supposed to have cleansing properties. In a spiritual sense." She paused, clearly expecting him to snicker at such a strange notion. Instead, he nodded vigorously, as if it made complete sense to him.

"Have you heard of using sage before?" she asked.

"Grandma Betty always had some around her house. I even tried it in high school when I started to become aware of my... my gifts. It didn't work so well for me, but I figured it was only because I was a sensitive. I assumed it might work for a normal person." He looked down at his lap and blushed, embarrassed.

She squeezed his hand. "You *are* normal, Matt."

He squeezed her hand back. "Thanks, Kate. Sometimes I forget to give myself a break."

"I know. I'm sorry I haven't been more supportive of everything you've been going through. I've been a self-centered jerk. Matt. I'm really sorry." She wiped a ribbon of fresh tears from her cheek with the back of her free hand.

"You have no idea how much that means to me," he said, wiping away a few tears of his own with his thumb. "I mean, look at me. I'm crying like a little girl." He laughed.

"A smart little girl," she said. "Should I finish my tale of woe?"

"Yes. Sorry. No more crying jags from me." He pretended to lock his lips with an invisible key and tossed it ceremoniously over his shoulder.

She smiled at his gesture and restarted her story. "So

anyway, Red gave me a bundle of sage to use at my house, which I did earlier tonight." Involuntarily, her body began shaking again. After a reassuring squeeze on her hand from Matt, she continued, "but the sage didn't work. I was in the basement prying bricks out of that weird extra wall-thing and I think I saw something move back there. It was like a shadow flitting by a window, but I could sense something was there. And then... I heard it." She gulped, clearly afraid.

"You *heard* it?" he said, his words exhaled in a frightened whisper.

"It was just horrible, Matt," she said. "It was sort of moaning or screaming. It started out kind of soft and then got so loud I just booked it out of there and came here. I didn't know where else to go." She sniffed.

"Well, I'm glad you came to me."

"Thanks, Matt." She exhaled loudly and leaned back on the couch.

"So, what do you think we should do next?"

"I think I'd like to call Red and tell him what happened. Maybe I did something wrong and he could tell me how to fix it. I just want this crap to stop. My life's been hijacked ever since I bought this stupid house." She groaned, clearly frustrated by the freak show her life had become.

"Let me get you the phone." He gently set her hand down on her thigh and got up to retrieve his portable phone from the kitchen.

She nodded and tightened the afghan around her shoulders.

Matt returned quickly with the phone and handed it to

her. She reached up and took it from him, her hand still shaking.

"Do you want me to stay while you talk to him or would you like some privacy?"

"Please stay," she whispered. She looked deeply into Matt's blue eyes.

He smiled and searched her face, puzzled by her sudden change in expression. He leaned down and kissed her gently on a clean spot on her forehead. She set the phone on the couch and reached up, allowing the afghan to fall in a heap behind her on the couch. With both hands, she held his neck and gently guided him down to his knees in front of her. She released his neck and lovingly brushed the hair off his forehead with her index finger. She leaned forward and rested her forehead against his.

"Thanks, Matt. I finally feel safe. Being here with you, I mean." She turned her face up slightly so she could look into his eyes.

"I do what I can," he said, nervously licking his dry lips.

"Do you think there is still a chance for us?"

"I know there is," he said. "And I'm psychic. I should know."

"Did you see this coming?" She pushed her face into his, kissing his warm lips. He leaned into the kiss, into her.

She leaned back on the couch and pulled him with her. To brace his fall, he set his hand beside her on the couch cushion. His hand landed smack on the portable phone and hit multiple buttons at once. It screamed piercing beeps of mechanical confusion.

He laughed and rolled off her. He grabbed the phone and hit a button to silence the irritating noise. Kate rolled her eyes. Clearly, she thought that even the telephone was working against her when it came to being intimate with Matt.

"I guess we should focus on other pressing matters first." He winked and handed her the quieted phone.

"Right. I guess I should call my Chief."

Matt nodded yes. *Could the Chief help her?* He had a sneaking suspicion or maybe more of a vision that the Chief was going to be out of answers. Matt had been sitting on an idea she could try, but she'd need to be convinced it was a good idea. He'd wait until she finished her call with Red. If the suggestions from him had dried up, he'd see if she was open to other, more drastic ideas.

She reached into her pocket and retrieved the sheet of paper with Red's phone number. She smoothed it out on her thigh and pressed the buttons carefully. She set the paper down on the coffee table when she finished dialing, crossed her fingers for luck and pushed the speaker phone button so Matt could hear. Matt nodded at her gesture and gamely crossed his fingers on both hands.

The phone rang once… twice… four times. She looked at the clock on the wall. It was 8:37 p.m. Probably, Red was still up.

"'Lo?" said Red.

He sounded fully awake, but mildly annoyed with the interruption to his evening.   "Hey, Red, it's Kate. Kate Hart from earlier today."

"Sure, Kate, of course I remember you. I may be old,

but I still have a memory like a bear trap." He chuckled.

"I'm so sorry to bother you twice in one day, but I really need some advice." On her lap, she kept her fingers crossed tightly.

"Of course, Kate. I thought I'd hear from you again."

"You did?"

"Yep."

"Oh."

"What did you need, Kate?" he said. By his tone, it sounded like he already had a good idea why she'd called him.

"I did the sage blessing as soon as I got home, and," her voice cracked, "it didn't quite go as planned."

"Did it get worse?"

"Yes," she breathed into the phone. "How did you know?"

"I suspected as much. Your property is extremely active with spirits. I'm guessing the sage kinda pissed somebody off." He paused. Kate heard him take a long puff off a cigarette.

Matt could see that Kate was angry. She rolled her eyes at him, clearly frustrated by the way the conversation with Red was going. She continued speaking into the phone, her face turning various shades of red. "You knew that could happen?"

"I was hoping it would work out for you, Kate."

Clearly irritated, she said, "So what do I do now?" Her shoulders slumped, obviously defeated and annoyed.

"You could try it again, but it probably won't help much. You're dealing with more than just benign spirits."

"Like what? The red-eyed man?" she said, her voice bitter.

Matt gasped loudly next to her. She looked over at him. He'd covered his mouth with his hand. She gave him the 'okay' sign with her finger and thumb. He nodded gratefully and let his hand fall down to his lap.

"I reckon so, Kate," said Red. "Now you know why our people keep off that land. We want nothin' to do with that creature."

"I thought I saw him on my driveway on the way home this afternoon." She looked over at Matt again. His eyes bulged.

"I bet he knew you were comin'," said Red.

"Knew I was coming? What? With the sage?" She shook her head.

"Probably." He took another long drag from his cigarette.

"So, do you have any other suggestions for me? Some secret Indian ceremony or something that could help rid my property of this red-eyed nuisance?"

For a long moment, Red was silent. Then, he spoke forcefully, "Get out of there, Kate. Get out and never look back."

Kate gritted her teeth, clearly agitated. "I'll take it into consideration, Red. I'll give you a call soon and let you know what I've decided."

"Don't wait too long, Kate. You don't want an angry spirit after you."

"Got it," she said curtly. Then, softening, she added, "Thanks for your help, Red."

"Good luck, Kate," Red grumbled and hung up his end of the line.

"Bye." She pushed the button on the keypad to end the call. She tossed the phone onto the couch and leaned forward, resting her face in her hands, obviously frustrated with the whole situation.

Matt watched helplessly as Kate fought burning tears that threatened to escape the corners of her eyes. After successfully blinking them away, she dropped her hands from her face and looked squarely at him.

"So, what do you think?" he said, unable to wait for her to speak, her determined expression making him anxious. Still worried about rocking the boat, he posed his next question cautiously, "Is moving an option now?"

She squeezed her teeth together, her temples moved in and out with the pressure. "I don't know."

"Do you want my advice?" He braced for an angry response.

She shrugged, clearly exasperated and tired. "Why the hell not?"

"Well, there is one more thing you don't know about me."

"Matt. If you tell me one more crazy thing, I think I'll really lose it."

He smiled at her. "I don't think it's too crazy. I promise."

She gave a dismissive wave with her hand. "Go on then," she said.

"Every Sunday, I go to the Sacred Heart Catholic Church. I think my priest there may be able to help you."

"I've already been baptized."

"I didn't mean that." He moved closer to her on the couch, reached over and grabbed one of her hands.

"Then what?" she said.

"What about having *him* perform a blessing? Maybe he could bring a little more juice to the party."

"Juice to the party?" Kate laughed. "You are too freaking much, Matt."

He laughed and looked down at their clutched hands. "In all honesty, he already knows a lot about you."

Her brow furrowed. "What do you mean by that?"

"I asked him for some counsel after we parted ways. I was too angry at Susan to talk with her or Marc about our problems. So, I went to Father LaCroix." He glanced at her face to see if she was angry with him.

Clearly unsure of the Catholic lingo, she asked awkwardly, "Like a confession?"

He laughed heartily. "No. Not quite a confession. We weren't in a little box somewhere talking about sexual urges or anything." He blushed and looked away from her again.

"Hmm." The new information seemed to be soaking into her exhausted brain.

"Are you mad at me?"

After a few seconds, she said, "No. I don't think so."

"Well, that's a relief."

"So, how much did you tell this guy?" she said, clearly embarrassed at the thought of a priest knowing her business. Or, lack thereof.

"Pretty much everything," he said with a gulp. "I was really freaked out by the man I saw in your window and all the other vibes I was getting from your house. And then to top it off, you ran me out of your house on our last date because I wouldn't..." He searched the wall for support, "Do the deed, so to speak."

She blushed and covered her face with her free hand. "Oh my God." She moaned. "He's going to think I'm some sort of psychotic slut or something."

He laughed again, trying hard to reign in the spastic guffaws that threatened to explode from his throat. After taking a minute to regain control over his twitching body, he tried his best to console her. "Don't worry. It was much more about me and my visions then about you and me and us, well, you know," he said. He wished he'd been more eloquent in his attempt to pacify her embarrassment.

"Great," she said sarcastically.

"He was interested in talking with you. He thought he could help. He's helped other people through stuff like this."

Quickly, she removed her hand from her face and gazed at him. "Really?"

"Yes." He nodded confidently. "He told me some re-lated stories and they're quite remarkable."

"Maybe you can tell me about them tomorrow, Matt. I'm suddenly feeling overcome with sleep. I just want to go to bed." She yawned involuntarily.

"I'm exhausted, too."

"Can I stay here with you?"

"Of course you can," he said, surprised she'd feel the need to ask. "You can have my bed and I'll stay out here." He pointed at the couch.

"Do you think you could handle sleeping with me? Just holding me. No monkey business?" She grinned. "Cross my heart and hope to die." She made an invisible cross over her heart with her finger.

"Well, it's not worth dying over." He smiled. "Of course we can snuggle, I'd like nothing more."

For the first time since she arrived, her face brightened. She stood and squeezed his hand. "Let me get cleaned up first, then it's off to bed," she said. She pulled his arm, guiding him from his perch on the couch. She led the way down the short hallway to his bedroom.

For the first time in a long time, it seemed they had a future together. An uncertain future. But that was good enough for now.

***

Kate awoke enveloped in Matt's arms. Her stirring woke him with a snort. He rubbed his eyes with the index finger and thumb of his free hand as if trying to erase a bad dream and glanced at her. After a look of confusion passed through his dark blue eyes, he smiled broadly and whispered, "Good morning, gorgeous."

"Hi," she said.

"I could get used to this," he said. He rubbed her back through the comforter.

"I was just thinking the same thing." She smiled and leaned into his caress.

"You were?" he said, unable to conceal the excitement in his voice.

"Yes. Does that shock you?"

He blushed and pressed a pillow into his face. "A little bit, yeah," he said, his voice muffled by the padding.

She scooted up the bed, her head over his and grabbed the pillow from his face. "You mean more to me than you know."

His eyebrows knitted together, questioning her words. "I do?"

"Yes, Butt-head, you do." She leaned down and kissed his lips.

He returned her kiss greedily. He loved her more than he'd ever loved anyone else. He wished he could make love to her right now. His body was responding quickly to her kiss, but the recent advice he'd received from Father LaCroix circled madly in his head. He knew now was not the time.

She rolled onto her back, clearly hoping he'd follow her lead.

Reluctantly, Matt stayed on his back. He didn't dare look over at her. She was lying expectantly next to him. He could feel her heart race through his arm still tucked under her back. He didn't want to look at her and see the disappointment of their unfinished deed in her eyes. He didn't think he could bear to ever see that look again. A part of him wanted to give in to the physical yearning they both felt, but his mind and spirit told him it would be dangerous to enter into such endeavors now. Too much was at stake. He hadn't revealed everything Father LaCroix had told him. He hadn't wanted to scare her last night. Her psyche was already fragile and used up by the time she'd arrived on his doorstep last night. He didn't want to put anything else on her that might cause distress.

Gently, he tugged his arm from under her warm body and sat up. He sensed her eyes boring into the back of his head. He still didn't want to face her and see her glaring disappointment. He swung his legs over the edge of the bed and planted his feet firmly on the beige carpet, and scrunched his toes into the soft pile.

He closed his eyes and said, "I'm sorry, Kate. As much as I want to be with you, I just can't. Not yet." He prayed she'd understand.

She sighed, clearly frustrated by his denial.

He sat, back curved and shoulders sagging on the edge of the bed. Kate leaned up on her elbow and rubbed his hunched back. "It's okay, Matt. I'll let you take the lead on this. Just don't forget to tell me when you're ready."

He turned around and scooped her up in a bear hug. "Thank you, Kate. That means more to me than anything else," he whispered into her ear.

She squeezed him back and took a deep breath of his manly scent. She burrowed her face into the skin of his bare neck, and rested her cheek on his warm shoulder.

He leaned his head to the side. He loved being wanted by her, needed by her. He hoped she'd be able to wait for him to come to grips with his hang-ups. She'd already quit on him once and he feared she'd do it again. He'd be cautiously optimistic and let things play out. He'd avoid reading too much into any visions that showed them apart. Quite frankly, he couldn't tolerate being away from her again.

He released her from his grip and softly set her on the bed. He kissed her forehead, stood, and turned in the direction of the bathroom. "I'll shower up first and call Father LaCroix. I think there's some cereal in the kitchen if you're hungry." He walked toward the door.

"Sounds good, Matt," she said.

"Okay." He hurried off to take a very cold shower.

Kate flopped down on the bed as he retreated into the recesses of the hallway. "This priest is going to think I'm a big, fat slut," she mumbled as she fought the urge to join Matt in the shower. She grimaced. "A big, fat, *horny* slut."

***

After calling sick into work, Kate fidgeted in her seat, peering into the small makeup mirror in the visor to fix her face with the meager supplies that were in her purse. She'd borrowed a button-down shirt from Matt's closet. She rolled up the sleeves to make it fit better and groaned when it slid back down her thin arm, clearly wishing she'd had the foresight to pack a bag of clothes and other supplies before she'd abandoned her house.

As he drove, Matt looked at her and laughed.

"What?" she said, obviously annoyed by his amused expression. "I'm nervous okay? So shoot me."

"I wish I could shoot you," he said with a broad grin, "with a camera anyway. You look gorgeous. There's something so sexy about a woman in a man's shirt." He wiggled his eyebrows.

"Great. You only want me when we're headed to see your priest."

He recoiled. He'd tried joking to calm her, but it was backfiring horribly.

"I'm sorry Matt," she said quickly, clearly recognizing she'd hurt him. "I'm just freaking out about meeting your priest. I've never been good with the religion-thing." She gave him a sheepish grin.

"Religion-thing?"

"You know what I mean." She groaned. "My mother used to be a different religion every other week. She'd be rubbing Buddha statues one week and attending wacky religious retreats the next. It's a wonder I was never kidnapped by a cult."

Matt laughed heartily. "Well, I can assure you that Father LaCroix is perfectly nice and professional. I bet he won't even ask you to join the cult." He choked back giddy laughter that threatened to force its way out of him.

"Funny. You are a funny, funny little man, Matt." She playfully punched him in the shoulder.

He rubbed his shoulder where she'd punched him. "Ouch! I'm taking you straight to confession!"

"I don't think Father LaCroix could handle my confessions."

He looked at her with wide eyes. "Let's not go there."

"Yeah. One issue at a time. So, how much does Father LaCroix know about my house problems?"

"Pretty much everything except for what happened to you last night. I thought it should come from you. You can tell him exactly what you were doing and what you heard. He's really interested in this type of stuff."

"He could probably write a book on the crap that's happening at my place." She stared absently out the car window.

Matt grunted in agreement. They pulled into the parking lot for the Sacred Heart Catholic Church. He drove the length of the lot and pulled into an open spot right in front of the rectory that was connected to the backside of the old stone church.

They climbed from their seats and shut the doors. She looked at the church, clearly marveling at the huge stained glass windows that adorned the walls. "Wow, this place is beautiful!" she said, obviously impressed by the delicate beauty of the multi-colored vignettes.

"Thanks." He followed her gaze to the vibrant panes of glass.

"I've driven by here a million times, but I've never been this close to it. The windows are just gorgeous."

Matt nodded, proud. He'd always loved this church. He was probably the only kid in the world who looked forward to Sunday services. When the priest gave his sermon, Matt would stare at the windows, and imagine stories that went along with the figures in the colorful glass.

"Are you ready?" He checked the time on his wrist watch. "We're going to be late if we don't go in soon."

"Yeah. Sure. Of course." She walked around the car toward him. "Let's do this," she said and grabbed his hand for support.

Matt walked to the entrance of the rectory and rang the bell. It clanged musically behind the door, summoning Father LaCroix. After waiting for a brief moment, echoing footsteps stopped at the other side of the heavy door. The old wrought iron handle bent downward and the door creaked open. Matt watched Kate as she greeted Father LaCroix.

Clearly, she realized Matt had left a few details about his old friend out of their earlier conversation. First of all, he was much younger than Matt had indicated, not much older than the two of them. He was handsome, too, with thick, sandy blonde hair combed neatly on the sides, framing his pleasant face. Piercing, joyous blue eyes capped off his appearance, clearly a priest that would make female congregants swoon despite his promised and permanent chastity.

"Hi, Matt," said Father LaCroix with a smile. "And, you must be Miss Hart," he added and shook her hand.

"Follow me, guys," he said cheerily. He led them down a dark hallway into a modest living room that smelled of scented oils and furniture polish. "Have a seat." He pointed to a well-worn, wood framed sofa.

They sat down on the old couch. Quite fragile, the blue and white French Toile fabric was worn in a few places. Most of the furniture in the book-lined room seemed old. The mix of scents and dark, mahogany furniture reminded Matt of his childhood.

He turned to Kate and overheard her quietly warn herself, "Settle down, kiddo." Clearly she was uncomfortable here. He grabbed her hand and gave it a gentle squeeze.

Father LaCroix pulled an ornately carved Victorian-style chair over toward the couch and sat down in front of them, their knees practically touching. Kate scooted back on the couch and looked at Matt. He was unfazed by the closeness of the priest.

"So, what can I do for you guys?" He first looked at Matt, then over at Kate.

Matt poked his thumb in her direction. "We're here

about Kate's house. It's gotten worse since I talked to you last week."

"I'm sorry to hear that, Kate," he said. "Can I call you Kate?"

"Yeah. Kate's perfect." She smiled, clearly shy.

"Why don't you fill me in on the new developments?"

"Okay. I met with Chief Redbird yesterday. He's a Chief with the Penobscot tribe." Father LaCroix nodded as if he knew who she meant. "He gave me a bundle of sage to do a blessing at my house, to rid it of the spirits who might be messing with things over there. But, when I got to the basement, I heard moaning and screaming. It was so horrible I just took off. I haven't been back, yet, to look in the daylight. Maybe it was an animal, but I don't think so. It sounded… human." She shuddered.

"I've heard of sage blessings making things worse in a house with paranormal issues. That's why the Catholic Church doesn't recommend them. We could try performing a religious blessing. Call out the spirits and urge them to leave. I think we should probably start there." He smiled at her, a comforting smile.

"And what if your blessing is as ineffective as the sage?"

"Kate!" said Matt, embarrassed.

"It's okay, Matt. It's a great question. If the religious blessing fails, we usually do something stronger, so to speak," said Father LaCroix.

"Like what?" said Kate.

Father LaCroix glanced at Matt. Matt nodded, solemn. The priest nodded back and turned toward Kate.

"Like *what*?" she repeated, clearly she'd noticed their odd exchange.

Matter-of-factly, Father LaCroix said, "An exorcism. Although, I hope it won't come to that. I'd have to get permission from the Vatican to perform one, but sometimes they're needed. I'm one of only a handful of priests in the Northeast who've completed a successful exorcism. I received special training from the Vatican. We'll just have to wait and see how things develop." He leaned forward and patted her shaking hand.

She nodded and tears bubbled over the rims of her eyes and streamed down her face. Her whole body trembled.

Matt pulled a crumpled tissue from his pocket and handed it to her. She dabbed tears from her cheeks and took a deep breath, blowing it out between pursed lips.

"Heavy stuff," said Father LaCroix.

"Yeah." She nodded and sniffed.

"It probably won't even come to that." He gave her a knowing pat on the back of her hand.

She looked at Matt and searched his face. His expression green, it was clear to Kate that he didn't agree with the Father's assessment.

Her voice trembled, "So, when?"

"How about this afternoon? I usually find the sooner these things get taken care of, the less likely they are to, um, progress," he added

"We don't want that," Matt said, his eyes pleading.

"Of course. I just want my house back. My life back." She nodded, clearly determined.

"Great. It'll take me a few hours to gather my gear and

get prepared. Do you want to meet outside your house after lunch?" He checked the time on his watch, "Say one o'clock?"

"Sure, sounds great, Father LaCroix," said Matt. He reached over and pumped the priest's hand.

"Thanks, Father," said Kate.

"Okay, then. I'll meet you at one. Just please don't enter the house without me."

Kate eyed him suspiciously and stood up from the antique couch. She pulled her key necklace from the collar of her shirt and gave it a quick squeeze. She felt calmer immediately.

"See you soon, Father," said Matt. He rose from the couch and put his hand on Kate's shoulder.

Father LaCroix walked them back down the darkened hallway to the heavy wood door and opened it for them with a loud creak. He nodded as they passed him, Kate first, then Matt. As Matt cleared the threshold of the door, Father LaCroix grabbed his arm and tugged him back to speak directly into his ear. "Remember," he whispered harshly, "do *not* go in without me."

With big, frightened eyes, Matt nodded obediently at the priest. He understood the warning probably more than Father LaCroix knew. He'd had visions all night about the house and wasn't planning on setting foot inside it without the protection of faith. A holy man wouldn't hurt either. He walked to the car where Kate had been waiting for him.

"What was that about?" she said after they settled into their seats.

"He just reminded me to not go in the house without

him," he said. He shrugged. "I think he's just playing it safe, Kate. Let's just do what he says. He's helping us for free, you know."

"Right. But, as soon as this is over, I'm done having people tell me what I can and can't do," she grumbled under her breath.

He smiled and patted her thigh. "You are a trouper."

"Humph," she grunted.

He laughed heartily. She could be stubborn as a mule, but he loved that about her. She was tough and bull-headed. Ironically, she reminded him a great deal of Grandma Betty. He wished she was still alive so she could meet his Kate. He'd also love to know her read of the situation. In the past, if he came across a sensitive situation, he'd dream of Grandma Betty and she'd give him advice. He'd hoped to see her last night in his dreams, but instead he had nightmares filled with fear, foreboding. He'd tried to shake off the anxious feelings he was having about being in Kate's house again, but the repeated warning from Father LaCroix made his stomach twitch nervously. He'd go for her sake. But, hoped it'd be quick. Quick and painless.

Kate waved a hand in front of Matt's glazed eyes. "Do you want to get some lunch and then head over to the house?"

He shook his head to clear it of frightening thoughts and turned toward her. He forced a smile and nodded in agreement, his voice momentarily lost.

She leaned toward him, clearly trying to read his odd expression. "Do you want to go to the diner?"

He nodded again and started the car. He swallowed

repeatedly to get his throat clear; he didn't want to sound like a teenage boy with a cracking, squeaky voice.

"Are you okay?" She inspected his ashen face. "You look a little green." With squinted eyes, she scrutinized his pallid complexion.

"I'm alright," he said. "I think I'm just hungry."

"Me, too," she agreed.

They sat quietly for the remainder of the ride to the diner. Matt sensed that Kate knew he'd lied about being okay. He worried she'd ask him the truth over lunch.

They entered the diner and were seated in their usual booth in the corner. He was grateful for the small amount of privacy afforded by the high-backed benches. He didn't want anyone in the diner to overhear them taking about ghosts or exorcisms or anything else of an unearthly nature. This was a small town, after all, and crazy traveled fast.

Kate plopped down on the puffy bench and leaned her head back on the cushion. She exhaled loudly, clearly grateful for the distraction of lunch. She ordered a roast beef sandwich and French fries. Matt ordered his usual turkey club on wheat with potato chips.

After he handed his menu back to the waitress, Kate reached over and grabbed both of his unoccupied hands. "Thanks for helping me with all of this, Matt. I know it must be especially hard for you... *with your gift*," she whispered.

"I wouldn't do it for anyone else," he said. He glanced at their hands cupped together on the table.

"Can I ask you something and you promise not to get mad?" she said.

"I'll try. It takes a lot to make me mad."

"I don't know. This may tip you over the edge."

"You're freaking me out, Kate. Just say it. Please."

"Is there something you aren't telling me?" She peered into his dark blue eyes, clearly trying to read his honest reaction to her question.

He leaned back, shocked. He'd thought he hid his fear better than that. She knew him well. Or, maybe *she* was gifted. Gifted at reading people and their emotions.

"What do you mean?" he said, trying to hide how flustered he was by her keen observation.

"I mean just what I said."

He sat for a moment, thinking how much he should tell her. He shook his head as he sorted through the information he'd been holding back.

"C'mon, Matt. I can take it. I'm a big girl." She squeezed his hands.

"I don't want to upset you, Kate." He squinted into her searching eyes.

"I'm sure I'll be fine. What can be worse than being run out of your house by a… *ghost*?" she whispered across the table. She looked over her shoulder, obviously worried that someone was eavesdropping.

"Okay, then. But don't say I didn't warn you," he said.

"Warning duly noted and accepted."

"Well, I've had visions of us being forced apart. And last night, well, last night the visions were just plain scary."

"Scary how?"

"It was about the house and what we have to go and do. In my vision, it didn't go well," he said.

She asked him, "Are your visions *always* right?"

"Usually," he said grimly.

"Oh."

"I know. But I think we still have to try."

"What about the other stuff? Us being apart? What do you make of that?" she said, her eyes welling with tears, clearly fighting the brewing sensation of becoming upset.

"I don't know what all that means exactly. I know, in my visions, I'm really sad and I can sense you're not there. I don't know if it means you move away or if we break up or if…"

"If what? Matt? If what?" she demanded.

He looked down at their clenched hands again. "If something bad happens to you," he whispered.

"Matt, *nothing* bad will happen to me. I'll burn the *fucking* place down before I let it come between us again." She spoke loudly and a couple at the next table turned their heads toward them. Kate broke her hold on one of Matt's hands and covered her mouth to stifle a giggle. She blushed.

He patted her hand reassuringly. "I'm sure you're right, Kate." He half smiled at her. Deep down, he didn't know what to believe. Usually, his visions and reality were one and the same.

The waitress approached with platefuls of food. Kate stuffed in her sandwich and fries. Matt picked at his food. He didn't feel any better after telling the truth. She didn't seem to understand the gravity of his visions. He'd need to explain it better. He crunched a potato chip under his finger. But, for now, he'd let her be happy. Her mood seemed lighter since he revealed most of his secrets and he didn't want to take that away from her. Not when he knew what they'd be walking into next.

Kate

They finished their lunch, piled into Matt's car, and left for Kate's house. Nerves were building quickly in Kate's stomach. She wished she hadn't forced herself to eat—with her growing anxiety about being in the house, she worried it might come back up.

After a few centering breaths, Kate became oddly serene. She had a modicum of control now that she had all the information Matt had kept from her. She'd decided that if this Catholic Church stuff didn't work out, and especially if they had to escalate it to the next level, she'd sell the house and never look back. There was a condo available in Matt's building. Maybe, she'd buy it and they could be close to each other. She was determined to disprove his vision. She was going to tell him what she was thinking, but decided to save it for later. His face looked green again and she wanted his full attention when she let him in on the good news.

They pulled down her rutted road. She surveyed the woods for any sign of the red-eyed man. Her search came up empty. *So far so good,* she thought.

Matt pulled to a crunching stop on the gravel in front of the house. He looked at her and was clearly surprised to see her smiling, almost blissful.

"It looks like Father LaCroix isn't here yet," he said.

She looked at the clock on the dashboard and pointed at

the green numbers. "Is that right?"

He glanced at the clock and saw it was three minutes after one. "Yeah, it might a couple minutes fast, but no more than five," he said.

"I hope we didn't miss him," she said, concerned.

"We didn't. He's always late for Mass so I think he'll be here soon."

"Do you want to wait outside?" She nodded to the welcoming porch.

"Um, no thanks." He gulped. "I think Father LaCroix would want us to wait for him in the car."

"You scaredy cat," she said. "Fine, we'll wait in the car."

Matt exhaled, obviously relieved she was so agreeable.

Kate knew he needed to get his head together to even allow himself to go inside her plagued house. She hoped he had the balls to walk through the front door. Even she could sense something had changed since she was here last. Despite in the relative safety of the car, she felt a distinct heaviness in the air. To her, it was like trying to breathe on the top of Mt. Everest, like she needed a respirator to help pull enough oxygen into her lungs.

"You okay, Matt?" She peered over at him, her eyes suspicious. His skin was pale green and now his chest was heaving. She reached over and grabbed his wrist. She turned it over and felt for his pulse. It raced madly under his clammy skin. "Whoa, Matt, you need to calm down."

He gave her a weak smile. "I'm just a little nervous."

She squinted at him, unsure if he was telling the whole truth. *Oh, God, is there something else?* "You can wait out here if you need to. I don't want you to go in if it's going to give you a heart attack."

"I'll be fine." He twisted his wrist away from her grasp. "I just need to breathe for a minute." He took in a deep drag of the thick, useless air.

"Okay, but as your nurse, if I see you looking weak, I'm pulling the plug on this whole thing."

He nodded in agreement. "Yes, Boss." He appeared to feel a bit better after taking several yawning breaths.

They sat in silence, alternately staring at the clock and the house. She thrummed her fingers on the dashboard. The minutes ticked by; it was ten minutes past one. Finally, the sound of wheels on the gravel drew up behind them. To their relief, Father LaCroix pulled his large black sedan to a stop next to Kate's passenger side window. He looked over and smiled at her through the dusty glass.

She waved timidly at the priest, still surprised by his youthful appearance. She'd always imagined priests old and stuffy, not young, vibrant, and handsome. *Were his parents disappointed he'd never provide them with grandchildren, being a celibate priest and all?* She blushed at the thought of Father LaCroix making grandchildren. She couldn't believe how dirty her mind could be at such an odd time. It was more evidence she needed to be with Matt. Soon.

The creak from Matt's door opening and closing brought her back. He was already around the car, ready to open her door by the time she'd shaken images of the naked priest out of her twisted mind.

She stepped from the car and nodded thank you to Matt for being a chivalrous gentleman. They waited for Father

LaCroix to gather the items he'd need for the blessing from the passenger seat of his car.

"That ought to do it," he said, a slim smile of obvious satisfaction spreading across his attractive face. He ducked from the recess of the car and shut the door firmly behind him. "So, this is the place, huh?" He scanned the dark windows with a thoughtful, curious gaze.

"Yup, this is it," said Kate.

"You guys ready?" He looked into their eyes, one set at a time. Kate nodded. Matt stood motionless, like a statue. A green, sweaty statue.

"Matt?" she said. She reached toward his left wrist. It hung limply by his side. She'd be damned if she'd let him have a heart attack or stroke at her expense.

Matt shook his head and pulled his arm away before she could grab it. "I'm fine, let's go," he said.

"Okay," said Father LaCroix. "Ladies first." He pointed the way with a broad sweep of his arm.

She dug the keys from the recesses of her purse, stoically walked up the front steps of the porch, and inserted the key. The door unlocked with a click and she pushed the door wide open, allowing the small amount of sunshine afforded by the tall pines to filter into the living room.

She was relieved when nothing rushed out at her. She hadn't known what to expect upon her return. The screaming from the basement had been so loud she'd assumed she'd released some sort of angry creature from behind the crumbling brick wall.

She turned back and smiled at the two men who waited behind her on the bottom step, clearly nervous. *They looked ready to run, too*, she thought as she turned her attention back to the open door. She sucked in a mouthful of pine scented air and stepped over the threshold into her living room. At least, it *had* been a living room when she'd fled yesterday.

Kate gasped. Her eyes bulged as they took in the upturned landscape that was the remains of ruined furniture. The room had been completely trashed. Trashed wasn't even the correct word. Destroyed was a better word. She covered her gaping mouth with a trembling hand and stepped over a large wad of stuffing from her couch and into the middle of the mess.

"What the hell?" said Matt as he stepped through the doorway, slightly ahead of Father LaCroix. "Didn't you lock up, Kate?" He said, clearly assuming only thieves or vandals could wreck a room so completely.

"Yes, I'm pretty sure I did," she said from behind her hand.

"I was afraid of this," said Father LaCroix from the doorway.

Kate and Matt whirled around, startled by the sound of Father LaCroix's voice. Kate had almost forgotten he was here. She was befuddled, shocked at the absolute destruction of her property.

"Afraid of what?" said Matt.

"When a spirit is very powerful and very angry, they can sometimes do this," said the priest. He pointed at the damage in front of them and under their feet.

"You mean a fucking ghost did this to my house?" said Kate.

"Kate!" said Matt, clearly embarrassed by her salty language in front of his priest.

"It's okay, Matt. She's in shock. It's really quite startling. I've never seen so much damage before. Not to this extent anyway." He kicked aside a large pillow casing, gutted of its foam center.

"What the *hell* is in my house?" sputtered Kate. She was pissed. More than pissed. Irate. Not only had an invisible force chased her from her own home, but now it had trashed her personal effects.

"I don't quite know yet, but I think we'll know a lot more after I start the blessing," he said. He bent down to pick up a broken picture frame that held a photo of Kate's deceased mother and shook the smashed shards of glass onto the floor. They landed on the hard wood with a melodic tinkle. He handed her the remains of the frame.

She grabbed the broken frame from his hand and set it on the coffee table she'd just righted. It was missing a leg, but it still stood, leaning sickly to one side like a three legged dog. She fished in another pile and picked up the remote control to her television set. The remote seemed to be intact, but when she looked where the television had been mounted on the wall, she shook her head with disgust. The screen had been smashed into a million pieces. Wires and electronic components dangled from the jagged holes left by her unseen enemy.

She threw the remote on top of the overturned couch. She remembered how difficult it had been moving it in here not too long ago. *How angry must the spirit have been to turn a heavy couch upside down?* She sighed and looked at the shredded remains of her life. "Let's get this thing out of my house," she said to Father LaCroix.

He nodded, set his kit on the skewed coffee table and unloaded his religious paraphernalia. To prepare, he carefully removed a purple silk vestment from his bag, kissed it and placed it over the shoulders of his black robe. He retrieved a tiny glass bottle containing holy water and a giant gold cross from his black kit. From a small velvet bag with a drawstring he removed a necklace of white rosary beads. They sparkled in a small wedge of sunshine that filtered through the partially open front door.

Kate continued to search the rubble for salvageable items. She saw Matt standing rigidly by the front door, soaking in the warm rays of light. Breathing unevenly, he watched her futilely look for unbroken treasures in the massive field of debris as Father LaCroix built his religious arsenal from the sad, tilted coffee table. She stopped briefly to watch his preparations. *Is this young priest strong enough to rid me of the vicious creature that has torn my life apart?* she wondered. At least now she didn't think she'd be stubborn about wanting to stay. Any creature strong enough to move full-sized furniture shouldn't be taken lightly. What if she'd been home alone when the extensive damage had occurred? Her skull could easily have been crushed by any number of items that had been thrown about. A vase, the coffee table, even the end of the couch could have instantly crushed the life out of her. *Was this what Matt's vision had warned him of? Urging him to get her the hell out of here before something physical and irreversible happened to her?*

"I think I'm ready," said Father LaCroix. He wrapped the glittering rosary beads firmly around his right fist and placed the heavy cross in the palm of the same hand. He held his open Bible in the other and turned it to the proper page, marking it with a strip of brown dimpled leather that matched the old cover.

"Where do we start?" she said, giving up her search for valuables. She walked carefully across the litter-strewn room and stood next to the priest.

"I think since you heard it in the basement, we'll start upstairs and bless the majority of the house before we have any sort of, um, confrontation," he said.

"Good enough," Kate said. She guided them to the narrow hallway leading upstairs. She crossed into the kitchen and gasped again at the carnage left behind by whatever was living in her basement. The kitchen had been equally ravaged. Pots and pans, once neatly stacked under the counter, were dented and tossed on the floor. Boxes of cereal she'd neatly arranged on top of the refrigerator were scattered across the room, plastic pouches ripped open and trails of crushed cereal in every direction. The refrigerator was pulled to the end of its cord, still plugged into the outlet, running furiously. The contents of the refrigerator were spilled on the floor near the door that dangled open, blocked by a pile of cracked eggs, curdled milk and smashed containers of leftovers. The ice cream from the freezer lay in a pool of soggy cardboard and water. Melted dessert oozed from the crushed lid into a sticky puddle, a swirl of chocolate and vanilla danced on her new linoleum.

She turned away from the mess. Her germ phobia started

to take root as she got a whiff of the spoiling dairy products. She clenched the railing of the stairwell and stomped up the steps. She didn't care if the asshole in the basement heard her, she was here to win. This thing had nearly cost her relationship with Matt and now it was costing her money in repairs, broken furniture, and wasted food. She'd go bankrupt before she let the stupid thing beat her.

Matt and Father LaCroix, mouths agape, stepped gingerly through the maze of scattered food and followed her up the stairs.

Kate was surprised at her own bravery. She was more pissed than scared. A pissed Kate meant a determined Kate. And, even though she knew she'd probably have to leave this place, the stubborn perfectionist in her wouldn't be able to leave rotting food on the floor ruining the finish. She was surprised she was able to walk by it right now.

Her bedroom and the spare bedroom across the small hallway were in just as much disarray as the downstairs. Whatever had been up here had done a thorough job. It hadn't left one piece of furniture or picture frame untouched. Everything was either broken to smithereens or turned on its side. Her mattress had been shredded down to the metal coils. Even the box spring was broken, the slats of wood torn from the frame, nails and all.

When the men reached her bedroom, they found her looking into the tattered remains of her closet. All of her clothes had been ripped from the padded hangers and thrown in a shredded heap at the bottom of the closet. Her shoes, once neatly lining the floor of the closet in an orderly row, were tossed around the room. One black high heeled dress shoe stuck out of the screen of her small television set that used to rest on top of her toppled dresser.

"What did I do to this thing?" she asked Father LaCroix when she became aware he had entered the room. She wiped tears from her cheeks with the back of her hand and waited for his response.

"Nothing, Kate. It's not you. It's the house… or the land."

"Everything I own is ruined. What do I tell the insurance company? I need everything replaced because an angry ghost trashed my crap?"

Father LaCroix chuckled. "I don't know much about insurance, but I'm sure we could come up with something. Maybe a wind storm?"

"Yeah. Maybe." She was only half listening. She was too distracted by the wasteland of her bedroom, her sanctuary.

"Do you want me to get started, Kate?" said Father LaCroix.

Venomously, she said, "Let's get this red-eyed fucker out of my house."

Matt's eyes bugged out of his head. Kate threw him a glare. He had better not even try to speak with her later about etiquette or any of that nonsense. The priest would get over it—it wasn't like he'd never heard it before. Besides, she was pissed—if there ever was a time to swear, it was now. She turned and began to pace heavily around the upturned room.

Father LaCroix walked purposefully around the room, sprinkling holy water in every corner, window, and doorway. He held up the cross and his rosary covered hand in the center of the room and repeated, "Holy Father, please reclaim this house for Kate and those who follow her. I banish any spirits from this home. Go into the light and leave this house. You are not welcome here. In the name of the Father, the Son, and the Holy Spirit. Amen."

He repeated the same mantra in both bedrooms upstairs and in every room on the main floor. After an hour of slowly covering every inch of the house with his holy blessing, it was time to reclaim the basement.

Kate led them down the creaking, narrow steps to her basement. So far, she'd been feeling left out of the ritualistic blessing. Matt seemed to know exactly when to say 'amen' and when to cross himself, but she had no clue. She felt like such a pagan. It was no wonder she had destructive spirits in her house.

On the center of the second to last step, she was surprised to see one of the bricks from the weird wall she'd started to take down. She bent down and picked up the brick, it was ice cold. *Why was it left on the steps?* She turned it over in her hands and searched it for any clues. She chalked it up to the ghost; it had put it there, probably as it trashed the basement. She set the brick back on the step and continued down the stairs, turning at the end to face the musty darkness.

At the bottom of the stairs, she stopped and surveyed the view in front of her. The basement was as she'd left it when she ran out screaming. Except for two things: the wall and the floor. The wall, the one she'd taken a few bricks from, was completely obliterated and the floor was littered with shards of brick and maroon dust, as if a bomb had been detonated in her basement.

To make room for Matt and Father LaCroix, she took a hesitant step forward. They descended the stairs behind her. Matt gasped. He'd seen the wall before and clearly he knew this was a change. A big change.

"What is it?" asked Father LaCroix.

Kate pointed at the crumbling remains of the wall. "That was a wall," she managed to croak. Any other words escaped her. Her throat, suddenly dry, felt as though it was peeling.

"Kate, did you do all that?" said Matt.

She shook her head and swallowed, urging her vocal cords to work. "No way. I only took out a couple bricks. That looks like it…"

"Exploded?" finished Matt. He stepped next to her, his eyes wide with fear and amazement.

"Right! It looks like something exploded from the wall. Look at how all the bricks fell this way," she said. She pointed at the broken pieces of brick and red dust covering the dirt floor.

"This isn't good," said Matt. He shook his head glumly. "Not good at all."

"Whatever's down here is very powerful, Kate," said Father LaCroix.

"I can feel it. Can you feel how heavy the air is down here?" Matt said. "I can barely breathe." He heaved and grabbed at the collar of his shirt, pulling it away from his neck.

"It does feel oppressive down here," said Father

LaCroix. "I've read about this sensation. I think I'll need to check in with the Vatican for advice." He nodded at the broken remains of the wall. "I don't think a blessing will cover whatever made that break."

"Just try it," she demanded.

"Are you serious?" said Matt. His eyes pleading, he searched her awed face for an answer to his question.

"What harm could it do?" she said, giving him a dismissive shrug. "The place is already a complete write-off. We might as well try."

Jabbing his index finger toward the crushed bricks, Matt said, "If a little bit of sage made this happen, what do you think holy water would do?"

"I want to see," she said, indignant.

"What do you think, Father?" Matt said, obviously hopeful his old friend would have the good sense to leave before things became dangerous.

Scanning the dingy, rubble-filled basement, Father LaCroix shrugged. "I don't see what it would hurt. Things already look pretty bad down here."

"Fine, then," she said. "*Please* continue." She clenched her teeth and glared at Matt. "You can go if you're too scared, Matt."

"Thanks for the offer, Kate, but I'll stay," he said.

She shrugged her shoulders dismissively at him again and turned her attention to Father LaCroix. She gave him a nod of encouragement, urging him to begin blessing the basement.

Father LaCroix took a hesitant step toward the ruined wall. When he was ten feet away, he sprinkled the remaining holy water in every direction.

Kate didn't know if she was imagining things, but she would swear the water sounded like it sizzled as it landed on the broken bricks and dirt floor.

Father LaCroix took a deep breath to ready himself for the speaking part of his blessing. Before he uttered a single syllable, a ghastly screech flew at them from the far side of the basement. It moved their hair and clothes as if they'd been hit with a strong gust of wind.

Matt trembled and turned to run for the stairs, clearly he expected the others to follow. "Kate! Let's get out of here," he called to her.

"I want to see it," she said. She lurched forward. To her own ears, she didn't sound right, she almost seemed to be in a trance, like she was being beckoned deeper into the dark corner of the basement by the screaming sound.

Matt turned back and pushed passed the immobile Father LaCroix who still held his rosary beads, cross, and Bible in the air. His body trembled although his feet seemed frozen in place.

Matt went to Kate first and quickly reached for her shoulder before she could stumble closer to the noise in the corner, toward whatever evil screeched defiantly at them. She pushed against his hand, still trying to move closer to the sound. He dug his fingers into the soft flesh of her shoulder and pulled her hard, turning her around. She blinked at him and shook her head dully. She wanted to see it, but felt that something was wrong. Maybe she should go with Matt after all. Her eyes burned as she tried to focus on his face.

"Kate! Move your ass!" he yelled into her confused

face, shaking her shoulders with his hands.

She nodded, and followed him towards the stairs. The creature in the corner shrieked a deafening, angry roar as they retreated from the center of the basement, moving toward the safety of the stairs. Kate watched as Matt left her at the base of the staircase and ran back to Father LaCroix. He grabbed him by one of his outstretched arms and physically turned his body toward the stairs. His feet shuffled on the dirt floor. Matt looked into his friend's dazed face and snapped his fingers inches from his glazed eyes. "Wake up, Father! Time to go!" he ordered and dragged him toward the stairs.

Father LaCroix shook his head dumbly. Then, fear obviously caught up with him, and he started to run with them up the stairs.

They burst out the basement door and ran toward the open front door, each of them tripping over the mess left by the invisible intruder. Only after they were safely outside by their cars did they stop to catch their breath. Kate breathed heavily as the fog that had overtaken her mind started to clear. The whole incident in the basement was a bit of a blur. All she could remember was broken bricks… and screaming. *Was I screaming? Or was it something else?*

Panting, Matt turned to face them. Father LaCroix was doubled over, leaning on his car for support. Between heaves for air, he said, "We must… call… the Vatican."

They nodded in agreement as they watched him wheeze into the metal hood of his car.

"We're going to need the big guns," Matt said to Kate.

"The biggest," she agreed, her eyes wide and unblinking. "We'll need the whole freaking army." She looked
back at the infested house she'd once considered hers. She
understood now she'd need to fight hard to get it back.
Harder than she could ever imagine. Harder than she believed she could. And there was no guarantee it would
work. Her once organized life was suddenly full of more
questions than answers.

***

Like an old married couple, they spent the week together at Matt's condominium. They would go to work, come
home, make dinner together, and then go to sleep. Just
sleep. Matt had discussed his choice with Kate before their
week together had begun to ensure she'd have no hard feelings or disappointments in regards to them making love.
He'd explained that with everything going on, he wasn't
ready, that he needed this craziness resolved before he'd
get intimate with her. He'd also pointed out that this was
direct advice from Father LaCroix, clearly hoping Kate
would aim a bit of her growing resentment at him instead
of focusing it all on Matt.

Kate had said she understood, but remained annoyed.
She'd never dated anyone who played so hard-to-get. She
tried not to take it personally and decided to let their week
unfold organically. She hadn't returned to her home since
the three of them had been chased off by the terrifying noises from her basement.

She tried not to think about her home being trashed.
She'd already written it off as a complete loss. She still

had a little money left from the sale of her mother's cottage. Maybe she could swing two mortgages for a short time, at least until she could sell her house. Of course, she still wanted to rid it of whatever was living down in her basement; no one could sell it with an invisible, shrieking creature scaring potential buyers, forcing them out the door. Not even Susan, the lying bitch. And, that was without mentioning the rotting food and broken furniture littering every room. The chaos alone would make a prospective purchaser turn and run and never look back.

Since she didn't have any clothes with her, she'd gone on a mini-shopping spree, buying new shirts, jeans, and one set of sexy lingerie, just in case Matt came to his senses. She hoped her presence for a week would break him down. So far, though, he was Fort Knox. In a weird way, she admired his restraint. She could have used that in college where she regularly enjoyed the company of cute frat boys and way too many Natty Light beers. She'd been a free spirit, channeling the hippie days of her mother with all her free love and excessive drinking. She was lucky to survive without a baby, a raging sexually transmitted disease, or a hideous tramp stamp on her lower back.

At Matt's place, on workdays, she'd leave the condo at 6 a.m. while Matt slept. She'd show up in street clothes at the hospital and raid the linen closet for scrubs. Marlene led the gossip parade and many nurses were a-twitter with what the unusual arrangement might mean. She'd overheard one person in the bathroom telling someone she and Matt were living together, shacked up, possibly she was pregnant.

She overheard three nurses wishing they were the ones

to have him and his undivided attention. They didn't know Kate and Matt had yet to "do it" but she enjoyed knowing at least they assumed they were.

She played coy with Marlene under a day of direct questioning. Kate knew the unspoken details were driving her insane. Nothing was funnier than watching the three hundred-plus pound Marlene red in the face and stomping around like a fat, angry toddler when she didn't get her way. Despite being practically homeless and not getting any boom-boom from her boyfriend, Kate was having a pretty good week. The stress of her infested house was slowly dissipating. She almost wished she didn't have to deal with the house and its spirits at all, but the wheels for a solution were in motion and she would feel guilty leaving a rabid ghost lurking around for the next owner.

While they had a relatively normal week, playing house and going to work, Father LaCroix was busier than ever. He phoned Matt to say that on top of his usual days of holding masses, visiting the sick and infirm, and spending hours preparing his sermons, he was in near constant contact with specialists at the Vatican. He told them that he had to relate Kate's story to tier after tier of gatekeepers, slowly working his way up to the ones who could make an emergency decision. So far, he'd convinced the first three levels of priests that this was a case for exorcism. Cardinal Henry was in the process of taking the information to a special meeting with the Pope and three other high ranking officials. Needless to say, Vatican City was buzzing about Kate Hart and her demon.

Clearly, Father LaCroix wasn't surprised the specialists

at the Vatican had considered her problems were caused by a demon. It fit the classic mold: the horrible screeching noises, the massive destruction of property, the sordid history of suicides on the property, and his research regarding the red-eyed man and the beliefs of the Penobscot tribe. He'd even made time to interview Kate's friend, Chief Redbird.

According to Father LaCroix and the internal writings by the Catholic diocese, the folklore of Native American tribes was treated as fact versus fantasy or a wild peyote trip because of the Indian's purported connection to the spiritual world.

Kate imagined a circle of richly clad, elderly holy men sitting shoulder to shoulder at the small, ornately carved antique table in the Vatican's 'Situation Room.' Father LaCroix told her and Matt that he'd been allowed in that room only once while he trained for this very situation. Every wall was covered with intricate tapestries. Small antique pedestals dotted the room topped with other treasures favored by the ruling Pope: hand-carved, gold-dipped busts of former Popes, angel sculptures by famous artists like Michelangelo and Donatello. He'd remembered a gold, jewel-encrusted chalice from ancient Rome and said he wished he could've spent more time in that room, but was whisked away to continue his studies.

He'd also told them that although he'd performed only one exorcism before, it had been successful and was confident he could do it again, even though he feared the ferocious monster in her basement.

He had to cut their conversation short, leaving his cell

phone to answer the rectory's landline, promising to get back to them with any news. "Hello?" he said into the phone.

"Father LaCroix? It's Cardinal Henry," said the husky voice on the other end of the crackling phone line. "You probably know why I'm calling. I've discussed the case with the Pope and his committee and they agree something needs to be done about the demon in Ms. Hart's house. Based on the description and subsequent research, it sounds quite serious, especially with the Native American piece added to it. The land may be a problem as well."

"So I can do the exorcism?" Father LaCroix said.

"Yes. But the Pope himself has some *very* strict guidelines for you to follow," Cardinal Henry said. "Do you have a pencil?"

"Yes, Cardinal. Go ahead. I'm ready." He pulled a blank orange sticky note from the dispenser on his desk and held his pencil above it.

"The Pope wishes you to be *extremely* cautious. He does *not* want you to antagonize the demon. Just banish it. Apparently, they'd had a case in England where the priest baited a demon into a confrontation and it did not go well."

Father LaCroix nodded, holding the phone in the crook of his neck.

"Secondly, Ms. Hart must be present for the entire ritual. The committee was concerned the demon might be particularly focused on her. She was the one who awakened it by disturbing its lair. Not that they fault her. There was no way she could know what was behind that wall. We imagine a previous owner of her property was compelled to build the wall, either by the creature or on their own accord, to keep it hidden away."

"Okay," he agreed and wrote the second instruction on his paper.

"Thirdly," the Cardinal said, "if you feel like you or Ms. Hart are in *any* danger, you are to get the hell out of there.

Father LaCroix thanked him and asked him to please thank his Excellence for his faith in his ability to perform the exorcism. "I'll do my best to rid the earth of the demon."

The Cardinal asked when the exorcism would take place.

"I think I could be prepared for tomorrow evening. I want to reread the passages and memorize them in case anything happens to my Bible. I've heard demons could get physical."

"You've heard correctly," said Cardinal Henry. "You should prepare to work under any conditions. Demons have been known to make the temperature of a room change, hot or cold. They can also mimic voices, sound like a lost loved one. They'll try every underhanded trick to interrupt the exorcism. It's up to you and you alone to continue. Even if Ms. Hart asks you to stop, *you must not stop* the blessing. If the demon thinks he's won, his power becomes even more potent. His Excellence would not like that."

"I imagine he would not." Father LaCroix gulped. A heavy, stress-induced pressure built in his chest. He held the phone's receiver away from his mouth and took a few deep, cleansing breaths.

"Continue your preparations, Father," said Cardinal

Henry. Neither spoke for a few moments. Then, "I'm sure you'll do just fine."

"I hope so, Cardinal."

"God bless you, Father LaCroix."

"Thank you, Cardinal. God bless you as well."

"We'll wait to hear from you. Good day," said Cardinal Henry. He hung up the phone with a loud shriek of static.

"Here we go," Father LaCroix said to the stack of anti-demon books on desk. "Here we go."

***

"Hi Kate, its Father LaCroix," he said into the phone.

"Hey, Father, nice to hear from you," she said. She worked to regain her breath. She'd been on a run and was jogging in the door when the phone had started ringing.

"How are you doing?" he said, clearly concerned by her heavy breathing.

"Doing okay," she said. She took a swig from her water bottle. "Really good, actually," she added. She wiped her wet mouth with the back of her hand.

"I'm glad to hear it, Kate."

"So, what can I do for you? Are you looking for Matt?" she said.

"Well, both of you, actually. I just heard back from the Vatican about your, um, your situation. They gave us the go-ahead," he said.

"Already?" She was dumbfounded. *Is the thing in my basement more serious than I'd thought?* She shook her head to make sense of everything. She'd worked so hard to ignore it for the last few days, she wasn't happy to have to revisit it so soon.

"Yes. They tend to fast-track these requests now since a delay recently… ah… not important."

"Oh?"

"So, are you guys available tomorrow night? I think I'll be ready by then," he said.

"Why not tonight?"

"Well, quite frankly, I need to rehearse."

"Rehearse? What do you mean?"

"Rehearse, like practice. Your spirit was classified a demon by the Catholic Church. Demons can be quite feisty as evidenced by the remains of your interior decorating. I need to memorize my Bible passages in case it gets, let's just say, gets close."

"Close? Like touching us?" That thought had never entered her mind. Obviously, she knew it was strong based on the size of the furniture it'd ruined, but she never imagined it would or *could* get physical with a person.

"Yes. I hope I'm not scaring you, Kate."

"I guess I should be scared. I wasn't fully grasping this as being a danger to *me*. I thought of it more as a nuisance."

"No. It's definitely more than that."

"So, you said they classified it a demon? Based on what?"

"Based on a number of factors such as the history of the property, Chief Redbird's account, and our recent experience. It's sort of a no-brainer for an experienced committee like the one you'd find at the Vatican. They were certain about it."

"Huh," she said. Slowly, she was soaking in the list of

strikes against her home starting with the missing keys and ending with the furniture smashed by the shrieking creature who'd taken up residence in her house.

"Are you following all this, Kate?" he said. "Should I call later and talk to Matt?"

"I'm not a child, Father LaCroix. I can tell him what you said. I'm just surprised they took it so seriously so fast. I thought we'd have more time."

"More time for what?"

"I don't know. Just more time to… ignore it, I guess. I'm sorry I snapped at you."

"It's okay, Kate. It's a lot to take in, I know."

"I mean, it's just that I've really been enjoying myself, staying with Matt. I'm just not ready to go home yet." Her face burned with embarrassment. She couldn't believe she told a priest she enjoyed living in sin.

"Matt's a wonderful man," he said. "I should know. We grew up together."

"I didn't know that! Matt never told me." *Why had he never told me?*

"We were altar boys together and used to rule our little neighborhood. We'd run through the woods, playing games and goofing off. We both had quite wonderful childhoods."

"Was he always so reserved and responsible?"

"Pretty much," he said. "We'd actually talked about going to seminary school together." He chuckled. "Then Matt discovered girls."

"You didn't?"

"It's not like that exactly. I've had a few girlfriends. But, I always felt pulled to the church. I can't explain it.

I've always wanted to serve God and this was the best way I knew how."

"Well, lucky for me, there were pretty girls in your elementary school," she said.

"And high school and college," he teased. "It probably didn't hurt that he was a handsome jock, too. I was more the bookworm."

"Well, I do appreciate your help. I'm sorry I was snippy with you. I've never been good around, ah... holy people."

"Oh, you're doing great. If it's easier for you, you can call me Roger. That's what Matt usually calls me."

"Well, thanks Roger," she said.

"So, will you get Matt on board for tomorrow night?"

"I'm sure he'll be there with bells on." She laughed hollowly. She hoped he'd go. She'd heard him thrashing about in his sleep the last few nights and he was looking haggard lately. She hoped he could muster the courage to go with her.

"Good enough. Five o'clock. And... try to stay outside. Agreed?"

"Yeah. No problem with that." Oddly, she laughed.

"Good. See you tomorrow."

Matt

"What are you so cheery about?" Matt grinned as he came into the condo and set down his large black sample bag and clipboard. He loved having Kate live with him. She was a great sight at the end of a long day. It was even better when she was in a good mood, like she seemed to be now.

"I just got off the phone with Roger and he said…"

"Roger?" interrupted Matt, a playful twinkle in his eye. "Should I be jealous?"

She smiled broadly. "He's your priest. You tell me."

"Go on," he said with a smirk and a dismissive wave of his hand. He was glad Kate and Roger were getting closer. He'd probably be the guy who married them.

"Anyway, Roger told me the exorcism is a go. We're to meet him tomorrow at five," she said. She grabbed one of his hands that had fallen limp by his side.

"Tomorrow?" His voice cracked and rose to a high pitch.

"Is that a problem?" She stared into his blue eyes for the true answer.

He looked away, wiggled his hand to loosen her grasp, and went across the room to the small kitchenette. He grabbed a beer from the refrigerator, twisted it open, and took a long swig. After setting the glass bottle down hard on the counter, still looking at his beer, he whispered, "I can't go."

"What?"

"I can't go," he said louder. This time he looked her squarely in her squinting, suspicious eyes.

Angry tears burned in the corners of her eyes. She tried to blink them away. "Why?" she demanded. "Why?"

"I just can't."

"Did you have a bad dream about it?"

Matt picked his head up sharply, grabbed his beer bottle by the neck and took a few steps toward her. She still stood by the open front door. "Why would you say that?"

"I've heard you groan at night. Felt you thrash around. I assumed it wasn't good." She shut the front door with a quiet click.

"Oh," he said. He looked down into his beer. He held the rim of the bottle to his lips and took another big drink, nearly sucking down half the bottle.

She closed the gap between them and grabbed his spare hand. "You can tell me," she urged. She peeled back his clenched fingers, exposing his palm and removed the bottle cap he had squeezed too tightly. She rubbed the indentation with her finger and looked into his eyes. "Please tell me what you saw." She continued to rub the angry red mark in the soft flesh of his trembling hand.

"It's not good, Kate," he said. He peered into her face to gauge her reaction. He didn't want to scare her. But, he knew she had to be warned.

"Tell me. Tell me all of it." She continued to rub the fading red mark in his palm.

"The thing in your basement isn't happy when I'm there. I sort of feel like it comes after me," he said, taking another gulp of beer.

"Is that it?"

"Pretty much. But, and I know this is weird, I could sense it was happy *you* were there." Confusion spread across his tired face.

"Weird? Yeah, that's very weird," she agreed. "But, will you at least think about going? I need your support and I'm sure Roger needs it, too."

He looked into her face, a smile creeping across his full lips. He knew she was hoping to bait him with old-fashioned Catholic guilt. He chuckled, "You are something, Kate."

She blushed, clearly embarrassed that he'd seen through her weak attempt to manipulate him. "I know."

"I'll think about it. But, no promises," he said. "Will you tell me what Roger told you?" He wanted to get off the subject of his visions.

"He told me our ghost is considered a demon by the Vatican," she said, an odd hint of pride in her voice.

"Really? That sounds serious."

"Yup. And Roger told me you were almost a priest."

"He did not!" He covered his blushing face with forearm.

"He did," she said and nodded knowingly.

"What else did Blabber-Mouth tell you?" he said and peeked at her above his elbow joint.

"Not much I could use against you," she said and pulled his arm from his face, careful not to tip his hand and send his remaining beer onto the floor.

"Thank God for that," he mumbled.

"Actually, it explains a lot." She put her hands on either side of his face.

"I'm glad," he said. He leaned down to kiss her.

"Me, too." She pushed up on her tiptoes to meet his warm lips.

The kisses they shared over the next few minutes were more passionate than any others since they'd been together. Finally, she left him to finish his beer and fluttered around the kitchenette making them a supper of baked chicken and salad.

Matt sat on a stool at the counter, slowly peeling the label from his warming beer. He had enjoyed their kissing, too, even considered allowing it to go further, but reluctantly changed his mind. He knew he'd only be doing it to keep her from being angry at him tomorrow. He had promised to sleep on her request to go to the exorcism, but already he knew his answer. Grandma Betty had come to him last night and told him, very clearly, to stay away from the house. She'd also warned him to have Kate and Roger stay away too, but he wasn't confident enough in himself and his gift to implore them to stay away. He shook his head sadly while he watched her happily prepare their dinner. She had no idea what was in store for her tomorrow, and her initial disappointment from his decision to skip the exorcism was just the beginning.

***

Matt's body twitched under the comforter. Instead of his usual dreams of infested houses and unexplainable occurrences, he dreamed of his friend Roger. Oddly, instead of seeing his dream like a movie, he was somehow, inhabiting Roger's body, seeing life through his eyes. Although he knew this was a little weird and a lot unusual, he was eager for it to play out, curious to see what a day in his friend's body would entail.

As dream-Roger, Matt's stomach rumbled beneath his black robe. Absently, he held a hand over his belly button. Another sharp pang caused him to groan; his physical needs were disturbing his studies. It reminded Matt of their years together in college when Roger's studying was impossible to interrupt. Not even the promise of a raging party or the prettiest of girls could pry the future Father LaCroix from his books.

Dream-Roger walked into the small, square rectory kitchen and carefully sliced a green apple with a small paring knife, covering each wedge with a thick coating of his favorite chunky peanut butter. He sat back in the wicker chair at the glass table, and savored each bite. He finished the last piece in two gulps and greedily licked the remaining peanut butter off the paring knife before putting it in the sink.

He wiped his mouth with a paper towel and went back to his office only to turn on his heel and return to the kitchen to pour himself a small glass of milk. He chugged the whole glass over the sink. Then, he poured a second glass and carried it with him back to his office.

In his bed, Matt smiled as he surveyed his friend, himself, humming cheerfully, and reentering the office with a respectable burst of energy. Crossing the Persian carpet separating the doorway from his desk, dream-Roger was startled by movement in the corner of his eye.

Immediately, the humming stopped. Matt shivered in his bed at the same time as dream-Roger. Still asleep, Matt pulled the blanket over his shoulder, his subconscious noting that the temperature in the office had dropped by nearly ten degrees.

Something moved in the corner of the room again.

Roger turned slowly toward the movement and was shocked to see a slight man sitting quietly in the corner on one of his extra chairs. Roger's hands trembled involuntarily, enough to make his milk slop over the rim of his cup, covering his hand.

The man in the corner stood silently and took a halting step toward the priest. "Hello, Father, I'm here to help you," he said. His voice was soft, soothing.

Milk dripped over the side of his hand, splattering onto his precious Persian rug. "He... h... hello?" said dream-Roger, unsure if the man was a hallucination. He shook his head.

"Sorry to startle you, Father," said the man. He took another step toward dream-Roger and held out a white handkerchief, nodding at the small puddle of milk slowly seeping into the rug. "You may want to clean that before it sets." He held the handkerchief out toward the confused priest.

Dream-Roger stared down at the white puddle, then back at the handkerchief. "Oh, shoot!" he said and grabbed the soft cloth from the man's outstretched hand and bent down to soak up the milk. "Thank you," he said and looked up at the man, his eyes curious.

"You are welcome, Father," said the man. He gave the priest a courteous nod. He took a step back and waited patiently.

When dream-Roger finished cleaning the mess, he stood and wiped his hand with the dry side of the white handkerchief. He also wiped the sides and bottom of his dripping glass and set it on the edge of his desk, then held the handkerchief out to the mysterious man. "Sorry it's so wet," he said. He grinned, embarrassed.

The man took the handkerchief from the outstretched hand of the young priest. He shrugged dismissively, carefully folded the damp handkerchief and placed it into the inside pocket of his black suit jacket, letting it fall closed after he removed his hand. "Happy to be of assistance, Father," he said.

"How can I help you?" said dream-Roger. He turned and leaned his hips against the edge of his desk, crossing his arms over his chest below the gold cross that glimmered brightly in the dim light of the office lamp.

"You have it backwards, kind sir. I'm here to help you," answered the man with a knowing grin that made Matt shiver in his bed. Dream-Roger shuddered involuntarily too.

The man's grin widened at the priest's obvious discomfort. His eyes twinkled mischievously when the priest blushed and wiped a bead of sweat from his furrowed brow with the back of a shaking hand.

Matt's stomach clenched as he watched Roger, *no, himself*, shake his head in confusion. Clearly, he, they didn't understand what this stranger was talking about, and he didn't understand how he could possibly be sweating with the office being so cold.

"Problem, Father?" The man's grin widened.

"Um, no. No problem exactly. I'm just… puzzled." Through dream-Roger's eyes, *his eyes*, Matt took a good look at the man who stood a few feet away. He was about six inches shorter than Roger. Dressed in a black suit and wearing a black hat, maybe a fedora, his style was decidedly old fashioned. It reminded Matt vaguely of a photograph Kate had showed him on her cell phone, one that she'd taken on her trip overseas.

"Take your time, Father," said the man. His tone bordered on sarcasm.

"Thank you. What do you mean you're here to help me?" he said, hoping for a straight answer, but suspecting he'd get more word games.

"I've heard you plan to perform an exorcism," the stranger said, nodding at the array of material spread out on the desk.

"How did you hear about that?" asked dream-Roger. Sweat started to break out over Matt's body as he lay helpless in his bed.

"Word gets around, Father. Small town, you understand?" The man grinned in a way that made both Matt's and dream-Roger's stomachs twist. The word "DANGER" lit up like a bright red neon sign and flashed across the scene as Matt watched, *no, lived,* his dream.

"Sure, I guess so. What about it then?"

"You need to leave Ms. Hart alone," the man said firmly.

"What do you mean by that?" said dream-Roger, insulted by the stranger's notion that he'd been improper with Kate.

"Keep your robe on, Father. I didn't mean to offend your sensibilities," he said, still flashing his knowing grin.

"Then, what *do* you mean exactly?"

"The exorcism cannot happen."

"Why the hell not? Who do you work for? Who are you?" Dream-Roger spit out the questions in rapid fire. A sick sensation gripped Matt's stomach. He curled on his side as he slept, hugging his midsection with his arms, his skin slick with nervous sweat.

"Who I work for is of no concern to you, good Father. Grant my request and I'll be on my way," he said, his eyes wide in anticipation of the priest's response.

"I will do no such thing," Dream-Roger said. "This exorcism has been ordered by the Pope himself. I *must* perform it."

"I implore you to reconsider," said the man without a hint of emotion in his voice, which gave both Matt and dream-Roger the creeps simultaneously.

"I can't. The wheels are in motion. There's no turning back." Dream-Roger shook his head at the man, clearly trying to emphasize his point.

"I'm sorry to hear that, Father LaCroix," said the man. "Very sorry." He shook his head slowly back and forth.

"Run," Matt whispered in his sleep. To Matt, the

stranger was like a Mafia Don, playing a sadistic role. He wanted dream-Roger to get rid of him, fast.

"Is there anything else?" Dream-Roger asked.

Run, Matt thought, wishing his friend could hear him, sense him.

"One more thing, Father." Suddenly a knife gleamed in his pale hand.

Dream-Roger gasped. The man held Roger's paring knife! The same one his friend, *No, he* had used not too long ago to make his favorite snack. The shimmering knife was in the hand of the man in black who stood statue-like in the corner.

"What in God's name are you doing here?" Dream-Roger barked at the man.

"I'm here for you, Father LaCroix." This time, the man's eyes were amused. Quickly, his smile became sinister, then transformed into a hideous grimace with bared teeth and squinting eyes that reminded Matt of a feral dog.

"Wh… what do you mean?" stammered Dream-Roger. To Matt, he sounded small and afraid.

Run, Matt urged, again wishing his friend would hear him and comply.

"I warned you. I told you *not* to help Kate." The stranger sneered, shaking his head at the priest. He took another step toward him and raised the knife above his shoulder, ready to strike.

"Okay. Okay," Dream-Roger said. He held up his hands and licked his dry lips with his drier tongue. "I… I won't help her." Matt knew he'd say anything to soothe this insane, malformed man.

"Too late, Father." The man scoffed at him through bared teeth. "You're too late." He grunted and lunged at the priest with his small weapon.

Roger stepped aside, and the small knife caught on his fluttering black robe, leaving a long tear in the thick fabric.

The man in black seemed unsurprised by the skilled move. Righting himself quickly, he glared at the priest. A twisted look of amusement spread across his warped face.

Why, he's having fun! Matt thought, his stomach instantly turning sour. He realized that Roger was the mouse, the creepy stranger was the cat, and they were playing a dangerous game.

Matt watched dream-Roger run behind his desk, using his chair as a shield and standing his ground. The man in black seemed larger now, almost filling the entire door frame behind him. The same sick grin was still plastered on his face.

The man paused and fixed his cold gaze on the priest. He grinned wickedly and took three large menacing steps deeper into the office, stopping in front of the desk.

"Come to *me*, Father," he beckoned. His voice rasped. He stared into the priest's eyes.

"Nuh. No," Roger mumbled, fighting an urge that was rapidly overtaking his body, his mind; Matt sensed his acceptance, as if his friend's brain, *his brain*, had already acknowledged his fate, subconsciously telling him he didn't need to put up a fight anymore.

"Father," said the man now in a soothing tone, "Be a good boy. Come to me." He stepped slowly around the side of the desk, his finger tracing along the edge of the dark wood.

Matt watched, horrified, as Roger's right leg, *his right leg,* took a small step toward the man. Internally, Matt screamed for him to stop, but his mind and his friend's body had no connection. Now the left foot followed the right, slowly bringing dream-Roger within arm's length of the man in black.

The man's face had softened considerably since his initial transformation. He now looked more like a disappointed dad getting ready to scold his naughty son. He held up a pale finger and wagged it back and forth in disapproval, inches from the face of the wide-eyed priest. "Now, that's a good boy," he said.

Matt tossed wildly in his bed, fighting his blankets as dream-Roger took another halting step toward the man.

"A little more."

Dream-Roger shuffled closer, nearly toe to toe with the man's shiny shoes. "What do you want?" he whispered. Matt hoped his friend would be able to summon some part of his own mind that was still aware of danger.

Still shaking his finger in front of the priest's glazed eyes, he said, "I told you before. I cannot have you helping Kate."

"I… I promise… I won't."

"I'm afraid, Father," said the man shaking his head as if in deep disappointment, "that is not good enough."

"I'm sorry," dream-Roger said, clearly trying to appease him.

"I'm sorry too, Father," said the man solemnly. "Now. Hand me the silver cross." He nodded his head toward the religious artifacts scattered across the desk.

"My cross?" Matt hated the way dream-Roger's voice sounded, flat and dopey, as if in a trance.

"Yes." He held out his pale hand. "Reach over and give it to me."

Dream-Roger, unable to break the gaze the man in black held on him, reached over toward the surface of his desk. His blind fingers moved on the desktop, searching for the cross. Finally, his fingers fell on the cold metal and closed greedily around it. He pulled his arm toward his body and set the cross gently into the stranger's clammy palm.

Matt watched as the man in black smiled broadly, exposing his crooked yellow teeth. His face suddenly morphed back into the awful, dog-like grimace he had seen during his initial attack. Matt met his gaze and was not surprised to see the eyes of the man glowed a bright, menacing red. The man's white fingers gripped the cross and he winced as if in pain when his fingers closed tightly around the sacrament. Quickly, he turned it upside-down, now holding it from the shorter end. Then, in one flowing motion, he…

Matt's eyes popped open. "No!" he yelled into the dark room. Panic gripped his chest, his heart raced madly under his sweaty chest. He took several deep breaths and slowly regained his bearings as his eyes adjusted to the darkness. *Just a dream*, he thought, taking another deep breath and turning to look at Kate as she slept soundly beside him, undisturbed by his tossing and turning. *Just a dream.*

He lay back in his sweat-covered sheets and shivered against the damp embrace. He closed his eyes and re-viewed his dream, recreating the sickening but necessary

play-by-play. In his soul, he knew that he and dream-Roger
had been in the presence of the red-eyed man, the same
red-eyed man who'd frightened people in the surrounding
area for years. For some reason, the creature was going to
leave the camouflage of the thick forest to find his friend.
As Matt fell back into an uneasy sleep, he sensed that the
man would go after himself and Kate next. The demon was
real and it was coming for them.

***

For the second time in the same horrible night, Matt
suddenly sat up, clutched his chest and gasped for air. He
threw the sweat-soaked sheet off his legs and squinted into
the dark bedroom to orient himself.

"What is it?" Kate said groggily. She lifted her head a
few inches off the pillow, but kept her eyes closed, waiting.

He inhaled heavily, his breath coming out slowly as he
patted her back. "Just a nightmare. Go back to sleep, Kate,"
he said.

"Okay. Good night." She pushed her head greedily into
the warm dent on her pillow.

He swung his legs over the edge of the bed and sat panting for another few minutes, trying to recreate the events in
his dream. They seemed so real, so vivid. What a relief to
wake in the safety of his bedroom.

With his mind abuzz, he let Kate sleep and went into
the living room to lie on the couch until he'd sorted through
his dream and, with any luck, would fall asleep.

He hoped Kate would get more sleep. She had a big
day coming up. She'd need every ounce of energy for the

coming day. He plopped down on the couch and pulled an afghan over his shivering body. He should have taken the time to write down the details of his dream, but it was too horrible and he was tired. Plus, he wouldn't want Kate to discover his notes in the morning and see the frightening things that had come to him in his sleep.

His vision started again the moment he closed his eyes. This was how he distinguished between a regular dream and a vision. Dreams were hard to bring back. Visions were always there, right below the surface, waiting for the chance to bubble up again. They were a gift and a curse.

The vision quickly took shape. He saw Roger. Based on the background, he was in his study or maybe another part of the church. Matt's heart raced when he saw that Roger had discovered a visitor in the rectory. The man was dressed in black. In Roger's confused eyes and weak posture, Matt sensed the presence of the man and his unknown purpose made Roger uncomfortable. In the vision, Roger's eyes were glazed, unnatural. Matt sensed something wasn't right. To his horror, the man in black attacked Roger and had evil, blood-red eyes. They seemed to stare beyond the vision, into Matt's own soul.

Matt shuddered under the bulky afghan. Even though it was the middle of the night, he yearned to call Roger and warn him to watch for any strangers coming to see him. Conversely, he didn't quite trust his vision or himself, nor did he know exactly what his vision was telling him, but he had an instinct it had everything to do with his association with Kate and the pending exorcism.

He squeezed his eyes tighter and ordered the vision to

vanish. He wished for Grandma Betty to come and tell him what to do. He wished for a new vision showing Roger happy and healthy. He wished for this whole damn thing to go away. No ghosts. No house-trashing creatures. No exorcisms. Nothing but a boring, normal life.

As the sun rose outside the kitchen window, he finally fell asleep. No more dreams or visions came to him in those few hours. This was good and bad. Good because he got some restorative sleep, yet bad because he didn't have visions that reversed what he saw happen to Roger.

He woke a few hours later, bundled on the couch under the heavy afghan. He smelled bacon cooking and heard Kate quietly moving in the kitchen.

She poked her head around the corner and saw he was propped up on one elbow, his hair sticking up comically in every direction. "Rough night?" she said.

"You could say that." He rubbed his chin and stretched his sore arm muscles. Sleeping on the couch was okay for young people, but an old man like him needed the support and softness of a pillow-top mattress.

"Anything you want to talk about? You were tossing around a lot last night. At one point you were whimpering. I almost woke you up, but I figured you wouldn't appreciate that."

"Probably not." He grinned at her sheepishly. "Sorry if I woke you up." He lifted himself off the couch with a grunt.

"I fell right back to sleep so no worries," she said. She walked over and kissed him playfully on the cheek. "I've got bacon on the stove so I've got to get back before it burns." She scurried back toward the kitchen.

"Thanks for making breakfast," he called after her. Why was she in such a good mood considering their plan for today?

"No problem," she yelled from the kitchen. "You have time for a quick shower if you want before this is done."

"Okay, I'll take one." He caught a glimpse of himself in the hall mirror. Now he understood why she'd been grinning at him. His hair poked up all over his head, he looked like a demented sea urchin.

The hot water washed over his body and loosened the stiff muscles in his neck and back. He tried to replay his vision for more clues. He wanted to call Roger, but worried that if Kate overheard his conversation, she'd be concerned. He finished showering, got dressed, and decided to wait to make the call. He knew he needed to have a conversation with her about the exorcism—no need to have two uncomfortable conversations. She wasn't going to like what he was about to tell her. Not one bit.

He looked in the mirror and fixed his hair, combing it carefully into place. Since he didn't have to work and knew she liked scruff on his chin, he skipped shaving. Maybe it would make her more forgiving. He left the bathroom and met her in the kitchen as she was plating breakfast.

"Order up," she said. She smiled and set his meal on the small table in the corner of the kitchen.

"This looks great! Thanks, Kate." He sat down to eat, smiled broadly at her, and shoveled a big forkful of scrambled eggs into his mouth.

"Take it easy there, slim," she said, clearly enjoying

that he was taking pleasure in her cooking.

"It really is good, Kate. Since when can you cook?" he said, surprised by her skill and eager to keep the conversation light.

"I'm just full of surprises, Matt." She took a bite from a crispy strip of bacon.

"I bet you are."

"So, do you want to talk about your dream yet?" She looked down at her quivering pile of eggs and absently jabbed them with her fork.

"I don't know yet." A nervous twinge tore through his stomach.

"Well… ah, well okay. Whenever you're ready."

He spoke slowly, carefully searching for words, "There is one thing we need to talk about."

"What?" She set the fork on the edge of her plate.

"Well, I don't quite know how to tell you this without disappointing you. Anyway, I'm just going to come out and say it."

"You're starting to freak me out, Matt," she said, her eyes worried, brow furrowed. "Just tell me what you're thinking." She put her hand on top of his and seemed surprised that it was trembling.

"Okay. Okay. Here goes. I can't go with you today. To the exorcism." He kept his eyes trained on her face.

She withdrew her hand. "What? Why?"

"It's kind of a long story," he said, his face turning red.

"Let me guess." Unable to keep the sarcasm out of her voice, she said, "A vision told you not to go?"

He searched her scowling face hoping for a hint of

understanding. "Basically, yes."

"Let me guess again," she said bitterly, "Grandma Betty told her little grandbaby not to go."

"Yes," he whispered, his eyes falling to look at his plate. He couldn't bear her judgmental eyes.

"Great. Just fucking great." She threw her napkin on top of her unfinished food.

"I'm sorry, Kate." What could he to say to make her feel better, to make her understand?

She shook her head. "Well, I'm sorry, too. Sorry I allowed myself to count on you for something so important."

"Don't be like that, Kate." He grabbed the hand that rested on her thigh.

She wrenched her hand from his grip. "Don't touch me!"

"Kate?"

"I'm done, Matt. Done." She stood. "Don't worry about me. I'll be at my place." She stomped out of the kitchen.

He sat at the table and covered his face with his hands. From the bedroom, he heard her yanking open drawers and slamming them shut, packing her suitcase. He pushed away from the table and quietly made his way to the bedroom. He found her sitting on the bed next to a half-filled suitcase, her head in her hands. Weeping, her shoulders shook with every sob.

He sat on the bed next to her and put his arm around her. She shrugged it off and squinted at him with wet, suspicious eyes. "How could you make such an important decision without even discussing it with me?" She seemed to search his blue eyes for an answer she knew wouldn't make her happier.

"I'm sorry, Kate. My visions are too powerful to ignore and this one was a biggie."

"So, you think your Grandma Betty is always right and she wants you to stay away?" she said.

"Yes. She's never been wrong." He patted her thigh.

"That isn't good enough for me, Matt. I can't have my life governed by a dead woman, your grandmother or not," she said and sniffed.

"Kate, please don't be like this. We can work it out."

"I don't know." She shook her head. "This is a huge thing today and you can't be part of it. What if Grandma Betty tells you not to be with me anymore or not to marry me or have kids with me? What would you do about that?"

"I honestly don't know, Kate." He retracted his hand from her thigh and rubbed the scruff he'd left on his chin.

"I know you don't and I can't live that way. I *won't* live that way."

"Please think about it. I need you." He wiped wet tears from his stubbly cheek.

"I need you, too, but if you can't be there for me when I need you the very most, what am I supposed to do?"

"I don't know," he whispered.

"Well, I need time to think and today isn't the day to make huge life decisions. I need to get this exorcism done with Roger and then I'll call you in a few days."

"A few days? Won't you even call me to tell me how things went?"

"I'm sure Roger can give you the play by play. I need to get my house back and then deal with this mess." She stood and tossed more clothes onto the growing pile.

Roger. He needed to call Roger. He watched helplessly as Kate gathered the last of her shirts from the bottom drawer and zipped them into her maroon suitcase.

"Can you stay at least until you need to go to the house?" He tried to grab her free hand but she stuffed it into her pants pocket.

"No, I can't." She pulled the heavy suitcase off the bed and set it on its wheels.

"Where are you going to go? It's still hours until you need to be there," he said. He needed more time to convince her not to leave him again, to forgive his betrayal.

"I'll think of something." She rolled her suitcase down the hall to the front door.

"Kate. Please stay." He sounded weak, beaten. He followed her to the door like a depressed puppy.

"No," she said sternly although tears welled in her eyes.

He reached out and grabbed her from behind, hugging her tightly. She struggled against him, tried to push him off, but he held on for a few moments. When he finally released her, her elbows shoved him back a step.

"Please call me," he begged.

She reached for the doorknob. "I need a few days," she said. She bit her bottom lip and kept her eyes on the door.

"Okay."

Not turning to look at him, she said "Bye," and opened the door, wheeling her suitcase behind her down the porch steps. Thump. Thump. Thump.

"Bye, Kate," he said. He wished he'd convinced her to stay, to talk. He shut the door and leaned his back on it, feeling wobbly and needing the strong wood for extra support. He shook his head. He'd known there was a good chance she'd take his avoidance of the exorcism badly, but he never imagined he'd get dumped over it.

He made his way to the couch and sat on the soft cushions. He leaned forward and held his head between his hands. He let his tears spill down his cheeks, onto the carpet, and watched them melt into the thick beige pile.

He cried for a long time before leaning back on the couch, putting an arm over his eyes to block out the emptiness of his condominium. It was quiet as death without her here and that set him to weeping again.

After allowing a while to grieve, he tried get himself together. *I must contact Roger.* He blotted tears from his face with his sleeve and stood, lightheaded from crippling sadness. He went to the phone, dialed the number for the rectory, and waited for an answer. An answer that never came.

Kate

Kate was beyond pissed. She was furious. She'd had a gut feeling Matt would back out. She could tell by the way he thrashed about last night in bed that he was having a bad dream or vision or whatever it was that made him "see" or know things. Even though she believed in him and his gift, she was still troubled by the decisions he made based on them.

She threw her suitcase into the trunk of her car and slammed it shut. She leaned on her car for a minute to think about where to go. She had nearly seven hours until she was due at her house to meet Roger. She was homeless until then. One option was going to work, but running into Marlene? "Ugh," she whispered. Plus, she'd have to come up with a reason for being there on her day off and she didn't know if she had it in her to lie convincingly.

She could visit Chief Redbird, but she didn't want to arrive unannounced. He probably was a ladies' man and she'd hate to interrupt any action he might be getting. God knew she wasn't getting any. A frustrated smirk spread across her puffy, tearstained face.

Well, at least she could go to her house and sit in the driveway. She'd be safe in her car. And, if she felt like taking a nap, she'd be secluded from prying eyes thanks to her long driveway and tree covered property.

She slid behind the driver's seat and turned the key. Her car purred to life. Putting it in gear, she said aloud, "At least I own my own home." She felt happy about going home even if she'd been instructed to stay outside.

The thought of not being allowed to go inside her house started to chap her already grumpy ass on the drive over. Even though Roger, Red, and all the other men in her life were trying to help her, she still resented the fact they told her what to do and when to do it. And, she'd given them that power.

Frustration marinated in her brain as she drove on the rutted driveway toward her house. With every bump and thump she grew exponentially more frustrated with the limitations placed on her by other people. She'd felt the same way when Mother used to let her old boyfriends, whomever they were, tell Mother and Kate what to do. Kate had always resented Mother's weak backbone, letting strange men dole out discipline to her, especially since she didn't even belong to them.

Some of the punishments she'd endured as a child were abusive: forced to drink Tabasco sauce for talking back, time-outs that lasted for hours, and her favorite stuffed rabbit gutted of her fluff and burned in the fireplace right in front of her. Mother never said a word against them, letting Kate take the brunt of whatever humiliation they decided to deliver.

Kate pulled into her familiar driveway. The tension and anger within her bubbled furiously to the surface. She put the car in park and punched at the steering wheel, hurting her thumb, which made her even angrier and more frustrated with the way her life was turning out.

She stepped from the car and took in a lungful of the fresh pine-scented air. The woods were still unusually quiet, but the heaviness that was in the air the last time she was here had dissipated. She almost felt safe. Leaning against the cold metal of her car, she listened intently for danger.

After a few minutes of silence, she calmed herself and decided she'd damned well make a move on her own. Yes, she'd be defying a direct order from Red, but she felt strong enough to wander into the woods and look for Devil's Chair. She'd had enough of sitting idly by and allowing things to happen. This time, instead of being a scared child wishing someone would save her, she'd save herself and face the foe in her own backyard. She had enough daylight left to be in the woods for at least five hours and still make it back in plenty of time to meet Roger.

She reached into her car and grabbed her reusable metal water bottle from the center console. She shook it gently; at least half full. The water was a day old, still good enough to drink. It only had her germs in it anyway. She grinned mischievously.

She slammed the driver's side door shut and unlocked the trunk. She fished her sneakers and a pair of socks from the mashed pile of clothes in her suitcase and put them on, throwing her ballet flats back into the dark recess of the trunk. Today was a day for taking charge. She'd be the one to make decisions. Not Matt. Not Red. Not Roger. Not Mother or Mother's miscreant boyfriends and certainly not the dearly departed Grandma Betty.

She shut the trunk and walked into the quiet woods.

The thick layer of orange, dead pine needles were slippery under her well-worn sneakers. She hoped they had enough tread left on them to get her out to the chair and back without falling.

She easily found a game trail in the woods and followed it. It seemed to lead in the proper direction, away from the house, deep into the woods. She was proud for being so bold and brave, like a suffragette on the verge of victory. She continued on her path, searching for answers to her questions, answers no one else could provide: *Why do I live life so timidly? Why do I allow others to mark my course in life? Why is my life such a mess?*

She continued on, purposefully keeping her mind off Matt. He'd worry about her if he knew where she was headed. Suddenly, she wished she'd remembered to bring her cell phone. Damn, she'd left it behind in her locked car.

"Screw Matt," she said to the woods. "Let him worry." She continued on her journey to find the threads of her missing independence. To find herself again.

Matt

Matt sat like a statue on his couch, unable to move. The strength he thought he'd regained had disappeared and now he was hollow and alone. He had a nagging urge to call Roger again, but it wasn't strong enough to get him off the couch.

After an hour of allowing himself to feel like an emotional zombie, he got up and redialed the number for the rectory. *Where could Roger be on such an important day?* It wasn't like him to not answer. Usually, he was available to pick up the phone or at least close by to return messages quickly, especially urgent ones. *Was my tone unclear when I'd left a message earlier?* He hadn't wanted to frighten his old friend, but maybe he didn't emphasize enough the importance of his call. It was hard for him to remember exactly what he'd said on the tape; he'd been reeling from Kate's sudden departure. He hoped he could lean on Roger for that issue later. For a man who'd never had a serious relationship with a woman, he was great at giving five-star advice. The rectory's phone rang for what seemed the tenth time.

He looked at the clock and saw it was nearly noon. Roger would have to go back to the rectory's kitchen soon for some lunch. Maybe if he left now, he could catch up with him while he was eating. He could tell him about his latest vision and what had happened with Kate. At the very least, he hoped for a shoulder to cry on. He also hoped to enlist Roger in getting her back, although he probably wouldn't broach that subject today. There were more pressing matters weighing heavily on his friend's mind.

He changed quickly from his tear-stained shirt, finding a clean-ish shirt on the bedroom floor. He couldn't bear to open one of the drawers for a fresh one and risk and seeing the empty spaces left behind from Kate's ransacking of their shared dresser. He felt a twinge of pain in his heart. He tried to push the image of her furiously packing her things from his mind.

He grabbed a wilted piece of toast from their ruined breakfast and gobbled it down, chasing it with a mouthful of warm orange juice. It left a bitter aftertaste in his mouth. He shivered and scolded himself for being such a wimp. Overwhelming pangs of guilt hit him hard. His aching mind pictured her working so diligently this morning, squeezing oranges by hand to make him juice. He hated himself for barely being able to stomach it.

He shook his head to clear it of the cobwebs of memories that threatened his ability to function. If he allowed the sadness to creep back, he might take to his bed and not get up again. He checked his reflection in the mirror by the front door and scowled at the broken man looking back at him.

"Time to cowboy up, Matty," he said to the scruffy man with tired eyes. He rolled his eyes at his pallid reflection and left.

***

Matt drove the short distance to the rectory hoping he'd find Roger eating his lunch. The small piece of soggy toast he'd eaten on his way out the door had awakened his stomach. He felt guilty for being hungry. He should be more focused on Kate's predicament and the vision he'd had of Roger's demise. Despite his shame, he still hoped Roger was sitting over cold cuts and wheat bread. And, he'd want to share.

He parked a few spaces down from where Roger's black sedan sat. *Roger! Thank God!* He rang the melodious doorbell and heard it chime down the long hallway, echoing back from the interior of the rectory. After waiting a moment, he rang it again. There was no way Roger wouldn't hear it. It was even louder inside. Matt had been visiting once when a parishioner rang the bell and he nearly jumped out of his seat.

He peered into the small peephole. His eye was met with darkness. He grunted disapproval at the door and decided to use the old fashioned, lion shaped door knocker. He picked up the wrought iron metal loop and banged it hard three times against the metal backing. He listened for a moment, certain he'd hear Roger's footsteps coming down the hall at a fast clip.

When the door failed to open, he grabbed the loop of the knocker again and banged it against the door as hard as he could, unconcerned if he damaged the aged metal or surrounding wood. To his surprise, the door popped open as if it hadn't even been locked.

He blushed for being a Neanderthal. Poor Roger was probably on the can and here he was, outside fighting with the door like a brainless ape. He shook his head and laughed. It felt good to laugh. It had been a long time since he'd had an honest to goodness good time. He'd been overwhelmed with his visions and Kate's house issues and now her leaving, he'd almost forgotten how to enjoy the simple things in life like a good chuckle.

He stepped inside the darkened hallway. It seemed darker than usual and it looked like no one was home.

"Roger?" he called. He hesitated, expecting him to come from the kitchen to his left or from his office a few paces down the hall.

"Roger?" he called again. "Father LaCroix, can you hear me?" It wasn't like Roger to be out of earshot when he was working. Something must have gone terribly wrong.

Matt gulped and instantly thought of Kate. *Had she had gone to her house early and summoned Roger? No.* He dismissed the notion, it didn't make sense. Roger's car was still here. He shook his head. Maybe she'd picked him up and taken him to the house. Maybe he was too late to warn Roger about his dream. Matt felt sick. Panic gripped his lungs, he could hardly breathe. His hands began to tremble and he squeezed them into fists, his knuckles turning white.

He stood frozen. *What should I do next? Should I call Kate or search for Roger?* He wished he could summon Grandma Betty to get her opinion. She always had a way of pointing him in the right direction.

The thought of Grandma Betty brought him back to his present situation. She'd always told him, just as a woman does, a man also has instincts and he needed to learn when to follow them. Right now, his instincts told him to find Roger. Find Roger fast.

He relaxed his fists and shook his numb fingers. He would check the office first, then the living quarters upstairs and finally the church itself. His friend had to be in one of those places.

He walked down the hall, turned into the dark office and peered inside. His stomach tightened. "Roger?" he called. He flipped the switch on the wall and the room illuminated brightly. On first glance, everything seemed normal.

Deeper into the office he could see an array of religious materials spread out on the desk. The Bible was open. Its leather bookmark lay to one side of the old, gold-trimmed book.

Feeling confident the room was empty, he walked to the front of Roger's desk and inspected the items, certain they were for the exorcism at Kate's. He leaned toward the Bible. A dark maroon drop dotted the opened page. He touched it. It had already dried and stained the page. He withdrew his hand and clumsily knocked a few pages of Roger's notes onto the floor.

"Crap!" He hoped he could put the handwritten pages back into some semblance of order. He got down on his knees to retrieve the scattered pages. Something strange caught his eye. *Was it hair? Yes, blonde hair.* Matt ignored the pages that littered the floor and reached toward the swatch of hair that continued around the corner of the desk. He crawled slowly on his hands and knees and poked his head around the edge of the desk, and braced for what he might see.

He gasped. His dearest friend in the whole world, his confidant, his male soulmate, lay in a sticky pool of congealed blood. Roger's glazed eyes and open mouth revealed the shock and fear of his last terrifying moments. Matt couldn't move. Frozen on the floor, he stared into his dead friend's eyes. He shook his head to make the horrifying image disappear. He desperately hoped this was another dream, not reality.

Crawling closer, he reached a shaking hand toward his friend and felt the hardened skin. He touched under his chin to find a sign of life like they did on the crime shows they'd watched together. He didn't quite know what he was looking for, but was certain he wouldn't find it in the cold flesh of his murdered friend.

Suddenly, he became very aware he might be in danger, too. The animal that had killed his friend might be lurking within the church. He crawled over to Roger's side, unable to leave and thought about what he should do. *Call the police? Yes, find a phone, call the police.*

Gently, he closed Roger's eyes and noticed the silver cross on his chest. *Had Roger pulled it on top of himself from the desk as he was dying, to comfort himself in his last moments?* Matt reached across Roger's torso and grabbed the cross.

His fingers closed around the smooth, cool metal. Immediately, he was sent reeling back, as if he'd been hit by a bolt of lightning. Although he'd never had a vision while awake, he knew he was having his first one now based on the speed of images rushing past his open eyes:

a man in black. The same man he'd seen outside Kate's window, possibly the same one from her cell phone photo gallery.

In the rectory with Roger, warning him, shaking his finger, telling Roger, "Stay away from her house." The man stabbing at him with a small knife. Oh God! It wasn't a dream, Matt thought wildly as the intense burst of information continued. *The man pursuing Roger in the office, coaxing Roger to hand him the silver cross. The man's eyes glowing red as he plunged the cross into Roger's chest. His expression: pure evil.*

Roger's ribs cracking as the cross passed through muscle, bone and organs. Roger falling to the floor, the man in black twisting and yanking the cross from his body. Roger clutching his chest, the killer wiping blood from the cross with Roger's robe, placing it deliberately on his bleeding chest.

Matt shook his head against the sickening vision. He'd never had a vision like this before. It was as if the cross had the information stored within its forged metal and his touch had brought the terrible truth out in a gut-wrenching rush.

He sat shaking on the floor next to Roger's body. My God, he was holding the weapon the murderer used to kill his friend. But, he was unable to release it. His body told him that he'd need this cross for something in the future. *But what?* He stared at the cross in his hand.

"Kate!" he yelled into the empty room. "I've got to get to Kate!" He pushed himself off the floor.

He bent down, quickly kissed Roger's forehead, not worrying about contaminating the crime scene. Anyway, he knew they'd never find the killer. Only he knew who had done it.

"Goodbye, my friend," he said. "I *will* stop him." He kissed Roger's forehead again, his lips pressed into his icy, unnatural skin.

He stood and held the sliver cross in front of his wet blue eyes. He tucked it through his belt and inside the front pocket of his jeans. He was running out of time. He didn't need a vision to tell him that.

Kate

Kate had been walking down the trail she'd scouted out for what seemed like hours. She checked her watch repeatedly to make sure she wouldn't be late to meet with Roger. She still had plenty of time.

She was sure she would've found the mysterious "Devil's Chair" by now. Red had made it sound like it was just beyond the woods, on the bank of the river that flowed near her house. She spotted a strange white birch tree with twisted, braided limbs, a number of times. It had to be the same tree, although everything started to look identical in the fading light. *Have I been walking in circles?* She'd forgotten how dark it could get in the woods with tall trees blocking the sun's rays. She kicked herself for forgetting a flashlight, her cell phone. Now, she clearly understood how people got turned around in the maze of trees, ferns and winding dirt trails. *Oh gosh, the dirt.* Her once-white sneakers were caked with mud and prickly burrs had embedded themselves in the laces. She'd definitely need a new pair now. Stubbornly, she continued on the path toward her goal.

Again, she passed a felled tree trunk that was all too familiar and shook her head, angry for being such a bone-headed fool. She took a short break and sat on the tree trunk, careful to avoid the mushy green moss covering the majority of the damp bark. She took a swig from her water bottle. *Oh God, it's almost empty.*

She sat very still and trained her ears to the surrounding woods, listening for anything that might help her find the river or better, the road. To her surprise, she heard a noise in the distance. It wasn't an animal—she'd yet to see or hear any creature scurrying about or flying overhead. Craning her neck, she concentrated, hoping to discern the sound. *Is it water? Moving water?*

She stood quickly and slipped in the thick carpet of moss that squished beneath her bald sneakers. "Keep your skirt on, Kate. It's not like it's going anywhere," she said aloud. Using the clean spot on the log for support, she regained her footing and headed in the direction of the water.

She trudged off the path and made her way through thick branches and huge ferns that beat at her legs as she pushed on. Her brain screamed at her to go back, but her stubborn, newly independent side wanted to go deeper into the woods and find the stupid chair that was the center of so much drama. She was sick of drama. She didn't want it in her life anymore and some imaginary chair wasn't going to force her from her house. If she could see it for herself, maybe it wouldn't be so scary. And, if she saw one of those wolverine creatures Chief Redbird had told her about, at least she could pin her fears on its furry little face.

The gurgling echo from the briskly flowing water grew louder with each step and the underbrush thinned as she neared the bank of the river. When she pushed through the last bit of thick growth, the water appeared, flowing rapidly over huge brown granite rocks that lined each side of the riverbank.

She peered over the edge. It was at least an eight-foot drop to the water. She walked along the edge of the rocks using jutting branches as handholds. As she made her way along the wall of rock, she peeked over the edge to see if the bank had become lower. It hadn't.

Realizing the danger she'd put herself in, she hoped she wouldn't sprain an ankle in the middle of nowhere. She'd also noted a change in the sky. Once light and clear blue, it was now full of dark, menacing rain-laden puffs of trouble. An ominous rumble growled in the distance. *How long do I have before the storm hits?* Luckily, she hadn't seen lightning yet and hoped to be off the river's edge before it started zapping around her. *Good God, I'm a sitting duck on these bare rocks. Why hadn't I thought to check the weather report? Dammit!* Her search for independence would probably cost her a good soaking at the very least.

She shuffled slowly along the edge for a few more minutes, looking down every few paces to judge if it was safe for her to jump or climb down. She neared a corner in the rocks where the river took a sharp left turn. Across the riverbank, something odd caught her eye. She squinted to make out what looked like random scribbles on the rock face.

She worked her way closer and squinted again at marks on the rocks. Finally, she was able to make out black words that had been spray painted on the flat granite. She read them to herself and tried to soak in the meaning of the strange phrase that a mysterious author had attributed to Shakespeare.

"Hell is empty and the Devils are here," she read aloud to the flowing water with an involuntary shudder. "What the hell does that mean?" she asked the woods with a confused shrug. *Who would have been out here to write such a thing? And be prepared with spray paint? Apparently, one little devil travels with a can of black Rust-Oleum,* she thought and grinned despite her predicament.

A loud rumble of thunder rolled down the river making her stomach twitch. It was closer now, much closer. She continued along the bank. Up ahead, the river bent again. She'd turn back after seeing what lay ahead.

She shuffled along the edge and tried to increase her speed as dark clouds roiled above her and black water surged below. She shook her head at the sky and rolled her eyes at the storm's rude interruption of her plans. *Dammit, I just can't catch a break today.* She edged closer to the bend as the first spattering of raindrops attacked the back of her bare neck. She hoped luck would finally be on her side and the elusive chair would be obvious to her tired eyes in the growing darkness.

Finally, she rounded the bend and squinted against the rain that sprayed her face. *Is that a structure on the far side of the bank?* She turned her body to face the water, holding onto the branches behind her to keep from falling from the edge that had become slick now in the heavy blanket of rain.

She peered across the river at a dark formation of rocks that must be the legendary chair. She shook her head in disbelief. "That's it?" she asked aloud. She had pictured the chair as ominous, huge. *This chair wouldn't hold an adult. It was a child's chair!* Of course, it would be bigger if she were on the other side of the riverbank, but from her perch above the rocky cliff, it looked like a bunch of flat rocks that were either deliberately piled on top of each other or left behind eons ago by a random glacier.

As rain pelted her face, she huffed incredulously at the chair. She couldn't believe she was literally risking her neck to see such a stupid thing. *What a pathetic disappointment!*

Lightning flashed above her head and a crack of thunder followed soon after, crashing its way down the river, making her heart beat faster. *The storm is scarier than that stupid chair*, she thought as she surveyed her surroundings for the easiest exit.

Lightning flashed a second time, making her head snap instinctively toward the sky. Mentally, she counted out the seconds until the thunder rumbled to estimate the storm's distance from her. Two miles.

"You idiot," she said aloud and shook her head for getting in such a ridiculous mess. Pride. It was her damn pride: the woman who could cope with just about anything that came her way was now stuck on a ledge in a driving rain storm with the added insult of thunder and lightning. Slowly, she picked her way a few steps from the edge, through a patch of prickly bushes to safer ground.

A third bolt of lightning struck the forest across the river making her jump. She searched the woods for smoke or flames. She glanced back in the direction of the chair as another well-timed flash filled the sky and was shocked to see something on the rocks that hadn't been there moments before. She froze in her sneakers, not daring to move. Her heart beat wildly in her chest. *Is my exhausted mind playing tricks on me in the bad weather?* She gulped. Horrid thoughts raced madly in her head. *If I were in a horror movie, this setting would be a perfect location for me to be proven wrong and rightfully taken away by woodland spirits—no, devils, Loks.*

Another flash of lightning, the brightest yet, brilliantly lit up the sky and rain-soaked rocks. She forced herself to look at the chair again, hoping she'd seen some sort of storm-induced illusion.

She gasped. This time, the figure on the chair moved, humping up from a fetal position. Instinctively, she backed further away from the ledge and into the underbrush behind her. She knew it wasn't the way she'd come in and hoped she could find her way back to her house in the dark, but she knew in her gut that she needed get the hell out of here, pronto.

A cracking barrel of thunder rolled down the white capped river followed by lightning a second later and she looked at the chair once again, hoping the figure hadn't moved in her direction.

This time, the figure was clearer in the fading jolt of lightning. *Is it a large animal? A man? My God, is it standing on two feet?* She squinted. The sky darkened again and in the musky haze, the creature's eyes glowed bright red.

Her involuntary scream was drowned out by a clap of thunder so loud it made the earth beneath her feet shake. She couldn't believe what she saw. Or, what she thought she saw. *Is it the fabled red-eyed man?* Her stomach twisted, an intense wave of fear washed through her body.

Her fight or flight instincts kicked in and this time, they told her to get the hell away from Devil's Chair. *Dear God, why hadn't I heeded Red's advice and stayed away from here?* Now, she knew there was no way she could stay on this land, in her house, with that creature or man or whatever it was, lurking, waiting to lure in its next victim.

The word "victim" swam heavily in her mind. She must never be a victim of this creature or anyone else. She had to act, to book it through the dark forest, as fast as her shaking legs and balding sneakers would take her.

Not daring to look back at the red eyes, she turned and pushed her way through a thicket of brush, the prickly bushes tearing at the skin on her bare arms. Somehow, she sensed the owner of the red eyes had already moved off the rock and was headed in her direction. But the creature had to get itself across the roiling river. *Please, let that buy me more time to escape*, she thought.

Kate ran. Using her hands and exposed forearms, she pushed branches and huge lush ferns from her path. Her delicate flesh was repeatedly ripped by thorny bushes and poking sticks. She fell. She kept falling and scolded herself for being such a cliché. *The girl in danger always falls down just in time for her attacker to finish her off*, she thought in wild frustration.

She searched the woods for any landmark she could recognize, but of course, she hadn't come in this way. Everything was different and the rain kept pouring down in the darkened woods. The lightning flashes did little to light her way with the thick canopy of leaves knitted tightly over her head.

She fell again, slipping awkwardly into a wet pile of moss. She sat still for a moment, and listened to the woods to determine if she was being pursued. Raindrops landing around her on the messy carpet of leaves and sticks and the intermittent rumble of thunder made it hard to hear anything other than her own heavy breathing and pounding heart that echoed madly in her ears.

She put her hand on the ground, and soggy moss squished between her fingers. She was about to curse the moss when a thought occurred to her. She got up and peered around at her surroundings in the gloomy darkness. *The moss I'd slipped on was right next to the log I'd rested on while trekking out to the chair! And that log was next to the braided white birch tree!*

The twisted tree loomed a few paces away. She probably would have run right into it if she hadn't slipped first. She quickly stepped to it and patted the trunk, thanking it for being a landmark she recognized and squinted into the darkness. A flash of lightning showed enough of the woods to reveal the trail she'd followed earlier in the day. Somehow, she'd stumbled her way in the right direction.

Stepping around her new favorite tree, she took a deep breath of the earth-scented air and jogged toward the path, and headed toward her house, now certain she was going in the right direction. While she was complimenting herself on being such a good woods woman, there was a distinct crack in the trees behind her.

She briefly glanced over her shoulder, but didn't dare slow for a good look. Now, as she jogged down the trail, she saw, *or did I imagine*, a menacing pair of red eyes following her. She screamed. Tears ran down her cheeks, mixing with the rain and dirt. She turned her head toward the trail and sprinted as fast as her traction-less sneakers would carry her, pumping her arms up and down like a gold medal track star.

I must not look back! Her psyche was fragile now. Imaginary or real, she didn't want to know if the red eyes were coming any closer. She ran faster, hopping over large sticks and jutting rocks. Again, she scolded herself, *Why hadn't I taken Red's advice? Why hadn't I waited in my car for Roger? Why had I been such a bitch to Matt? How could I have been so stupid, stupid, STUPID?*

The storm raged on but a glimmer of light appeared in the foreground. *Is it the edge of the woods?* She pushed her tired and muddy legs as hard as she could. She fought against the burning in her overworked lungs that screamed at her to stop.

Finally, she neared the entrance of the trail. A wave of relief washed through her body. And there was her car, in the driveway, the metal glinting brightly in the near constant flashes of lightning.

She hurried to her car, slowing only to greedily feel her pants pockets for the bulge of her keys. But her pockets were empty. She slapped at the two pockets as if she might have somehow missed them and even knowing the keys wouldn't fit in the small pocket on her blouse, she slapped it, too. She ran around her car, and searched the soaked ground to see if she'd dropped them as she left for her hike in the woods.

No keys. She dropped to her knees on the gravel. Small rocks poked into her scratched knee caps and shins. She swept her hands lightly over the rocks feeling for the steel jumble of keys, hoping they were camouflaged by the grey rocks. A horrible thought loomed in her mind. *Had I tossed the keys into the trunk before I changed my shoes? How could I be so careless?*

She circled her car and pulled on each handle, hoping the automatic door lock had failed to seal one of them. She yanked fiercely on the driver's side door, wishing brute strength would will it open. She caught a brief glimpse of her reflection in the rain soaked window as a flash of lightning flared above her. She looked crazy; Wet hair stuck to her face and neck, her eyes puffy with tears and fear. Her forearms and legs were dirty and streaked with blood. A fresh scratch on her forehead was bleeding and her matted hair was stuck in the wound. She was oddly optimistic that her ghastly appearance would be enough to frighten away any predator that might be searching for her, following her out of the woods.

She shook her head at the pathetic image that melted away in the dark. A loud rumble of thunder brought her back to her current task of searching for safety. It dawned on her, *I have a whole house of relative safety just a few feet away.* Hastily, she weighed the pros and cons of going into her destroyed, spirit-infested house versus staying in the driveway like a sitting duck, waiting for the red-eyed man to drag her kicking and screaming back into the woods.

Quickly, she opted to take door number one and bolted up the three steps of her porch in one giant leap. On Matt's suggestion, she'd hidden an extra key in one of those ridiculous fake rocks and had left it somewhere on the rain-soaked porch.

She shoved a heavy rocking chair out of her way
and bent down to retrieve the plastic rock, hidden in the
gloomy shadows and concealed by two flower-filled pots.
She turned the baseball-sized rock over in her hand and
searched for a way to open it. She shook it hard and it rattled metallically. *Good, the key was still inside!*

She pressed her thumb against a seam on the rock that
looked like it could be a hidden lever and growled angrily
when it remained shut. *Why did I let Matt place the spare
key in the fake rock and hide it on the porch without asking
him how to retrieve the damned thing?* She hadn't given
him credit for his idea when he brought it home to her one
day. He'd been so proud to give her such a unique and
handy gift. *Why did I laugh at him for being a worry-wart,
a dork?*

Worried about wasting time, she decided to smash it.
She picked up the large, geranium-filled ceramic flower
pot and held it a few inches over the rock. She slammed it
down three times, as hard as she could, squeezing her eyes
shut in case the pot shattered.

The deed done, she was surprised the sturdy pot was
still intact, although the geraniums now leaned sickly,
stems bent. She nearly cheered when she set the pot to the
side and saw the broken pieces of plastic lying in a sad heap
on the wet floorboards of her porch. Carefully, she picked
up a large piece of broken grey plastic. A flash of lightning
lit up the house key on the floorboard. A strange feeling of
calm that she couldn't quite explain washed through her
body. *Is it hope that things might turn out alright after all?*

She retrieved the key and took a quick survey of her

driveway and the surrounding woods. No skulking creatures. No Mr. Red Eyes. She unlocked the front door and
stepped inside. The putrid stench of rotting food and sour
dairy products instantly made her gag. The smell had at
least warned her to watch her step in the living room. *I
mustn't tumble on the broken remains of my furniture, my
life.*

She reached for the light switch on the inside of the
door and flicked it up. Nothing happened. She flicked it
again, down this time. Nothing. She jiggled the switch up
and down repeatedly, hoping to force some spark of electricity. Still nothing changed in the dark room. She huffed
angrily at the switch. Of course: the storm had knocked out
the power.

She crossed the room and pulled the string attached to
the tattered remains of her Venetian blind. The dark sky
provided a bit of light. It wasn't quite evening yet and if the
storm cleared out quickly, as they often did, she might even
get a tad of sunshine in here. She pulled open the second
blind on the window that faced the driveway.

A flash of lightning illuminated the room. She turned
reluctantly to face the carnage, almost wishing the lightning would hit her home and burn the whole mess to the
ground. She crossed the room again and got down on her
hands and knees and rooted around in the rubble.

"Gotcha, you little sucker," she said to the small, green
flashlight she'd seen hidden within the debris a few days
before. She turned it over briefly in her hand, hunting for
damage, and finally clicked the black button on the side. A
bright, wide beam of light cut through the hazy darkness.

The flashlight had been another of Matt's ideas. He'd put a flashlight in every room in case the electricity in the old house went kaput.

She flashed the beam around the room, her eyes taking in the work that would need to be done to make the room livable again. She shifted her eyes to the kitchen, audibly groaning when she again smelled the spoiled piles of food working their way into the creases of the floor.

A shuffling noise to her left, near where she'd righted the coffee table about a week before, caught her attention. *Is it a mouse or squirrel or God forbid, a skunk, attracted by the food?*

She turned toward the noise, aiming the flashlight at it.

The culprit sat quietly on the edge of her tilted coffee table with both feet planted on the floor, arms crossed, grinning at her. She gasped and nearly dropped the flashlight in the rubble. She tried to suck enough air into her lungs to allow herself to scream.

"Hello, Kate," he said pleasantly, still smiling calmly, looking quite comfortable as he sat on his uneven perch in the destroyed room.

"Heh… hello," she croaked. She recognized this man from somewhere. *But where?*

"Aw, don't you remember me?" He feigned disappointment.

"Yes. Yes, I do," she said, stalling as she filtered quickly through her memory bank of faces, trying to place him and to figure out why he was sitting in her living room. Her fight or flight instincts were kicking in again, making her dizzy.

"Want a hint?" said the stranger.

She sensed he was working overtime to appear playful, but… her mind raced… *how did he get in? What did he want?*

"Okay," she agreed. She worried she wouldn't be able to remember the man quickly enough to appease him. She wanted him to identify himself, state his purpose, and leave.

A loud clap of thunder rumbled and a bright flash of lightning lit the room. The man grinned broadly at the window. He seemed to be enjoying the violent storm.

Slowly, he turned his head back toward her. A shiver crawled down her spine. She shuddered involuntarily and hoped the stranger didn't notice. She wanted him gone, but at the same time, she didn't want to appear fearful. She sensed the wrong attitude might set him off.

"Remember the key?" said the stranger. He nodded in her direction.

"The key?" Did he mean the key to the house?

He took a long, deep breath and shook his head slowly as though unable to hide his disappointment. "The one I gave you as a gift," he explained and pointed a bony finger directly at her drenched chest.

"Oh." She blushed, embarrassed. She grabbed the key that hung loosely over the front of her shirt on its long chain. It must have freed itself from the safety of her bra when ran like a maniac through the trees. She shuddered again against her wet clothes and the memory of her recent escape from the forest.

"Remember now?" he said, evidently trying to coax the memory from her.

She looked down at the intricate gold key in the palm of her hand. She snapped her head back up and squinted at the stranger, training her flashlight directly on his face. "Adam?"

He clapped his pale hands together, clearly pleased. "You do remember me!" He stood and took a deep bow toward her, removing his hat in an antiquated gesture.

"Adam?" She tried to wrap her mind around this sudden, weird turn of events. "What the *hell* are you doing here?"

"Exactly," he answered and chuckled at her obvious confusion.

"What?" she asked as alarm bells echoed in her head. His demeanor was downright spooky. She couldn't remember giving him her address. She couldn't have given him the address to this house; she didn't even own it when she'd met him in Jerusalem. *But, did I give him the address to my old place? Maybe the new owners had pointed him in my direction?* She couldn't remember. It didn't seem like her to give private information to a virtual stranger. Although, when she was in Jerusalem, she wasn't quite herself while grieving the sudden passing of her mother.

He straightened his torso and replaced his black hat. "I'm sorry I'm confusing you, Kate."

Her flashlight beam shook over his pale face, but she had to keep him in sight. "Do you mind filling me in?"

"Of course," he nodded. "Might I just say that you still look beautiful?"

His comment instantly made her stomach sour. "Um, before you go on, I want you to know that I have a boyfriend. I hope I didn't lead you on back in Jerusalem. I was... I don't know... searching for something... so to speak." She thought back to their encounter at the wall and wondered how he could've taken their brief interaction so wrong and now assumed that she liked or wanted him.

"I know all about your boyfriend." He pursed his lips as if he had just tasted something bitter. "The priest, right?" his voice was venomous.

"He's *not* a priest."

"Right," he agreed, his expression softening. "Let's not get too ahead of ourselves, shall we?"

She tried to strengthen her voice. "So, why are you here exactly?"

"Hmmm." A playful glint came into his eyes.

Suddenly, in a sickening wave of realization, she sensed... no... *knew* things would not end well.

"Please," she mumbled.

"Don't be frightened, Kate," he said, his voice unctuous. He took a short step in her direction, easily missing the debris on the floor that surrounded his black shoes.

"Just tell me what you want," she whispered, uncertain she wanted the real answer.

"Let me tell you about Jerusalem." He took another small step toward her. "I was searching, too," he said. He stared intently into her unblinking eyes.

"Searching?" *Move*, she screamed at herself, *get the hell out of his path.* But she was trapped in his gaze like the proverbial deer in the headlights.

"Yes, Kate," he soothed. "I'd been searching for you." He took another step toward her.

She lowered the flashlight now, pointed the faltering beam toward the floor. "Me?" she whispered. Her body trembled.

"Yes. It's time to claim your birthright." His grin turned ugly, menacing.

Kate frowned at the man. "Birthright? What do you mean by that?"

"I've been waiting years for the right person. The one born with the purest of hearts. That's you, Kate," explained the man.

"What?" She shook her head from side to side, tried to break her eyes away from his, to make sense of what on earth he was saying. Nothing made sense. *Why can't I will myself to run out the front door? Roger! He should be here soon, maybe he could help me,* she thought, her hope fleeting.

Adam's eyes followed hers to the front door. He smirked knowingly. "Are you expecting someone? Your friend, the priest, maybe?"

"How'd you know that?" *How could he possibly know?* Roger wasn't supposed to mention it to anyone and she knew he wouldn't blab.

"I just know," he snapped. "And don't expect him to rescue you. He's already been… dealt with." He grinned broadly again, showing his yellowing teeth.

"Dealt with?" she asked, her sour stomach almost ready to boil over.

"Never mind that now, Kate," he said. He took another small step in her direction.

Doing the math, Kate realized that if he took two more

steps toward her, he'd be within arm's reach. She gulped and stepped back. "Just tell me: Why are you here?"

He seemed annoyed by her lack of understanding. "Like I said before, Kate, it is time for you to claim your birthright."

"Enough games, Adam," she said to the floor, her own annoyance growing. She realized that if she didn't look directly into his eyes, she could concentrate, begin to plan an escape.

He bobbed his head around in the dark to get her to look at his face. He seemed to understand that she'd figured out his power of persuasion and was trying to avoid it.

"Fair enough, Kate," he said. "You need to do something for me."

She looked over his head, careful not to get sucked into his hypnotic gaze. "What could you possibly need from me?"

"You were pre-destined by birth to help me."

"Pre-destined. What does that mean?" she huffed, her strength growing every second she kept her eyes away from his. In addition to sensing his intentions, his condescending air had started to irritate her. *Another man with orders for me*, she thought.

"Come downstairs with me," he ordered. His chin jutted toward the basement door.

"Downstairs? No freaking way!"

"Don't be frightened, Kate." Another sinister grin crossed his face. "*I* won't hurt you."

She shuddered. "I can't go down there, there's a ghost or spirit, something evil's down there. I can't go down."

She knew she sounded lame and false, although it was the stone cold truth.

"Nonsense, Kate. If you complete your task, you can leave." He spread his hands open wide in a gesture of goodwill.

"I… I don't believe you," she stuttered. She took another step back and glanced quickly around the room, searching for a way out. She'd be damned if she'd let him lure her into the basement. Her mind flashed to an episode of The Oprah Winfrey Show her mother had made her watch when she was in high school. A safety expert advised women not to allow an attacker to take them to the second crime scene. Her living room was scene one and the basement would be scene two. According to the expert, nothing good happens at scene two.

"Now, be a good girl, Kate. Please don't make this any harder than it needs to be."

"Please. Just leave," she begged. She hoped some shred of their brief friendship would echo in his brain and allow her to leave unharmed.

"Sorry, Kate." He shook his head rhythmically from side to side. "The time is now." Quickly, he closed the space between them with one giant leap and grabbed her upper arms. He squeezed them in a vice-like grip, painfully pinching her skin and muscles.

She screamed and tried to wrench her arms free. She twisted and pulled against the force of his cold hands. Easily, he turned her around so her back was against his body. He lifted her from the ground as if she was a sack of laundry and half pushed/half carried her to the open door of the basement stairs.

"No!" she screamed. Her vocal cords burned with terror and exertion.

"Don't be difficult, Kate," he said calmly, and tried to shove her through the threshold of the door and down the stairs into the basement. He barely seemed winded despite their struggle.

At the top of the steps, she managed to wiggle her arms free and clawed at the frame of the door, digging her fingernails into the wood to keep from tumbling down the narrow staircase to the dirt floor below. The hard wood tore her fingernails from their cushy beds; excruciating pain shot through her hands like the lightning bolts that had haunted her earlier.

Using the door frame for leverage, she managed to squirm around so she was facing him again, her mouth and nose buried in the folds of his musty-smelling suit coat. She took one hand off the wood frame and clawed at his face, hoping that any remaining scraps of her ruined fingernails would harm him, cause him to stop.

He hesitated for a moment, long enough for her to squint into his face and try to give him one more giant scratch. She met his gaze and screamed. His eyes burned a bright, angry red. His blood-streaked face had morphed into the dog-like creature she'd seen in her nightmare about the market in Jerusalem. Any remaining fight in her body evaporated.

Adam caught her limp body before it could slide to the floor. He grabbed her under her armpits like a toddler and prepared to heave her down the stairs to the basement.

Summoning one last ounce of strength, she grabbed a handful of fabric from the lapel of his black suit. "If I'm going down, you're going, too!" She spat angrily on his growling snout. She pulled on his jacket with all her might.

Shock spread across his distorted face. He fell toward the open void above the staircase and tumbled down the wooden stairs.

Kate's body twisted and somersaulted beneath him. The weight of his falling body pushed her flesh and bones into the hard wood steps. Searing pain exploded on each impact. Her left collar bone hit a step with a sickening crack that made her want to throw up.

They landed in a broken heap with a puff of dust at the end of the stairs. Oddly, she remembered that first time she'd laid eyes on Adam, there had been puffs of dust then, too.

After a few moments of stillness, Kate realized he wasn't moving. His full weight pressed heavily on top of her broken body, constricting her chest, smothering her. *Is he unconscious? Maybe dead?* She used her right arm to push his body and rolled him down her bruised legs like a heavy log.

After pulling free, she leaned against the rock wall, panting heavily and grimacing in pain. *I must summon enough strength to get back up the stairs and out to my car.* She didn't know if she had that much strength left, at least not at the moment.

She glanced over at Adam, lying a few feet away, still unmoving at the bottom of the stairs. Thankfully, his freak-ish visage faced wall. His chest didn't appear to be moving up and down either. The nurse in her wanted to lean over him and check for a pulse, but he'd tried to hurt her, maybe even kill her. She shouldn't risk get close enough for him to grab her, just in case he was pretending. She looked around in the dark basement for something to help her get up.

She reached over her head toward a stone that jutted out awkwardly from the old wall and used her bleeding fingers to drag her body upright. Still weak, she stood, certain she had a badly sprained ankle and perhaps more serious injuries yet to be discovered.

She glanced over at the ruined brick wall, remembering the menacing sounds that had emanated from the far corner the last time she was down here. Cautiously, she moved each limb, testing them for functionality, with the exception of her left arm. The pain in her collar bone was almost too much to bear when she moved it. She kept it immobilized against her aching side, which helped a little.

I must leave the basement, pronto. She turned back toward the base of the staircase and reluctantly shuffled toward Adam's body. She searched for a way to step over him without touching him.

As she neared his body, her injured foot kicked up small puffs of dust as it dragged behind her. A pale hand darted from under Adam's body toward her working ankle, trying to trip her.

She hobbled a few steps back, deeper into the basement. Now her only escape route was closed. Slowly, Adam rose from his crumpled position on the floor, appearing taller than he'd been before. It seemed as if his disfigured animal-like head almost touched the ceiling. He

growled angrily and limped toward her, forcing her to retreat toward the danger that probably still lurked near the
obliterated brick wall.

Frantically, she looked for anything to protect herself.
The gargoyle. Her eyes fixed on the statue of the gargoyle
that had been cemented into the wall so many years ago
and was suddenly struck by the similar forehead, and long,
pointed snout shared by both Adam and the ugly statue.

She tore her eyes away from the sneering gargoyle and
stared at Adam's hulking frame, certain she was about to be
finished off by the angry man-creature. His eyes glowed a
brilliant red, giving her a bit of light that helped her search
for a weapon: a rock, a hammer, anything to fend him off.

Adam continued his lumbering approach. In the ruddy
light from his red eyes, a glint of metal on the floor by the
remains of the brick wall caught her attention. Her heart
leapt in her chest. It was the pickaxe she'd used the first
time she tried to take down the brick wall. She'd dropped
it where she stood in her haste to leave. The explosion of
bricks must have pushed it against the edge of the floor
where it met the old stone foundation.

She lurched forward and bent crookedly to grab the
pickaxe, hoping to avoid further injury to her throbbing
collar bone. She hoped he'd think she was falling, off balance from her obvious injuries. Her bloody fingers grabbed
their target and she cupped the pickaxe handle in her right
palm, grateful her dominant hand was available to defend
herself against his inevitable attack.

She turned quickly, leaned her back against the cool
stones that made up the basement wall, and braced for his

lunge. A thick stream of saliva, muddied with blood from broken teeth, drooled from his dog-like mouth.

He smiled grotesquely at her. His smug red eyes seemed to assume victory over his weak competitor.

Hot surges of anger welled in her chest. She sensed the putrid creature believed he'd already won. Again, he started toward her and she steeled herself against his attack and the knowledge of what she'd have to do to him to survive.

He drove forward, threw his weight at her and tried to pin her to the wall. His breath was hot on her neck as his gnarled, blood-streaked hand grabbed her face by the cheeks and turned her head to face him.

She fought hard, straining every tendon in her neck as he continued to force her head, her eyes toward his hideous face. She squeezed her eyes closed and in one quick motion, plunged the hidden pickaxe into his bulging neck directly above the white collar of his shirt. Blood spurted from the wound and covered her face in a dark splash of hot fluid. She was relieved she'd closed her eyes against the horror that unfolded inches from her face. His grip loosened, releasing her neck. Behind her closed eyelids, she sensed that he was backing away. His rank breath retreated quickly from her blood-drenched face.

Finally, she dared to open her eyes. In the miniscule amount of light that trickled into the basement from the small rectangular window above his head, she saw him desperately clutching his neck, holding a trembling hand over his wound. The pickaxe dangled sickly from between his fingers, still inserted into his pulsing flesh.

He dropped to his knees. A blood-filled growl escaped

his curled lips, his red eyes dimmed in the dark basement. Unable to use his hands to brace the downward motion, he fell. His exposed face hit the dirt with a sickening thump.

She covered her eyes with her injured hands. She didn't want to see any more. Even though she had defended herself, she felt unimaginable guilt for taking a life, as hideous as it was.

She slid down the wall and held her knees to her chest, grimacing in pain with every anguished cry. It was over. There was no way Adam or anyone could survive a direct hit like that. She took deep, calming breaths to stop her blubbering, worried she might hyperventilate.

After a few minutes of slow breathing, the small light bulb at the bottom of the stairs flickered alive. She looked at the bulb, confused. *How had it turned on by itself?* Then, she remembered. When they'd fled a week ago, they'd left the light on. So, the power, lost to the storm, had been restored.

She glanced over at Adam's drained body. A dark pool of blood had spread underneath his head as it lay crooked on the floor, angled cartoon-like away from his large frame. Without warning, she began to giggle hysterically. She clapped a blood stained hand over her mouth, embarrassed by her surge of joy at such a hideous scene. She couldn't fault herself too much. At last things were finally going her way.

She pushed herself back up the wall, using the old, protruding stones for support. She was determined to leave the basement forever when something behind the wasted brick wall caught her eye. *Funny, I hadn't noticed anything over there before.*

She winced and limped toward the freshly exposed stone wall, previously hidden from view by the bricks. A large abscess was now visible in the wall.

Kneeling, she grimaced with pain and peered cautiously into the dark hole. Her heart thumped nervously. She squinted into the gloom, willing her eyes to see beyond the shadows. Instead, her eager gaze was met with empty space.

Still kneeling in front of the opening, she hesitantly put her head inside. She ran her hands along the smooth sides just inside the threshold, hoping to find a spring or catch, some trick that might expose another hidden compartment or perhaps a secret cavity laden with valuables.

Unsuccessful, she sat back on her heels. Disappointed, she was hit with another wave of pain and was suddenly very aware there was a dead body laying a few feet away. She shook her head. *How could I be such a greedy fool?* She needed to get the police and get to the hospital. The fracture in her foot throbbed as she rested her weight carelessly on her heels.

Getting up again, every bone and muscle in her battered body ached. *This must be how a marathon runner feels after running a tough race. The only difference was I'd lost fingernails instead of toenails,* she thought. This repulsive fact had been told to her by a runner friend after she'd competed. She surveyed her grimy, bloody nail beds. The sight of them made her feel weak; her stomach churned sourly. She shuddered, remembering how she'd lost her fingernails.

She needed to get up the stairs and out to the road to search for help, assuming the upstairs telephone was still knocked out from the storm. When she turned away from the door to begin her odyssey of climbing the narrow stairs, a strange whooshing emanated from deeper in the void. She turned, taking a painful step toward it, and peered inside.

Hearing the noise again, she leaned in closer, wondering if she was in shock or had a brain bleed and was starting to hallucinate. She closed her eyes and trained her ears toward the dark recesses beyond the wall's opening.

An overwhelming urge to find the source of the noise gripped her. It was ridiculous given her current circumstances, but the intense desire to know more outweighed any of her injuries. She stood motionless and assessed herself. She had no fear, only awe and nagging curiosity. She worried for a brief moment that if she hadn't been in shock before, maybe she was now, which might explain her irrational need to continue investigating the void, the strange sound and whatever lay beyond it.

She peered anxiously into the void again. This time, instead of complete darkness, she was greeted by something even more shocking—there was a light, far in the distance. The hole in the stone wall was an opening to a tunnel! An extremely long tunnel.

Quickly, she weighed her options in her head. She needed to call the police, Matt, and Roger. But the strange tunnel beckoned and she sensed that whatever she'd find at the end of this mysterious passageway would be amazing, possibly change the world.

Fighting through her pain, she bounded up the narrow

steps of her basement to find another emergency flashlight. The one she'd dropped in her struggle with Adam was broken, but she knew Matt had stored another one in a kitchen drawer.

In her haste to find the flashlight, she pulled open a number of drawers, not caring some of the contents were spilled on the floor. On the third drawer, she had success. She found the flashlight she needed and ran swiftly down the stairs, taking them two at a time, a fresh surge of adrenaline doing a fine job of masking her pain.

She ran past Adam's lifeless body and clicked on her flashlight, shining the beam into the tunnel. The small light didn't help as much as she'd hoped, but it would do. It illuminated a few feet ahead, allowing her to make her way into the dark.

Crouching, she walked deeper into the tunnel, touching the cold, wet stones on the wall with her free hand. She smiled broadly in spite of everything that had just happened. She couldn't believe this excellent turn of luck. She went from potential victim to probable hero. She continued moving forward in the tunnel, forcing herself not to whistle a happy tune while she carefully made her way along the slippery, damp stones under her feet.

Matt

Matt drove around town like a possessed lunatic. He'd searched all Kate's known hideouts hoping to locate her before something awful happened. Already, he'd struck out at the diner, movie theater and library. He tried the hospital thinking perhaps she went in to work a shift. He found only her co-worker Marlene toiling over a pile of patient files at the nurse's station. A half-eaten bag of chocolates lay on the desk next to the teetering stack.

"Have a lover's quarrel, did ya?" she asked with a snide expression.

"Something like that." He didn't want to give her more gossip for the rumor mill he knew was alive and well within the walls of the hospital.

"Too bad," she said. "I always thought you were too good for her anyway." Her eager eyes searched his stressed face for a hint of agreement.

He rolled his eyes and walked away without answering. He'd been hard on Kate in the past when she'd complain about Marlene, defending Marlene's actions as those of someone who probably didn't have many friends and not much of a chance at a love life either, but he didn't have the patience for her rudeness today. He made a mental note to apologize to Kate for being Marlene's secret cheerleader. Really, she *was* a rotten bitch. He left the hospital in a huff, planning his next location to search.

Sitting in his car, he nervously tapped the steering wheel. *In Kate's angry state, where else would she have gone?* "Red!" he yelled into the bug spattered windshield. Maybe she visited Red for more advice. He started the car and turned up the road toward Red's trailer park, glad Kate had pointed it out to him the other day on their way back from the grocery store. Otherwise, he'd have to stop somewhere and ask for directions, wasting precious time.

He sped toward the trailer park, not worrying about speed limits or hidden patrol cars, getting more desperate to find her by the minute. The day was fading fast and she was due to meet Roger at her house soon. He wanted to catch her before she made a dangerous mistake.

He pulled into the Winding Winds trailer park and tried to heed the slow speed limit posted on the narrow drive. The last thing he needed was to run down some poor kid on his bike in his urgent quest to find Kate.

He pulled to a stop in front of Red's dingy trailer, got out of his car, and slammed the door hard, hoping the loud noise would summon him to the door, possibly saving a few valuable seconds. As he suspected, Red was already peering suspiciously from the top of the screen door at the lanky stranger who was fast approaching.

"Whatch'ya need, son?" he said through the screen, a small amount of ancient toughness in his tone.

"Hi, sir. My name is Matt. I'm Kate Hart's boyfriend. I was wondering if she'd been by here today. I've been looking for her all over the place." He heard the growing panic in his own voice.

Red scratched his stubbly chin with a nimble hand. "Kate's missin'?"

"Sort of," said Matt, wishing Red would answer his question so he could move to the next location.

"Hmm," he grunted through the screen. Thinking slowly, he chewed the skin on the inside of his cheek.

Matt, a bundle of nervous energy and anxiety, couldn't appreciate the old-fashioned charm that had wooed Kate upon her first visit with him. Red's thoughtful contemplation of Matt's simple question was pushing him over the edge of his usual patience. "So, has she been here?"

After scratching every part of his wrinkled body, Red finally answered, "Nope. Not today."

"Ok, thanks anyway," he said and turned quickly back to his car.

"Hold up a minute," Red called out.

"What?" said Matt, trying to hide his frustration at the whole situation, not just the slow-thinking Red.

"You don't suppose…? No, never mind."

"Suppose what? Please tell me what you're thinking." Matt softened his tone. "I'm running out of ideas here."

"Well, I reckon Kate's a bit of a rebel. Not too keen on following orders or recommendations, so to speak. Do ya think she'd do something I specifically told her not to?" He raised his thick salt and pepper eyebrows quizzically at Matt.

Matt nodded his head. "Probably, she would," he said, knowing in his gut Red was on the right track.

"I warned her to stay away from Devil's Chair. I was firm on it. I could tell it stuck in her craw a bit. I'm a gambling man and I'd put money on it. You'll find her in those woods stirring up God knows what." His dark eyes echoed sadness at the prospect of Kate's disobedience and the trouble that was certain to follow.

"Oh my God! I hadn't even thought about her going out *there*!" Matt slapped his forehead with his right hand. "Do you really think she'd be *that* stupid? To go out there alone?" But he already knew the answer.

"You know her better than me. But, yes. I think she would," he said. "Without hesitation." Red shook his head woefully, his dark pony tail swishing rhythmically on the back of his plaid shirt.

"Thanks, Chief," said Matt and he ran to his car.

"Go save her, Matt," he called as Matt slammed the door shut. "She'll need saving if she's at the chair."

Kate

Kate shivered. The air in the tunnel was cold, the walls and ceiling wet and dripping icy droplets of condensation on her hair and shoulders, making the journey slippery under her sneakers with their worn treads. Her emergency flashlight's equally useless beam only illuminated a few feet ahead. She'd taken a good spill a few minutes before, tripping over a loose rock, reawakening the pain in her collar bone and ankle, a fresh reminder of her violent altercation with Adam.

Kate continued to crouch and shuffle deeper into the tunnel that had started at the hole in the wall of her basement. It was narrower now and she still couldn't believe how long it was. She'd been walking for what seemed like forever.

Occasionally, she'd stop to listen for clues indicating where she was in the world. Based on the direction of the tunnel and how long she'd been walking, she thought it would eventually lead to the river. The same river she'd been to earlier in the day. The same river where she saw the red-eyed creature-man. She swallowed her fear. Since Adam, with his menacing red eyes, was dead in her basement, she was probably safe from running into the creature again. *Unless he wasn't the only one,* she thought and shivered again, wishing she'd thought to grab a jacket when she'd gone back upstairs to get the flashlight.

She shuddered again when she let her mind wander back to Adam and how viciously he'd attacked her. Vivid images of him and those glowing red eyes flashed in front of her in the dark as she felt her way along the tunnel. *What time was it? It has to be close to five, doesn't it?* Roger would arrive soon. She'd feel horrible if he entered her house, concerned for her whereabouts, and stumbled on the grisly scene in the basement. He'd certainly call the police. She quickened her pace, wanting to get to the end of the tunnel and back home before he was scarred for life because of her inexplicable curiosity, stubbornness and her innate belief that she was so clever she could cope with anyone, any problem.

She wished Matt were here with her. Somehow, she believed that whatever she'd find at the end of the tunnel would change her life. She knew it deep in her broken bones. *Is it possible I'm having a vision of my own, much like Matt's gift of foresight?*

She smiled. She pictured him proud of her strength and fearlessness in the face of such horrible and abnormal circumstances. Surely, he'd love her again. Things had to work out between them. "So long as I don't end up in jail," she said aloud, thinking of the lifeless man who'd bled to death on her dirt floor.

She paused again and strained her ears to listen to her surroundings. She blocked out the constant drip of water and her own rapidly beating heart and thought she heard rushing water. *Am I finally getting close to the river end of the tunnel?* She hoped the storm that had just passed through hadn't swollen the river too much. *What if the tunnel filled with water?* She'd drown. Quickly, she tried to calculate how high or low she'd come out on the river bank.

Focusing her energy on the saturated rock floor, she scuffed her sneakers along the surface to keep a decent pace. She peered ahead, hopeful the dim glow she saw was the end of the tunnel.

When she passed around the next bend, the light grew. Her heart leapt with joy. She squinted and saw the wide open mouth of the tunnel. *I've made it!* The tunnel continued to expand and now she could stand upright. She hobbled to the end and stood on a patch of dirt that had sprouted grass tall enough to block the tunnel's opening from the river below. Her body was sore, some parts still throbbing, but she'd made it.

The rain had stopped and the sun had forced its way through the clouds. She narrowed her eyes toward the setting sun that shone brightly behind the undulating grass. A blaze of red-orange streaks filtered through the tall pines that littered the river's edge.

Still at the mouth of the tunnel, she parted the grass with her damaged hands and looked down. She was high over the river, about eight to ten feet above it. The far bank was lined with trees and seemed familiar to her. *Is this where I was earlier today?* She leaned through the grass to confirm her suspicions.

Craning her neck upward, she saw a protrusion of rock above her and a little to the right. She gulped. *Oh God! The tunnel led me directly to Devil's Chair!*

Suddenly gripped with fear and irrational thoughts, she

could hardly breathe. *Is Adam still dead in my basement? What if I was wrong? What if he'd magically come back to life?*

"You idiot," she scolded herself. "Idiot! Idiot!"

Night was swiftly coming to the woods, and here she was, alone, a stone's throw from Devil's Chair, with only a weakening flashlight for a weapon. *What if Red's folklore was correct? The red-eyed creature was some man-eating, check that, a woman-eating wolverine?* She took quick steps back into the tunnel to shield herself from the prying eyes of the forest, its furry inhabitants, and any nearby horrible creatures.

Oh God, she thought, *the sun's setting.* Now she probably couldn't make it back in time to meet Roger. He'd see the carnage in the basement and contact the police. They'd be waiting for her when she returned, ready to slap on the cuffs. She shook her head to clear it of the terrifying images that swirled in her brain, confusing her, making it hard to determine her next move.

Finally, she decided she'd head back as quickly as possible, through the tunnel, and intercept Roger before he called anyone. She had to explain what had happened to her and get a well-loved priest on her side before the cops showed up. Maybe if she showed them the tunnel, they'd believe it was how Adam had been coming and going from her house for who knows how many years. Maybe, just maybe, she'd be lauded as a hero for solving a decades-long mystery of the red-eyed man. She'd caught him and killed him. All by herself.

She turned, leaving the darkening woods behind,

determined to move faster on her way back to the house. She took a few steps into the tunnel and slipped on a slimy pad of thick moss, landing with a wet thump on her backside. In her flailing attempt to keep her balance, she dropped her faltering flashlight, and sent it spinning wildly deeper into the passageway.

"Crap!" she yelled into the tunnel. *Crap, crap, crap,* the echo mocked her.

The flashlight, she saw, was still spinning slowly a few feet from where it had landed. She stood cautiously, mentally surveying her body for further injury. She felt a stab of pain in her back when she straightened up and held a hand cautiously over her tender tailbone, certain it was badly bruised. She loped toward the flashlight happy that it had miraculously survived its inaugural flight.

She bent over to grab the handle of the flashlight and winced from the pain emanating from her lower back. Now, the tiny bulb flickered, barely able to show the way. She groaned at her bad luck. With the growing pain in her back and the lack of a light source, she knew she'd never make it back in time to fix things. She hoped they'd notice the tunnel and come find her; she could use a ride on a stretcher.

She took a tentative step toward home and immediately slipped again. This time, arms swinging wildly, she managed to maintain her balance. The cost: a fresh burning sensation sizzling within her wounded collar bone. She grumbled at the wet cave floor and shined her light on the blameworthy spot that had caused her near-fall, to curse the moss that had dared slow her departure.

As her flashlight moved down the wall, toward the

floor, the light caught a glint of metal that stopped her mid-investigation. Curiously, she saw a small, child-sized door nestled within the wall of the tunnel. "What the hell?" she said aloud and immediately tried to find a way to open it.

She grabbed hold of a leather strap nailed into the door and pulled hard, ignoring the burn in her wounded limbs. It wiggled slightly, but remained firmly closed. Her curiosity for the strange door was overwhelming, as if she was drawn to the mysterious entrance that had been lying dormant in her basement, hidden carefully away for all this time.

She forced her aching body onto the damp floor and sat in front of the door, putting her feet on either side of the hole. Using the wall for leverage, she pushed with her feet and pulled on the leather strap with her good arm. The fracture in her foot cracked when she pushed against the stones. She screamed and stopped, realizing the door hadn't budged.

In the gloomy recesses of the tunnel, she got on her knees to make a closer examination of the door. It was made of wood, ornately carved. *Mahogany?* She ran her hand over its smooth lines and brushed off years of dust that covered the coffee-colored wood.

Is this what Adam had been looking for? What he wanted my help with? Why he wanted me in the basement? Things started to make sense for the first time in a long time.

Had he been following me? Wanting whatever lay beyond this door for himself? It didn't explain their initial meeting in Jerusalem, but he might have been the one making the sounds in the basement, trying to scare her off. *Why didn't he just open the door and take whatever lay beyond it?* She'd been gone for more than a week. That would've been more than enough time to steal anything of value and be gone forever. She would've been none the wiser.

Then it dawned on her. She realized why he'd tried to lure her into the basement and why he'd attacked her. *He needed the key!* She grabbed the key from her chest. She marveled at the ornately etched key that had hung from her neck nearly every day since she'd met Adam all those months ago.

She thought about his words from earlier, "the purest of hearts," and her last name was Hart. At the time, she'd thought it was a ridiculous notion, almost as ridiculous as Grandma Betty's warning, "beware what Kate Hart brings," before she'd even met Matt. But still, it made sense in the oddest way. He used this tunnel to repeatedly enter and "haunt" her house, demolish the brick wall, trash her belonging and he needed her to open this door. *Could it be he was cursed and she was special in some way?*

She squatted next to the door and ignored the pain that seared in her foot and burned wickedly in her collar bone. She ran her hand along the door again, searching for a lock. She blew a puff of dust from a metal plate near the bottom of the door and found a keyhole previously hidden from view by a thick layer of grime and cobwebs.

She caught a glimpse of her hand and cringed. Bloody and covered with dirt, it was ghastly. The dust from the door clung to the empty wet spots where her fingernails used to live.

She lifted the key from around her neck and let the

chain hang loose over her battered hand. She turned the gold key over in her palm and compared its intricate carvings to those on the newly discovered metal locking plate.

Her heart surged. When side by side, it was impossible not to see the glaring similarities between the two relics. Both had intricate etching in the same flowing pattern and the lock was encircled by the same molded swirls, identical to the head of the key. In her uneducated opinion, they appeared to be a spot-on match. In a wave of giddy excitement, she laughed.

She slid the key firmly into the lock's black hole. As they met, the metal key scraped against the metal lock, sending a ripple of chills down her back. The key moved easily toward the back of the lock despite all their years apart. She hesitated briefly and then turned the key to the left.

A satisfying click and the lock disengaged. The seal on the door popped, reminding her of a set of Tupperware she'd bought years ago from a desperate coworker at the hospital.

She released the key, leaving it twisted inside the lock and put one trembling hand on the leather strap. Slowly, easily, the door lifted.

Standing now, she lifted the door so it was wide open. Oddly, the door opened not on the left or right, it opened from the top, the hinge hidden by the stones that jutted from the tunnel wall. She ducked under the door and peered into the void behind it, expecting to see hidden treasure—diamonds or cash, something amazing that would take her breath away. Instead, her eager gaze was met with empty space.

Kate entered the small chamber and was able to stand. She surveyed her surroundings for clues, still puzzled why Adam would want or need this opened. With the weak flashlight beam trained on the ground, she saw a small puddle in the center of the floor. She bent over and reached a hand toward the slick spot and touched it with her fingers. The liquid she found was amazingly slippery between her fingers. She held her damp fingers to her nose and sniffed. It didn't smell like anything she recognized. Standing over the small puddle, liquid from above dripped into her hair. She touched the back of her head and her hand came back covered with the same slippery fluid.

"Ugh!" she gagged and tapped her dimming flashlight against the palm of her hand, hoping to fix it. Luckily, the beam grew stronger. She trained the light on the ceiling, squinting against the dark shadows, to see what was making the slippery mess on her and the floor.

When her flashlight revealed the horror on the chamber's ceiling mere inches from her head, she gasped and immediately clapped a hand over her mouth. A hulking black creature hung bat-like above her. Jagged teeth protruded grotesquely from black, hairy lips that oozed clear mucus onto the floor from its perch over her head. It took long, garbled, sucking wet breaths in its slumber.

She continued to hold her hand over her mouth afraid even the smallest sound would wake the creature. Her heart raced madly in her chest, as if trying to pound its way out of her body and escape. *Would it be safer to go back to the tunnel's edge and jump into the river? Or, should I continue to sneak past the sleeping creature and hope I got through the tunnel before it wakes up?*

Despite her shock, she quickly calculated her options: The drop into the river might sprain or break both ankles. Her only plausible choice was to exit the chamber and escape toward home, and pray she made it before things went horribly wrong.

Not daring to shine her flashlight onto its sleeping face, she took a last hesitant look at the repulsive creature. Its long talons gripped a large, protruding slab of rock, holding it motionless above her like a disgusting, mucus-dripping zeppelin.

Careful to avoid the growing puddle of drool that lay like a booby trap on the slick rock floor, she shuffled out of the chamber and into the tunnel, hoping to get to the first bend without making a sound. She neared the bend and glanced back, relieved to see the tunnel was still empty behind her. She knew night was minutes away, not giving her much time to retreat if the creature was nocturnal.

Turning to flee, her knee connected with a rock protruding from wall. She grunted and bit her lip to keep from reacting. Momentarily, she stopped, rubbed her injured knee, and had to look back once more before she disappeared around the bend.

The creature's giant head poked out from the chamber's small opening and Kate saw its hairy ears twitch. *Shit!* She hoped her eyes were playing tricks in the growing dark. *Did it hear my pained grunt or the smack of my bone against the rock?* The creature's huge pointed snout opened wide and it screeched loudly, like a bald eagle squawking in a canyon. The eerie noise echoed madly through the confined space and reminded Kate vividly of the noise that had initially frightened her from her basement. Kate clapped her blood-covered hands over her ears. Her body shook involuntarily. Frozen, she was too frightened to turn her back to the stirring creature.

The creature screamed again, louder this time, the vibration of its call echoed through every fiber of Kate's shaking body. It somersaulted from its stony tomb and landed with a thud on the floor of the cave, its feet pressed into a fresh puddle of sticky mucus.

She flashed her faltering light directly at the creature hoping to confuse or scare it. Her usual instincts had gone out the window. She didn't know what else she could do at this pivotal moment.

The creature shied away from the light and turned its head toward the dark wall. *Would it fly out the tunnel's entrance and disappear?* Kate willed it to be so.

The creature seemed to read her thoughts. It turned toward her. Grinning viciously, its jagged teeth gleamed brightly in the arc of her shaking light. A glop of mucus dropped from its massive jaws onto the floor with a sickening slap.

She took a step back to get as much space between herself and this horrible creature, suddenly very certain of its intentions. Her backside hit the wall of the tunnel and she pressed herself into it.

The creature, sensing her fear, took a big, greedy sniff of the cool evening air. It seemed to enjoy the smell of her fear-induced sweat. It tilted its large head toward her and started to rise. Before, it had been hunched down, its legs bent nearly in two. Now, it rose to full height. Veined brown wings spread out grandly, touching either side of the cave walls, blocking any scrap of light from the dimming sun.

She trembled violently, aimed her flashlight at the creature, taking in its full height and girth, both amazed and terrified at its awful magnificence.

She lifted her light to the creature's gnarled face. The creature flicked open its heavy-lidded eyes revealing huge irises. *Oh God!* They glowed bright red. Kate screamed.

The connections in her brain fired furiously. The creature standing before her bore a strong resemblance to Adam. They had the same dog-like snout, jagged teeth, and menacing red eyes. Now, she understood he'd been here to release this beast from the door. But, it was she who'd released it. She'd brought all this on herself and it had started with that damn trip to Jerusalem when she first met Adam and accepted his gift of the key. Everything else: buying the house, the haunting, and the rest of the craziness had brought her to this one terrifying moment.

As her mind churned, the creature crept closer, carefully stalking its prey. She shook her head. Her anger at her own stupidity overwhelmed her fear as the beast inched toward her.

The beast was now ten feet from her. She estimated that it had to be more than eight feet tall. She didn't stand a chance. The creature continued its cautious approach.

"Please don't," she begged weakly. She searched the creature's eyes for any shred of compassion.

It stopped a foot in front of her. It breathed heavily, dripping mucus on its furry chest and feet. A sickening odor of rotted meat and death emanated from its body. Remnants of food hung in tattered clumps in its teeth. Again, it grinned wickedly at her. She pressed her body deeper against the cold stone wall, wincing in pain as the stones pressed roughly into her bruised flesh.

Stronger than before, she yelled at the creature, "Leave me alone!"

The creature's grin widened. It tilted its head to the left and peered into her wide eyes. In its huge red irises, she saw her own reflection. She looked very small and very afraid in the mirror image. She blinked away the tears that had welled up in her eyes, blurring her vision.

She racked her brain for anything she could do to save herself. In a last act of desperation, she pulled her arm back and heaved the flashlight at the creature's face, hoping to make it leave or at least recoil long enough to give her a chance to escape.

The flashlight bounced harmlessly off the creature's muscular chest. It fell, useless, clattered onto the hard stone floor and went dark.

The creature grinned even more viciously, as though amused by her feeble attempt to protect herself. She cowered against the wall. The creature lifted its head and opened its enormous mouth, exposing rows of fangs. It growled deeply. The sound reverberated off the stone walls.

Trembling, Kate screamed and turned to run.

Matt

"Move your ass!" Matt bellowed at the car lollygagging in front of him. He raised his hands angrily at the windshield to show the driver how irritated he was. Matt was driving from Red's trailer to Kate's house, but the pace, thanks to the old lady in front of him, was painfully slow. He'd been kicking himself the whole way for not thinking Kate would be stupid enough or angry enough to go to the house alone.

The dawdling driver finally turned into an entrance of a shopping plaza allowing him to pass. The old woman looked over at his passing car and shrugged at him apologetically. Instantly, Matt felt his cheeks burn hot with embarrassment. The driver was probably eighty years old and here he was, a young whippersnapper, riding the bumper of her pristine silver Volkswagen.

He gave the woman a small wave, pressed hard on the gas pedal and sped ahead. He flew toward Kate's property on the edge of town, making up time now that the traffic had thinned. He turned quickly onto her rutted driveway, not slowing on the bumpy trail. His body shook in his seat and his chest bounced painfully into the steering wheel.

Gingerly, he rubbed his ribs where they'd met the steering wheel. He flinched at his own touch, cursing himself for being so careless. *Did I crack a rib in my haste to rescue*

Kate? He hoped it was just bruised. She'd easily know using her nursing skills. He'd rescue her and then she could rescue him. He smiled when he pictured her babying him and his wounded chest back at his condo, safe and sound.

He neared her house and held his breath. He prayed silently to anyone who would listen to find her there, hopefully waiting patiently in her car for her meeting with Roger. When he turned past the last stand of trees, he released the air he'd been holding in his lungs. His heart jumped with happiness. *Her car was in the driveway! She was here!* He couldn't believe his luck. *Should I call Red to thank him for the idea? No. Don't waste one second.*

He leaped from the driver's side door and rushed to her car, searching it for any information that might help him locate her.

He circled the car, searching frantically for clues to her whereabouts. Through the glass, he saw her purse resting neatly in the passenger seat, much as he would've expected. He swallowed hard when he looked in the back seat and saw one of the bags she'd packed when she'd left his house this morning, so angry at him.

He rounded the car, stopping at the back end. Imprints from her feet were visible in the gravel, a sure sign she'd stopped at the trunk at least for a moment to perhaps grab something from her suitcase.

He went to the edge of the woods and searched it for any sign of her. The grass and, further in, ferns were flattened. Was this from her forging a path or from a gust of wind? *Why hadn't I paid attention when I was a Boy Scout, learning to identify animal tracks in the woods?*

Desperately, he searched the tree line. Giving up, he went to her car and leaned back on the trunk, resting a weary hand behind him for added support. As soon as his hand made contact with the cold, damp metal, he was seized by a flash in his brain. It was the flash of a vision, much like the vision that had come to him earlier when he had touched the cross on top of Roger's body.

He closed his eyes and focused his energy on the flash, to make sense of the pictures that flew behind his lids: Kate, right about where he was standing although, now she was turned the other way, digging for something from the trunk.

She pulled a pair of sneakers from the suitcase, replacing her dress shoes, in preparation for a trek into the woods. Then she set off, angry at him and the long list of other people who had let her down. He groaned. His heart ached. He was the cause of her pain and frustration. He shook off his bubbling emotions and refocused on the vision that continued to unfold.

She headed confidently into the woods and found her way to the river. Her disappointment washed over her like a hot wave when she found Devil's Chair. She was bored by its diminutive size and lack of foreboding.

Suddenly, she saw a figure on the rock following her every move with burning red eyes. She ran, sprinting frantically through the woods, running for her life.

He exhaled, relieved, when he saw her make it back to her house without being badly injured by a fall or attacked by the figure in the woods. He saw her search her pockets and then the ground for her keys. He experienced her numb realization that she'd locked them in the very trunk that was mere inches behind his back.

He squeezed his eyes tighter. The vision unfolded faster and faster, challenging his ability to keep up. *She smashed the hidden plastic rock he'd given her, now using the emergency key to get herself safely inside.* Desperately, he wanted to open his eyes and look up on the porch for the broken pieces of plastic, to verify his vision, but if he did so, he'd risk breaking his connection to his speeding thoughts.

He refocused his energy and pressed his hand harder into the wet metal of Kate's trunk. *She groped around in the dark living room, trying to turn on the lights. She sighed, frustrated when she realized the storm had knocked out the power. She picked up the flashlight from the floor and smiled, claiming it like a trophy.*

Suddenly, the beam of her flashlight illuminated a stranger's face, sitting quietly in her living room, waiting patiently to be discovered. She tried desperately to place the man's face, to figure out if he was friend or foe.

"She knows him," he said aloud, surprised by the sound of his own voice. He clapped his free hand over his mouth to prevent further distraction. Definitely, he must not lose his vision now.

The man approached her slowly, like a cat teasing a frightened mouse, playfully luring it into submission. He sensed the evil intentions of the peculiar man. The man wanted something from her. *What was it?* He gulped. His mind raced with horrid thoughts of what a strange man might do to a woman, alone, in a dark, desolate house.

The vision continued to unfold, Matt, helpless to aid her in what had already happened. He felt like a sick voyeur watching a lurid video. He wished he could force his way into the vision, make his body burst through the door at just the right moment, tackle the menacing stranger and save his love from harm.

She lifted the key on her necklace from her chest and held it out quizzically to the man, wondering why he needed it or needed her. The man took menacing steps toward her.

Suddenly, the man lunged at her and dragged her toward the basement. She cried out, scared and in pain. Her fingers bled from her struggle against the man at the top of the stairs. The acid in his stomach rose to his mouth when he saw, through Kate's eyes, the man's eyes burned an angry red. *Then, they tumbled down the stairs in a flailing heap of entangled arms and legs.*

Matt bent over and threw up on the gray stones at his feet. Hastily, he wiped his lips with the back of his free hand. He squeezed his eyes closed again and tried to regain the vision that had flown away with his violent regurgitation.

Now his vision clouded. Unable to regain his clarity, he cursed himself for not being able to control his body. The last image he saw before the vision disappeared entirely was Kate and the strange man lying in a broken pile at the bottom of the basement stairs. Faintly, he felt the burning pain of fractured bones and bruised muscles. He squeezed his eyes tighter yet, willing the vision to return to its full strength. To his shock and surprise, he was awarded one more image before it dissipated for good. He saw blood. *A large pool of dark blood soaked into the dirt floor of the basement.* He didn't know if it was Kate's or the stranger's.

Without hesitation, Matt bolted up the three steps to

the porch and pushed open the front door. He crossed the mess of the living room in two running leaps and landed in droplets of blood that stained the wood floor at the opening to the basement.

The rotten food-scented air from the ruined kitchen made him choke, but he took two steps at a time into the basement, steeling himself for what horrors he might find.

Kate

The creature lunged at Kate, crushing its huge jaws around her neck, her bones and tendons snapped easily under its tremendous strength.

A spurt of blood spurt shot straight from her neck and into the prickly fur of the creature. In her shock, she realized how similar it looked to Adam's blood spurting through his fingers when she'd hit him in the jugular with the pickaxe. The creature's fangs must have punctured the same artery in her neck. Oddly, she was happy knowing her death would come quickly and hopefully with little pain.

Despite her predicament, she was calm. Pain had yet to hit as a surge of adrenaline sped through her veins. The creature slightly released her neck only to bite down again, taking more of her face into its jaws. It crunched her cheek bones easily, like a child stepping on a wayward cracker. A burning sensation crawled across her face and down her neck, but she was unable to scream. With her broken bones still engulfed in the clenched jaw of the creature, she knew it was killing her. She was dying. An overwhelming wave of sadness swept over her. Her life wasn't flashing before her eyes as many people report in the throes of death. Instead, she had flash forwards which were even harder to take. She was being shown snapshots of a future that would never be.

First, an image of marrying Matt floated in her mind's eye. Then, them in a hospital, having sweet babies; enjoying a long life together; raising their brood and growing old together. A future that would never happen was her punishment for releasing this creature. An intense wave of grief washed over her: grief for Matt, for herself, and for her unborn children. Tears flowed from her broken eye sockets.

The creature released her from its massive jaws and stared into her blood-speckled eyes. She sensed the creature had seen the same images she'd seen; saw the future it had stolen from her.

Darkness spilled into the corners of her vision, blurring away to nothingness. The last thing Kate saw before her eyes went black was the sinister creature licking its ebony lips and grinning at her, clearly satisfied, her blood oozing from the corners of its twisted mouth.

Matt

Matt barreled into the basement, surprised the lights had come back on at some point in Kate's fight for her life.

Instantly, he was confused and horrified by what he discovered. By the way the dirt floor was scuffed and disrupted, he could tell there had been a mighty struggle. His stomach clenched when he spotted a dark puddle on the floor midway through the basement. He closed his eyes and prayed it wasn't Kate's blood.

He made his way slowly to the puddle, peering suspiciously at every shadow, making certain nothing moved aggressively toward him.

Finally, he stood over the puddle, swallowed hard, and forced himself not to vomit. He squatted down and touched the drying puddle with two fingers. He pulled them toward his face and reluctantly sniffed the fluid that stained his fingers. His nose crinkled as it recognized the coppery stench of fresh blood.

He gagged, stood quickly, and backed away from the puddle so he wouldn't contaminate any more crime scenes as he had done at the rectory. He shook his head to clear his mind and sucked in the fresher air from above his head, desperate to forget the odor of the obviously grave injury.

His head cleared. Lying near the bloody puddle, he saw the probable weapon that had caused the damaging injury to Kate or the stranger. He shuffled closer and gasped when he saw the small pickaxe lying in the dirt, the wood handle stained with blood.

He couldn't bring himself to touch the pickaxe. He knew if he touched it, he'd probably have all the answers he needed. He just couldn't do it. He couldn't bear to see if Kate had been stabbed with it. It would kill him to know she'd suffered so badly at the hands of someone she'd once considered a friend.

Matt's knees were weak. He worried he might faint and be unable to help Kate. *What if she was only injured?* He tried to fill himself with hope and purpose. He convinced himself that she was merely injured and needed his help. *I must find her. But where?*

Refocused, he followed droplets of blood that led to the old brick wall. He took a few steps toward them and was overjoyed to see footprints in the dirt. By the size of them, they were probably Kate's. Recently, she'd complained the absence of a decent tread on her sneakers, and the dusty, in-distinct footprints led him to believe they very likely were hers. She might have survived the initial attack upstairs, won a battle in the basement and went somewhere else, fighting to live.

He followed the trail of footsteps and droplets of blood to the stone wall on the far side of the basement. The foot-prints ended and an opening was now evident. He gasped and knew she'd entered the wall here in her attempt to escape.

He marveled at the hidden tunnel. *How long had it been down here?* He mused that it must've been hidden by the old brick wall. Scanning it hastily, he checked the entrance for structural integrity.

Quickly, he decided if he were to save her, he'd need to follow the tunnel and hope she was hidden inside it, waiting for help. He crouched, bending at his waist and entered the tunnel. Although he sensed it would be slow-going and he'd have to battle a slight case of claustrophobia, he hoped she knew he was coming for her and he prayed desperately for her life to be spared.

Kate

The creature stood over Kate's drained body, grinning fiercely at her crumpled remains. She had served her purpose and was no longer required. It waited patiently for the arrival of his keeper.

The creature cocked its head to the side and listened keenly to the variety of sounds echoing within the tunnel. Its large, sensitive ears filtered out the echo of dripping water falling from the ceiling and walls of the tunnel. It heard the dull roar of the swollen river beyond the tunnel's entrance and the distant grumbles of thunder from the retreating storm. It grinned viciously. Her blood still dripped from its pointed jaws when faint, familiar footsteps made their way slowly toward it in the dark.

The footsteps grew closer. The creature lifted to its full height, clearly wanting to show itself in all its glory to the approaching keeper, letting him know he'd survived his years of confinement only to grow larger, stronger, and ready for battle.

The footsteps stopped abruptly, a shocked gasp filled the tunnel.

"Hello, Master," said Adam, breathless as he took in the huge size of his released master. "You appear very strong," he said with obvious pleasure. He took a step closer, and his red eyes seemed to search the creature for any signs of injury.

Through rows of jagged teeth and leaking mucus, the creature garbled, "I am well, Keeper."

"I'm sorry it took so long to find her," Adam said, nodding at Kate's lifeless body on the floor between them. "Pity we couldn't keep her." He shrugged indifferently.

"She fulfilled her destiny," said the creature, nodding at her body with reverence. "She will be remembered for that."

"So she shall," agreed Adam with a solemn nod.

"What do we do now, Keeper?" Its red eyes searched Adam's face for answers.

"We wait, Master," Adam told him matter-of-factly.

The creature nodded somberly. It knew who was coming and he'd have the fury and power of God with him.

"We should hide ourselves while we wait," Adam said, pointing to a dark corner. "He'll have much ire towards us for harming his woman." He nodded at Kate's unmoving body on the dank tunnel floor.

The creature nodded obediently and disappeared into the murky shadows on the ceiling, returning to its stony perch above Adam's head. Adam stepped quickly into the gloom beyond her body, happy the sun had set, allowing him better cover.

It wouldn't be long now.

Matt

Matt continued his shuffling steps down the long tunnel from Kate's house. His emotions wavered between intense fear for her safety, hope for finding her alive, and marveling at the very existence of the tunnel, which he estimated, was close to half a mile long.

Who would've had the idea to make it? Why did it lead to Kate's home? Obviously, the tunnel was old and from the bends it seemed to take and the noises he started to hear, he figured it would come out at the river that was set back from her property.

He slipped on the wet floor for the umpteenth time and smacked his shin hard on a protruding rock. Searing pain shot up his leg as if a firecracker had exploded in his bone.

"Shit!" he said in a harsh whisper and grunted. He'd been trying to follow Kate's trail silently in case she was still in the clutches of the intruder he'd seen in his vision. He wanted the element of surprise on his side if he needed to jump him.

He stopped for a moment and rubbed his throbbing shinbone. He cocked his head to the side to gauge his distance from the river. He knew he was getting close. The stream was roiling and loud, as if it had filled up considerably from the recent storm.

He soldiered on, expecting to see the end of the tunnel

around the next bend. He hoped for a full moon to light the remainder of his path. If Kate wasn't down here, he'd try to head back through the woods. He figured he'd have a decent chance of finding the house, even in the dark, if the moon were agreeable.

He rounded another bend and was overjoyed to see the exit. The mouth of the tunnel, although partially blocked by vegetation, was huge. He was surprised no one else had discovered it yet, although the mystique of Devil's Chair was probably enough to keep the majority of locals out of the woods. The unblocked portion of the tunnel's mouth afforded him a bit of light from the clearing evening sky. He started forward, shuffling quickly toward the opening. The veil of claustrophobia he'd been fighting started to lift when he caught a slight breeze from the rain-cleansed air.

With his eyes trained on the opening of the tunnel, he'd forgotten to look down to ensure he was on solid footing. In his distraction, he tripped over an obstruction and nearly fell. He caught his balance by grabbing onto a rock that jutted from the wall. He waited for the searing pain that had been accompanying his bumps to begin, but this time, he realized the obstacle that stopped him was almost... *soft?*

He peered down in the darkness, squinting against the shadows, and made out a figure lying directly below him. He'd tripped over a body.

His stomach lurched as he squatted down to search the face of the unmoving figure. He grabbed at a shoulder shrouded by the dark and was horrified when his hand touched hair. Long hair. Long, flowing hair. *Kate's hair?*

He fell to his knees and scooped her onto his lap. He

wiped matted hair from her face with his hand and tried to feel if she was breathing. He held her tightly against his chest.

"Kate!" he yelled into her ear. "It's Matt. Kate? Can you hear me?"

Her head lolled loose on her neck, not a normal way for a head to move. His stomach churned, bitter with acid. He touched her cheek with his hand, turned her pale, blood-streaked face toward his own and searched her blank eyes for a sign of life.

"Please, Kate," he begged softly through burning tears, his throat tightening with overwhelming grief.

He held her ruined head close to his chest, stroked her hair, tangled with dried blood, and rocked her slowly on his lap. Using a hand to support her weak neck, his fingers easily found the lethal injury, a gaping hole, gooey with congealed blood.

His body was getting cold. *I must be going into shock.* He didn't care. Right now, he wished *he* were dead. He'd failed her and she'd paid the ultimate price. He wept into her blood-stained shirt and moaned her name over and over, not caring if the murderer was still close. *Maybe,* he thought wildly, *if he were lucky, the killer would finish him off, too.*

Slowly, his sobbing abated and he suddenly became aware of another presence in the tunnel. Reluctantly, he lifted his head from Kate's still chest and looked toward the opening of the tunnel.

"Who's out there?" he said, his voice strong with anger.

A figure in a black suit stepped from the shadows. He

removed his hat and bowed toward him.

"Who the hell are you?" Matt asked.

"My name is Adam. I am the keeper of the Master," he said without emotion. "We've been expecting you." He gave a grin that revealed a glimmer of amusement within his red irises.

"Who the hell are *we*?" Matt demanded, never suspecting two murderers.

"Myself and my Master," he answered, rolling his red eyes toward the ceiling of the tunnel.

Matt's suspicious blue eyes followed his gaze and made out a dark shadow on the ceiling that appeared to be moving. Matt's heart raced madly in his chest. His urge to live suddenly outweighed his previous desire to die along with Kate.

Keeping one eye on the flutter of movement on the ceiling, he slowly slid Kate's body from his lap and laid her gently on the tunnel's floor. He hated putting her on the cold, wet ground, but he needed to be able to fight. Quickly, he kissed her hand, placed it on her chest and closed both of her glazed eyes with his fingertips.

He stood to face the man in black. He had youth on his side and knew he could take this older man down relatively easily. *Unless he has a weapon*, a voice in the back of his mind told him. His gaze shifted momentarily to the open wound on Kate's torn neck.

Adam didn't move or speak as Matt expected. It was almost as if he were giving him a moment to grieve for her before continuing his assault.

Matt walked carefully around her body, still trying

to protect her even though it was too late to save her. He planted his feet firmly on the slippery floor and placed his hands on his hips, trying to appear unafraid of the slight man standing less than ten feet from him.

He bellowed, "Who is this Master you speak of?" He surprised himself at the strength in his voice. His words echoed from the tunnel walls, sounding ancient and foreign, as if spoken from another era, in another language.

Adam stood silently. A mischievous grin spread across his pale face. His red eyes rolled back up to the ceiling playfully, as if he wanted Matt to see for himself.

Matt grunted at Adam. He had no tolerance for playing games. He wanted prompt answers, and he was ready to kick some major ass. Kate's death was sinking in hard and fast and he felt less anguish and more anger with every passing second. He needed to retaliate, *had to*, and this clown was a good place to start. He took a small step toward him, clenching his fists, ready to tear him apart with his bare hands.

Adam's eyes left the ceiling. He looked back at Matt and seemed oddly excited by his aggressive stance. He smirked. "The Master is ready to reveal himself to you, Matt."

Matt was taken aback. *How did this strange man know his name?* Kate must have mentioned him. Maybe she'd begged to see him one more time before she had her throat removed. He shuddered and fought the urge to turn around and look at her again, still unable to believe she was really dead and there was nothing that could bring her back.

Adam, seeming to read his thoughts, clucked his tongue

lightly. "The Master will explain." His eyes glanced to the ceiling once again.

This time, Matt followed his bright red gaze. The shadow on the ceiling *was* moving, he was certain of that now. He gulped a mouthful of musty air. Suddenly, he felt dizzy, his bravery quickly fading in the face of the unknown looming above him.

The shadow dismounted from its perch above like a limber gymnast and moved rapidly to the floor. It made a strange swooping sound as thick wings brought it down.

Matt stared in horror as the creature landed a few feet in front of him. The beast's face had a snout, like a large pig or a dog, with wayward black hairs poking out in every direction. It grinned viciously at him, showing many rows of dangerous yellowed teeth. The muzzle of the creature was stained a dark maroon and Matt's stomach clenched when he realized the thing standing before him had ripped Kate's throat out with its strong jaws.

The creature spread out leathery, bat-like wings. They touched either side of the tunnel with its massive size. Matt gasped, unable to hide his fear. He was certain this was it, he'd suffer the same fate as Kate and they'd be lost forever in this dank cave.

The creature peered directly into Matt's watering eyes, almost hypnotizing him with its flickering red irises. It grinned again and cocked its head to the side. It seemed to be listening to Matt's thoughts or the pounding of his heart within the walls of his chest. It flapped its huge wings, covering Matt with a puff of air that smelled of rotten flesh. Matt shuddered involuntarily, unable to move.

Now, the beast wrapped its wings around its torso, hugging itself tightly into a hairy brown cocoon.

Was this how it began an attack? Matt wondered, *making itself small only to spring forth in all of its freakish power?* Matt watched in horrified awe as the creature writhed within the closed wings, as if it was trying to beat its way out of them. Adam stood behind and to the side of the creature, a pleased grin on his thin lips. *The bastard's enjoying the show!*

Suddenly, a loud crack shook the tunnel. Matt wondered if the storm had returned and a clap of thunder had found its way into the tunnel's entrance or if a lighting strike had brought down a tree close by, but when he saw smoke rising from the creature, he knew the sound had come from within the cocoon made by the beast's wings. He hoped the evil creature was on fire, burning its way back to where it had come.

The smoke grew thicker by the second, filling the small space of the tunnel with a black cloud-like blanket. The stench of scorched hair seared Matt's nostrils. He could barely see in the haze. He waved the smoke away from his face with his hands not wanting to be taken by surprise if the creature was using smoke to trick him.

Finally, the smoke began to clear. Matt caught his first glimpse of what had happened in the black blur. The terrible creature was gone. In its place was a naked man who rose from a fetal position on the ground. Relatively handsome, he appeared to be in his late thirties, maybe early forties. Mounds of wasted leathery skin smoked around his feet. He stretched his taut body in all directions as if he'd just woken up from a long nap.

The nude man turned toward Matt, seemingly unembarrassed by his exposed, muscular silhouette. He reached a well-manicured hand to his mouth and wiped a smear of blood from his mouth and flicked it to the ground in disgust. Matt realized it was Kate's blood on his lips and felt anger well inside him again when he saw his new enemy was human, flesh and bone.

Behind them, Adam had fallen to his knees and gazed up at the stranger with an odd reverence. "Welcome back, my Master," he whispered to the naked man's backside.

The man turned and nodded at him, silencing him with his expression. Then, he turned back toward Matt, clearly ready to address his questions. "I'm sorry for your loss, Father," said the man in a strong, clear voice. He nodded at Kate's body behind him.

"Did you kill him, too?" Matt asked, assuming the "father" reference was in regards to his friend Roger, who'd also been brutally murdered today.

The man nodded his head solemnly and pointed a finger toward Adam who still kneeled behind him.

"Why?" Matt asked. Angry tears burned his eyes. "Why in God's name did they have to die?" Hot tears rolled down his cheeks.

"It was their destiny," the man said matter-of-factly. "They served their purposes and were released." He nodded as though implying he'd done them a favor.

Matt racked his brain to make sense of the garbage and lies he was being told. Finally, through gritted teeth, he asked, "Who *are* you?"

"You know who I am, Father," said the man. He smirked at him, his red eyes clearly amused.

"*What* are you?" Matt asked, clarifying his question for the evasive man.

"We were once what you strived to become, Father," Adam said from behind the naked man.

"We realized there is no shame in wanting to lead rather than follow," added the naked man. "Unfortunately, the Lion and his herd felt differently. Does that fact make us so bad?" he sneered, then smirked wickedly at Matt.

"Are you the... the *devil*?" Matt asked, his voice shaking.

The man chuckled. The corners of his red eyes smiled along with his mouth, still filled with jagged yellow teeth.

Matt yelled, "You're an evil, murdering son of a bitch!" Instinctively, he pulled Roger's silver cross from his belt and held it toward the naked man and Adam. He hoped his faith would keep him safe from the man-creature and his devoted minion.

The man's face contorted, pained. He shielded his red eyes from the cross, now glowing bright in the dim tunnel.

"Answer me," Matt demanded. "Answer!" His confidence was buoyed by the man's reaction to Roger's cross. Holding the cross toward the two men, Matt took a determined step forward. Adam let out an ear-shattering, eagle-like screech.

The naked man gnashed his rows of serrated teeth and spit out his words. "I've waited nearly a thousand years to return to this realm. Now it is *my* time!" He nodded toward Adam who looked at him expectantly, like a soldier awaiting an order. "Arise and be ready. We have work to do. The war is coming." Adam stood, nodded vigorously at the naked man and turned toward the entrance of the tunnel. He jumped soundlessly into the black void of cool night air and disappeared.

The naked man carefully averted his gaze from the gleaming silver cross Matt held toward his red eyes. Instead, he stared directly into Matt's face and grinned viciously.

"Father, the Lion weeps for you," he said smugly and nodded toward Kate's body. "But rest assured, I *will* return and my kingdom will not be denied." His red eyes burned.

Matt held his position, pushing the luminous cross as far as he could toward the man, straining every muscle in his shoulder.

The man hissed angrily and turned toward the mouth of the tunnel. He glanced back once and sneered at Matt. Blood laden drool still dripped from his chin when he, too, jumped silently into the black night.

Matt stood motionless and waited to hear him land on the rocks below, but the sound never came. He held the cross in front of him for another ten minutes, frozen, uncertain if it was safe to let down his guard.

Finally, he believed the two had left. He dropped to his knees, exhausted and spent. He crawled toward Kate to retrieve her lifeless body.

Although he felt crushing sadness for Kate, his love, and deeply mourned the loss of Roger, he now had a solid purpose. He knew what he had to do. Those creatures wanted a war, and they were going to get one.

Hell hath no fury…

About the Author

Stefanie Jolicoeur left the world of finance in 2008 to raise her four children and to write books. This is her debut novel for adults. In addition to *Devil's Chair*, Stefanie has published three books for children and a novel for middle school children.

When Stefanie isn't busy writing, she enjoys reading (Stephen King is a special favorite), creating art in many forms and spending time with her family. She also enjoys visiting schools to share her books and her love for reading and writing.

Stefanie's books and much of her artwork is available for sale on her Etsy.com store - HappyHeartStudios.

More information can also be found on her website:
www.thehappyheartstudio.net.

Author's Photo credit: By Richard Guptill and Marsha Guptill

CPSIA information can be obtained
at www.ICGtesting.com
Printed in the USA
JSHW061352120922
30293JS00002B/10

9 780996 212137